ACCLAIM FOR T...
CECELIA H...

Titles by Cecelia Holland

THE SECRET ELEANOR
THE KING'S WITCH

The King's Witch

C E C E L I A
H O L L A N D

BERKLEY BOOKS, NEW YORK

THE BERKLEY PUBLISHING GROUP
Published by the Penguin Group
Penguin Group (USA) Inc.
375 Hudson Street, New York, New York 10014, USA
Penguin Group (Canada), 90 Eglinton Avenue East, Suite 700, Toronto, Ontario M4P 2Y3, Canada
(a division of Pearson Penguin Canada Inc.)
Penguin Books Ltd., 80 Strand, London WC2R 0RL, England
Penguin Group Ireland, 25 St. Stephen's Green, Dublin 2, Ireland (a division of Penguin Books Ltd.)
Penguin Group (Australia), 250 Camberwell Road, Camberwell, Victoria 3124, Australia
(a division of Pearson Australia Group Pty. Ltd.)
Penguin Books India Pvt. Ltd., 11 Community Centre, Panchsheel Park, New Delhi—110 017, India
Penguin Group (NZ), 67 Apollo Drive, Rosedale, Auckland 0632, New Zealand
(a division of Pearson New Zealand Ltd.)
Penguin Books (South Africa) (Pty.) Ltd., 24 Sturdee Avenue, Rosebank, Johannesburg 2196,
South Africa

Penguin Books Ltd., Registered Offices: 80 Strand, London WC2R 0RL, England

This book is an original publication of The Berkley Publishing Group.

This is a work of fiction. Names, characters, places, and incidents either are the product of the author's imagination or are used fictitiously, and any resemblance to actual persons, living or dead, business establishments, events, or locales is entirely coincidental. The publisher does not have any control over and does not assume any responsibility for author or third-party websites or their content.

PRINTING HISTORY
Berkley trade paperback edition / June 2011

Library of Congress Cataloging-in-Publication Data

Holland, Cecelia, 1943–
The king's witch / Cecelia Holland.
    p.   cm.
  ISBN 978-0-425-24130-1 (pbk.)
  1. Richard I, King of England, 1157–1199—Fiction.   2. Crusades—Third, 1189–1192—Fiction.
3. Witches—Fiction.   I. Title.
  PS3558.O348K575   2011
  813'.54—dc22
  2010054212

PRINTED IN THE UNITED STATES OF AMERICA

10   9   8   7   6   5   4   3   2   1

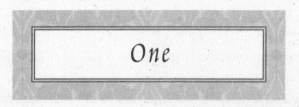

One

CYPRUS

Early in the morning, when the other women had gone to Mass, Edythe went into the conquered town.

The air was cool and bright, the sun just risen. The town was quiet and empty. She guessed that all the local people fled when the Crusader army swept in. Now the army itself was gone, chasing the Cypriot king into the hills, and in the whole town nothing seemed to stir.

She went up and down streets strewn with the garbage of the townspeople's flight, broken jars, trampled food, on one corner a wagon with the wheel off, the harness lying in front like the hollow outline of a horse. She saw no sign of what she was looking for.

Surely they were all gone and she would find no one. But then, through the corner of her eye, she caught the motion of a window shut abruptly as she passed. An overturned bucket lay by the well, the spilled water drying on the stones. Flies buzzed everywhere. Beyond a high wall a cock crowed. There were still living souls here.

So she sauntered along, swinging her basket; walking by herself still delighted her. For years, living in Queen Eleanor's court, she had been shut in, locked up, watched over day and night. Now going where she wished, as she pleased, was a joy.

She felt the strangeness of this town, white and quiet in the morning sun, and the airy freedom of being away from home. But then she missed Poitiers, the familiar place, the faces she knew. Where she knew how to live. Her mood sank. Suddenly she pitied the local people, forced to flee their homes. *But we are Crusaders*, she thought. *We come on God's cause, and everyone should help us.*

She repeated that to herself, uneasy. *I am a Crusader.* She wasn't sure it was true. She was only trying to see her place in this. But she hadn't chosen to come, and maybe that made a difference.

Beyond the next street, past a row of beached ships, the sea muttered up and down the shore, and at the upper edge of the sand she went through a deserted marketplace. Her steps slowed, although there were no merchants here, no one buying. She served Queen Johanna now, and the Queen of Sicily and her women all loved the potions and philtres, for which Edythe needed honey, herbs, and vinegar. She had brought some from Sicily, but the storm had soaked in and ruined most of her store.

That same storm had blown them here to Cyprus, where, their ship wrecked, they had asked for help, and instead the king Isaac and his people had tried to capture Queen Johanna and hold her for ransom. So the Cypriots deserved what they got, the fury of the Crusaders.

She wondered if she deserved what she got.

Deserving should mean having a choice, and she had little enough to say about any of it. Eleanor never asked anyone's leave. "I trust you, Edythe—watch over my children. And keep me informed. You can use the Jews for that; they have connections everywhere." The children being Johanna and her brother King Richard, both actually older than Edythe, and now also the King's bride, the Princess Berengaria of Navarre. Of course he had yet to marry the bride.

Having pronounced her will, the old Queen had gone back to sweet and lovely Poitiers, and King Richard announced he was taking them on the Crusade with him, sister and bride and all, and Edythe should pack and be ready at sunrise.

She told herself she should accept her place, that it was a good place, after all; most women would envy her. Widowed Queen of Sicily, Johanna was greathearted, truly Eleanor's daughter, and she kept a fine court, even so far from home, in a conquered hall. Edythe should not resent being told to spy, but it felt low, and now this, the search for a Jew to convey the message, opened deep old wounds. Eleanor should have known better.

She felt guilty for thinking that. She loved Eleanor, who had saved her; she owed everything to the Queen Mother, and she could suffer a little for her sake. So she would obey.

The sun grew stronger. The day would be hot. She had walked all over the little city without finding what she looked for. She went along a narrowing path past the walls of houses, the ground paved but cracked and sandy. This way ended at a wall, only a few stones deep, tufted with grass; on her right, as she stood before it, the wall rose away, steadily higher, climbing toward the landward side of the town, but on her left it tapered away entirely, as if the builders had lost interest.

Just beyond it, a trail led up through low, dusty brush. Birds called, out there. She climbed over the low stones and followed the path.

The worn dirt trace wound up the green hillside toward the headland that stood over the bay. The air grew warmer as she rose. Swallows flew dipping over the brush ahead of her. A flock of goats browsed the steep slope inland of her, a bell jingling.

Against the sky up there, she made out a confusion of shapes, walls, branchless tree trunks in among a scrubby overgrowth that constantly shivered in the wind. She passed a block of white stone, and on it was strange writing, graven into the surface. She slowed, looking around her, understanding.

This was the ruin of an ancient town, half-buried in the sea-runneled brush; the branchless trunks, all in lines, were columns of marble, some fallen into round drums jumbled on the ground. Ahead of her the brush yielded to a stone floor, vines crisscrossing the white steps leading up.

She climbed onto it and from its height looked out over the broad sea, a glinting surface pleated with little waves, unbroken to the misty horizon. When she turned her gaze downward, the lower town spread out at the foot of the hill like a jumble of boxes.

Once the town had been up here. And there were still people living up here. Another trail led inland, past more broken walls. Footprints and hoofprints muddled the dust. She passed an old empty building and came to a street of houses.

The four houses stood in a line, each sharing a wall with the next, and as soon as she saw them she knew this was what she sought. Beside the right-hand post of the doorway was the little box that said these were Jews. She gathered words in the old language and went up to the first doorway and knocked.

No one answered the door, and she went to the next. She was full of nameless dread; her heart was pounding and she hoped no one answered and she could go back, shrug, say it was no use. Then the door opened slightly.

She said the few words she had memorized. "Peace to us all. I have a message to send to a friend of the Jews." She reached into the basket for the letter.

The door opened slightly wider, and the servant who had first answered backed away. Behind him was a man in a dark unadorned gown, a small cap on his gray hair, which hung down in curls past his bearded jaw. He said, "Very well," and put his hand out. He said more, asking in the old tongue who she was.

She stammered. With the letter given into his hand she was already backing away, but the urge broke on her to go to him, to walk inside, to be home again. This was impossible. She had no home here. She could not remember that language anyway. She shook her head at him. His gaze was keen, as if he understood, but he closed the door.

She hurried down the path back to the town, and like a swarm of wasps the memories rushed after her. She remembered her mother's voice, singing, and her father, who had worn a small cap over his dark hair, who had been a doctor, as she was. A better doctor than she would ever be. She broke into a run, pursued. A little girl in someone else's clothes. The cold, lonely flight, afraid. Hungry. No one wanted her. Standing on the doorstep of the captive Queen of England, clutching the letter, shivering, crying.

The light of the lamp, and the kind hand that drew her in.

The gentle voice: "Forget. Forget everything. You are mine now. We'll say you are Saxon. You fled from a nunnery. This is your new name." This alien, old woman's name, like a misshapen mask.

Ahead lay the little town and the court where she could bury all this, wall out the memories, and she slowed, and settled herself. She would forget. She would bear the name, she would be Edythe. She would go forward, forward, and leave the past behind forever.

A great throng of men was pouring in through the gate at the top of the main street, cheering and galloping their tired horses. Many of them were waving long pieces of cloth, banners and robes. She went by a lane toward the Queen's compound, but when she came out onto the main street the screaming horsemen cut her off; she dodged into a gateway to keep from being trampled.

Now she was trapped. The army flooded past her, stirrup to stirrup, brandishing their trophies overhead. She groped behind her for the gate handle, but it was locked. The men crowding by were beginning to notice her. One grabbed at her. Then suddenly a horse stopped in front of her.

She recoiled into the corner of the gateway. From the saddle a big man in mail looked down at her. With a leap of hope she realized she had seen him before, at court: Johanna's cousin, whom they all called Rouquin for his bristling red hair.

He looked down at her and said, loud over the uproar, "Aren't you that woman of Eleanor's—the doctor? What are you doing out here alone?" He reached his arm down to her. When she didn't immediately seize his hand, he said, "Hurry the hell up, will you? I'm rescuing you."

She realized she had no choice; she gripped his forearm, and he hoisted her effortlessly up behind him on the horse. She sat sideways, as women were supposed to do, and took hold of the high square cantle of the saddle with one hand and the horse's crupper strap with the other. Rouquin nudged the big horse out across the push and shuffle of the passing crowd.

Her breath came easier. He was only trying to help her, after all.

Around them the other Crusaders were whooping and waving their trophies, and his horse snorted and shouldered its way through them. She said, "Did you fight?"

His back was to her, his body massive in his mail. The hood was down; his shield and helmet hung on his saddlebows. His dark red hair stood up in spikes. He said, "Not that much. We ran them right into the ground in one charge. Lots of prisoners, lots of loot. Nobody beats us. Isaac got away, the little King. You're stupid coming out here alone. You think this is Poitiers?"

"I wanted to see the city," she said. The horse banged into something and half-reared, and she slid sidewise on the wide back; she clutched tight with both hands to stay on.

"There's nothing to see. Stay where you belong."

She gritted her teeth together. He was rough as tree bark. She began to dislike him. She said, to turn this aside, "Was anybody hurt?"

"No, it happened too fast. Johanna should take better care of you. Does she know you're out here alone?" He stabbed a look at her over his shoulder. His face was dirty and a scar creased his cheek above his scruff of beard. His eyes were slate gray. "Eleanor sent you, didn't she? To spy?"

She met his eyes, thinking he was one of the family, and so well versed in family ways. She said, in stately tones, "The Queen saved my life. I do as she bids me."

He turned straight forward again. Finally they were out of the crowd, going down a side way between a wall and an orchard. He said, "The Queen Mother's against the Crusade. All the world knows it."

She said, "Eleanor may be against the Crusade, but she would do nothing to hurt Richard, would she?" Ahead was the hall, its front gate bustling with people waiting to get in. "I can go alone from here." She slid down from the horse.

He said, "That's what I'm telling you; you can't go around by yourself."

On the ground, she turned toward him and said, "Thank you."

"Do what I say. Stay inside."

She smiled at him. "Thank you." She turned and started off. Behind her she heard him growl, and he cantered away down the lane.

.   .   .

Johanna said, "Did you get all the treasure back? Where is Isaac?"
The lord of Cyprus, Isaac had tried to take her prisoner; now she
wanted to see him chained.

"He ran as soon as he saw us." Richard kicked at the treasure
chest, which stood in the middle of the floor. "He doesn't deserve
Cyprus. I think I'll take it away from him." He walked up and down,
a cup in his hand. Fighting always made him restless, and he had
come back spitting orders. He needed this hall, now, he wanted a
throne, now; the treasure chest would sit under the throne, which
was to be raised up on blocks. "Before I'm done with Isaac, I'll have
money to pay for the whole Crusade."

"And I talked to the Bishop about marrying you and Berengaria;
we can do it tomorrow, in the little church here." She gave him a narrow look. "You can't get out of this, you know. Lent's over, no more
excuses."

"Oh," he said, and turned to face her, a head taller than she, who
was tall, brawny as a lion, her splendid, bewildering brother. The
door was shut, but they could both hear the people outside pressing
loudly to get in. "I mean to marry her. Her father's the King of Navarre; he has a large army with no wars to fight in a good position
to help me fight mine. But there will be no wedding night. Tell her
that."

"What? Then you won't even be married."

"I'll do enough. I'll lie down on a bed with her. But I am chaste—
the Crusade requires me to be chaste."

Johanna lifted her cup; she realized she was a little drunk. But
the first part of her mother's orders looked easier to fulfill than she
had expected: Richard would marry the girl after all. "Chastity. I
suppose it has to start somewhere. As Saint Augustine said."

"Don't try to distract me," he said. He walked toward her, put the cup on the table, and put his booted foot up on the treasure chest. "That wasn't half what Augustine said."

"So you'll be chaste for the Crusade? How long will that last?"

He gave a bark of startled laughter. His eyes were so intense, even the irises seemed blue. "This is the Crusade. We're bringing in the Kingdom of Jesus. What higher calling is there? It lasts until we win. Maybe it lasts all our lives."

She hoped not. She said, "This new chastity of yours. Is that why you made that confession in Messina? All but naked in the public square in front of most of Sicily? Do you know what Mother said about that?"

He smiled at her. He seemed pleased. He loved to shock their mother. "Mother told me, although I don't remember she got so worked up when Papa had himself whipped for killing the Archbishop. And I told her, I did it to cleanse my soul for the task to come. And since—"

"As if everybody didn't already know you have the morals of a billy goat."

Richard sat down beside her on the couch. "And since then I have not touched a single white buttock, nor pressed my lips to soft sweet lips—" He began to sing a little, on the last words, part of an old song, his hands holding an invisible lute.

Johanna said, "Female or male?"

"Man, woman, boy, girl, or goat." Abruptly he stopped smiling. "This is my offering to God, Jo. Myself, free of sin, to do His greatest, most glorious work."

Johanna realized that he meant this, that it was no mere proper face that he put on when it served him. She saw the second of her mother's orders becoming even harder than she had expected.

Get him married. Get him home, where his real duty was.

He said to her, "Christ will come when we are worthy."

Johanna said, "Yes, but you must have an heir. What if something happened to you? What if you do spend the rest of your life out here?" She ran out of wind; even she could see that against the lure of King Jesus a baby was nothing.

"I'll attend to that in good time. And there's an heir. There's John. The family will go on. The Crusade is more important than anything else, even us."

"John is not good. Even I don't like John."

They were quiet a moment. Johanna thought they were thinking of the same man, and what was never said about him. Richard broke the silence.

"Who will marry us?"

"Evreux, of course. Nothing fancy."

"Good. Just get it done. I can lie down on the bed with her." He got up. His foot nudged the treasure chest again. "You need to get busy. Make this room over so I can hold court here. Put this where it belongs." He raised his hand and the two guards by the doors leaped to open them. The men gushed in, shouting, cheering Richard, who went in among them, his arms out. They all massed together, smacking and banging together as men usually did on meeting, especially after a good fight.

Johanna turned, her temper bridling up. This was why he had brought her along, to keep his household for him. She wished she were a man; she would show him how to rule. Her women were waiting, over at the other side of the hall, and the new girl, Edythe, had come in among them, which pleased her. She liked Edythe, who was sensible and capable and did instantly as she was told. She was good with potions and tonics, and Johanna's mother had said she had healing hands. If she was a spy for Johanna's mother, at least they were all working to the same end. Johanna went to collect them and go and tell the Princess Berengaria she would soon be the Queen of England, although with a difference.

⋅ ⋅ ⋅

Berengaria looked up; her face was bright with relief. "No, I mind not. How noble. He is noble."

Noble, Edythe thought. From what she had seen, Richard cared no more about her than a chair to sit on, or a horse to ride, and everybody knew why he did not want to bed with her. The little princess's chamber was stuffy with the heat, but the girl still sat bundled into her gowns and shawls. Johanna said, "Then you shall be married tomorrow, and made Queen. Will you like that?"

"Oh, yes, much." The girl smiled at her. "I then have my own palace, and my own court. I then do much good, I hope." Her voice grew silky, and her head tipped, so she watched Johanna through the corner of her eye. "Do I precede over my lady Sicily?"

Johanna grunted in surprise. "We will have to find a herald, and see."

"I ask my lord," Berengaria said. "But I have to make ready."

"We will do that," Johanna said. "Only heed your maids. The wedding is tomorrow."

"Yes, my lady."

As they went off, Johanna said, "Well, the little priss. He will never love her." Her voice was salty with anger.

Edythe said, "She doesn't much care about him." There was a merciless balance in all this. She followed Johanna out the door.

⋅ ⋅ ⋅

Berengaria had brought a gown to be married in, but during the storms at sea the chest had leaked, and now the matted cloth looked and smelled awful. Johanna gave her another dress, and all the women passed the night taking in the seams and raising the hem, and clipping the gold embroideries and jewels from the ruined dress and stitching them onto the new one. In the morning, yawning, Johanna watched as the princess's Navarrese women tucked her into the gown, and smiled.

"You look very fine."

Berengaria's lips moved without sound. Her eyes were wide with terror. The women moved around her, brushing and plucking and straightening, and the girl lifted her gaze to Johanna. "Please."

Johanna kept on smiling. She began to see this as a fit revenge. "Please what? Come, your bridegroom awaits you."

She thought for a second the girl would need to be carried, but then she moved woodenly toward the door. The other women fell in around her and they went to the chapel. The day before, a fleet from the Holy Land had brought some of the Christian lords to see Richard, and so the place was jammed with witnesses. When they saw the women they began to cry out and wave their arms, and as Berengaria trudged by them, they threw flowers at her, so that she seemed to wade through a river of rose petals.

Inside, by the altar, Richard waited, the candlelight glinting on his golden crown, his long pale hair. The Bishop of Evreux stood beyond him. Johanna stepped aside, and Berengaria plodded into the blaze of the candles; Johanna could see her shaking, the little fool.

The Queen of Sicily glanced around the chapel, its walls and square columns plastered with icons in the Greek way. Arrayed around her were her own women, and Richard's court, but behind them stood the crowd of newly come strangers. She looked them over curiously; the King of Jerusalem was supposed to be among them, and she wondered which of these elegant men he was.

She had heard a lot of gossip about the King of Jerusalem, even as far away as Sicily. Then Evreux was speaking, and she turned forward.

Berengaria stood there rigid, her face white as salt. When Richard took her hand to put the ring on, she started all over as if he had struck her. Richard did not seem to notice, all his attention on fitting the ring to her finger.

He never lifted his eyes to the girl's face. She mattered nothing to him. Johanna found herself smiling. The priest said words, and the whole crowd made the response and crossed themselves.

Then Berengaria knelt before her new husband, her hands together as if in prayer, and he put a gold crown on her head and said something in French, and she was Queen of England.

Her lips moved. She shut her eyes, Richard moved back, and for a moment she knelt there, crouched forward, as if the weight of the crown forced her down. Then she shivered and straightened, her head rising, and her eyes opened.

Johanna felt a sudden pang of sympathy for her. She herself had married a man she had met first at the altar. She reminded herself that that had worked out well enough. She thought she should be kinder to Berengaria. With the rest, she knelt and prayed for the long life and many children of the King and Queen of England.

. . .

The feast began at noon and proceeded very briskly, like the wedding itself. The King and his new Queen appeared in the hall for a moment, where the whole crowd could see them. While they were there receiving bows and cheers, Edythe went across the courtyard to the royal chamber, to make the new Queen's bed ready.

Berengaria came in almost at once. With the other women, Edythe helped the girl into a long white gown, sat her in the big open bed, and brushed her hair all around her. The girl was rigid, her eyes staring, her lips pressed together, as if she faced some ordeal. They scattered flowers around her, so Edythe put a white rosebud in her hair. The new Queen had wispy pale hair, so Edythe went out to the garden and got a red rose instead.

The King walked in with fifteen people on his heels. Edythe drew off to one side, out of their notice, but where she could watch. Richard greeted Berengaria with a proper bow and the right words, and sat down on the bed to let a squire take his boots off. After that, he lay down on his back next to his new bride and touched his bare foot to hers. Immediately after that he got up, bowed to her, and left.

Edythe let her breath out. Everybody else followed Richard away, except the Queen and the two old Navarrese women who waited on her. Berengaria sat up straight; the rosebud fell unnoticed in the sheets; her women closed around her. Edythe came and kissed her. The Navarrese women would care for the little Queen, and she wanted to go back to the feast. She said, "God bless you, my lady."

Berengaria looked at her, her face slack with relief, the pure white froth of lace and silk all around her. "When will I have the baby?"

Edythe choked a little, and glanced at the other women, barricaded behind their own language, who only stared back. "After the Crusade," she said, and patted Berengaria's hand and left.

She went across the open space to the hall, where Johanna and the other women sat chewing up the good meats. The great room was splendid. Johanna had hung it with the silken banners and rugs looted from Isaac's camp, so it seemed like a tent, the silks fluttering softly, continually, in the drafts. All around, the fading sunlight spilled in through the opening in the center of the roof to glow on the floor. Around the walls, on the hollow square of the stone couches, newly softened with Isaac's cushions and scarves, sat Richard's lords

and the great men of the Holy Land who had just arrived. Edythe
went in and stood behind Johanna, who was seated on a bench with
the curved paws of a lion, and the Queen smiled and got her wrist.

"Sit. You've done well with all this, I'm pleased with you."

A flush warmed Edythe's throat; she sank down, her hands in
her lap. She had her place here and she would be glad of it. Yet this
ate at her. She lifted her eyes to the court, a broad loud splash of
silks and jewels all around her, wishing she belonged here.

Two

CYPRUS

Philip de Rançun, who was called Rouquin, slouched against the wall, bored. Down the hall another of the great lords rose, hoisted his cup, and shouted a salute, and all around everybody cheered until the stone walls rang. So far they had agreed that the Crusade was God's work, Saladin was the devil, and Jerusalem was surely theirs now that Richard was come, and they looked to go on agreeing until the wine ran out. Rouquin shifted his weight, his hands behind him. Richard meant to take Cyprus now and had given Rouquin the charge of running down the fugitive King Isaac; he was itching to start. He loved having his own command.

The thunderous chanting faded. Richard was sitting back on his throne. Rouquin saw him glance over his shoulder toward him and stepped forward and sank down on his haunches at his cousin's elbow.

"What do you make of this?" Richard said. He drained his cup and handed it off to a page. "Why did all these high lords come to Cyprus? We'll reach Acre in a few weeks. They're that excited at seeing us?"

Rouquin let his gaze wander along the rows of drinking, shouting men. "Getting to us first. Making sure we line up with them and not somebody else."

"As usual, you see my mind," Richard said. "This doesn't argue well for the general condition of the kingdom, does it? Now look."

Rouquin stood; the man approaching them clearly outranked him, older, anyway, draped in creamy velvet figured with gold thread, many jewels about him, a crown on his graying tawny hair. The herald bawled, "Guy de Lusignan, King of Jerusalem!"

Rouquin looked keenly at him, all the stories coming to mind. Guy bowed, and Richard inclined his head. "My lord, I welcome you."

The King of Jerusalem's voice boomed, meant for everybody to hear. "I welcome you, my lord, who will help me recover what is rightfully mine, and bring us all revenge for the evil of Hattin and Saladin." He went on like that for a while. Rouquin noticed he avoided mentioning that the disaster at Hattin had been entirely his fault. Richard reached down into the treasure chest beside the throne and produced a ring, said some proper words, and thanked the King of Jerusalem for taking the gift. Guy bowed himself away.

Rouquin said, "So that's the King."

"Maybe," Richard said. "Maybe not. But Guy is one of us; he's Poitevin. That should count for something."

Rouquin scrubbed his hand over his face. He thought in the Holy Land they would need the best men they could find, and Guy was famously hapless. Son of a great family in Poitou, he had gotten in trouble there as a boy and been exiled. Coming out here to the east he had managed to marry a princess and become king when the Leper died. Then at one toss he lost the whole Crusader kingdom to Saladin in the stupid battle at Hattin.

"He sounds like a fool to me. He led his men to their deaths."

Richard said, "Here come the Templars."

Two of the black and white knights had arrived from Acre, and now Robert de Sablé, who had sailed with Richard, was approaching the throne; Richard introduced them. De Sablé was the new Grand Master of the Order, elected in Paris. The knights shook hands and bowed and said some pieties. De Sablé blessed them, which everybody took with a straight face. Richard made no move to give them anything, and eventually they sat down.

"They dress very well for monks." Rouquin watched de Sablé walk away, one hand on the heavy silver hilt of his sword.

"Poverty, chastity, and obedience," Richard said.

"Besides," Rouquin said, remembering something else. He sank down on his heels again by Richard's throne. "How can Guy even still be the King? I thought his wife had died."

Richard gave a dry chuckle. "She did die, and their children with her, but first she hounded him into laying siege to Acre. She saw it clear enough: Recovering the kingdom starts with recovering Acre. She and Guy led the way. Which is why we're here, to help him finish the job of taking Acre. So he'd better still be King."

The herald said, "My lord Humphrey de Toron."

This was a slight man in neat plum-colored brocade, a silver belt, a single amethyst at his throat, fine silk slippers. He wore no sword. His hands were long and white, and he seemed never to have shaved. After their greetings he said, "My lord, you alone can save Jerusalem. Whatever I may do in our cause, command me. Like King Guy, I depend on you to help me get my honor back."

Richard mouthed some compliments and gave him another ring. Rouquin said, "De Toron. There was a de Toron who was constable."

"This one's father. This Humphrey's another man who could have been King. He was married to the sister of Guy's princess, but he refused the crown. So they took his princess away and gave her to somebody else."

Rouquin watched Humphrey go, wondering how he could have let that happen—how he could still keep his head up after that had happened. How he could expect ever to get his honor back. "Who married her?"

Richard said, "That would be Conrad of Montferrat."

"Oh. The Italian."

"Yes, a small prince in a big world, who is not here, you'll note, but at Tyre, where we are supposed to go next. And I'm afraid he has a better claim to be King than our friend Guy, since his princess is still alive and seems to be the rightful queen. This is a difficulty, maybe. Go find out what you can, while I gild our way down."

Rouquin straightened. Another gaudy jewel-encrusted man was appearing to receive presents and make his promises and vows and pledges. Rouquin shrugged it all off. He would be on the march soon, the true work, and better. He drifted away across the room, looking the other men over.

From the midst of her maids Johanna smiled at him. The woman he had seen out in the street, the doctor, sat beside her, looking toward Richard. He had heard her name, but forgotten it. Some lispy Saxon name. He paced around the room, watching Richard take homages and give out rewards, gold and silk and swords and cups. At the far corner Rouquin came upon Humphrey de Toron.

He spoke his name and bowed, and Humphrey bowed, and they said the usual things when first meeting. The young man made Rouquin deeply confused; he did not know how to speak to a boy who should have been a girl. The look on the young lord's face said this was not new to him. His father had been a Crusader legend who had saved the King's life in battle. The son had never even been dubbed a knight.

"I suppose now there will be a wild dash to get Isaac Comnenus," Humphrey said.

Rouquin saw no reason to tell him. "Richard has some plan."

They were of the same rank: Humphrey was a baron of Jerusalem as Rouquin was of Aquitaine. Thinking that, Rouquin felt himself move onto solid understanding again. Humphrey went on, musing.

"Cyprus is ready for a good king. Isaac had a very tenuous grip here in the first place. I don't know what the Emperor will think of it, but Constantinople hasn't had much to say about Cyprus for thirty years." A servant came forward and poured Humphrey's cup full, and then another took the cup and sipped from it, nodded, and put it on the table before the Lord of Toron. Rouquin watched this, absorbed.

He said, "I think my cousin is already talking to the Templars about buying Cyprus. He needs the money." Richard always needed money. He glanced at the two black-cloaked knights sitting down the table. Robert de Sablé sat among them, more a smiler and a nodder than a fighting man. A banker, a merchant in power. People like that complicated everything. He turned back to Humphrey, so knowing and so willing to talk.

"The Templars will be hard masters," Humphrey said. "They have not been the same since Hattin. The best of them were slaughtered at Hattin. And even the Master de Ridford is gone now."

"Who are the captains at Acre?"

"There are many noble fighting men at Acre; I can hardly list them. Crusaders have been coming to join Guy since he went down there. It was a noble act, a kingly act, he and Sibylla, with a few hundred men, riding against a huge city like Acre."

"But the other King. Conrad. He's in Tyre."

At the mention of Conrad of Montferrat, Humphrey's eyes gleamed and he smiled, not pleasantly. "Yes. He has the French King's support. You should know that the King of France, Philip Augustus, has few good things to say about your cousin Richard."

Rouquin scratched his beard. Richard and King Philip had been friends once, when it suited them, but now they hated each other, which suited them better. Richard called Philip the Gnome. "He's at Acre," he said.

"Yes. But he cannot win it by himself. I promise you this eats him like a canker, and King Conrad, too. They need Richard, even as they hate him." He smiled at Rouquin and lifted his cup. "To the Crusade," he said, and drank.

They spoke a little longer, about the wealth and condition of Cyprus, and Rouquin wandered away, his mind full. He saw the purpose in Humphrey's chatter. He thought, *That's why he's here. Not just to get us behind Guy. To make sure we know that the Gnome is on Conrad's side, and so to pit us against Conrad.*

He turned, looking for Richard, and saw him all the way across the room on his throne, one foot up on the treasure chest, laughing.

Rouquin got a cup of wine from one of the army of servants. Everything had seemed much simpler back in France: the prize, the glory, what they would have to do, who would be their friends, who their enemy. The closer they got to the Holy Land, the more it all opened up like a nest of snakes. Now already he saw two sides among the Crusaders, and they hadn't even gotten there yet. Likely by the time they reached Acre, there would be more sides than two. All of these men were honing their own swords. In his mind his thoughts shifted. He scanned the room and found Humphrey, now standing by the table, talking to a gaunt old man in blue silk.

As he watched, Humphrey's head turned, and he looked across the room toward Richard, and just for an instant, over by the throne, Richard raised his head and looked back.

That's why, too, Rouquin thought, and drank the wine down in a few gulps.

•   •   •

Later, when he had gone out to check on his horses, he came back into the hall and Richard called him over. Everybody else was gone and the servants were cleaning up; all the lamps but two were out.

Richard said, "Listen, Rouq', I want you to take Guy de Lusignan along when you go after Isaac."

Rouquin jerked up his head in a surge of temper. "He outranks me."

"Yes, well, I need to do something with him. You take care of the work and let him—"

"You promised me this command."

"That was before he came."

"He's a fool! He admits it!"

Richard shrugged, undisturbed. "You aren't. You'll catch Isaac. Just—"

"And he'll get all the glory."

"Rouquin." The King's voice slapped across his angry outburst; he stared him in the eyes. "I want you to do this. That's all." Turning on his heel, he walked away.

Rouquin bit his teeth together, a baffled fury roiling in his belly; when they were boys, he would have knocked Richard down and rubbed his face in the dirt for something like this. Instead his face was in the dirt, because now Richard was King, and he was nobody. He stood for a moment, as if he had no will, as if he meant nothing and was nothing. He went off to find something to hit.

•   •   •

Johanna's nursemaid Gracia had gone with her when they were children to Palermo and considered it her privilege to fuss around her still, straightening her skirts, and bringing cushions for the hard bench. They were sitting on a wagon by the city gate to watch the army leave. Richard had already sailed that morning with the fleet to conquer the coasts of Cyprus, and the rest of the army would soon ride out to chase down Isaac. Edythe felt useless and in the way, pushed herself into a corner, and watched the others.

Gracia was a round little woman with a baggy face, always smiling. The other maid, Lilia, who was younger and slim and very pretty, leaned out over the wagon's side to look up the street.

Already a crowd was gathering along it, more people pushing up every moment; these must be the Cypriots, come back into the town. Of course they could not stay away long. Edythe wondered what this looked like to them, what she and Johanna looked like to them.

Lilia cried, "Where are they? Oh! I can't wait."

Gracia gave a little cough. "Get yourself busy, that will help. Bring me the basket there. Yes, that one, Lilia, don't be a giddygadder, please."

Lilia brought her the basket, full of food and wine. "Gracia, you are such an old woman." She fished out a cup. "My lady, may I give you to drink?"

Johanna sat straight on her bench, her hands in her lap and her cheeks red with excitement. "Yes. I think the men are coming."

Edythe, in the corner, craned her neck to see down the street. A noisy pack of horsemen was striding toward her, in the lead a knight in a helmet with a tall red plume and a crown, a yellow banner floating above. Lilia was trying to pour wine and see the oncoming parade at the same time, and Johanna took the cup from her.

She did not drink of it but leaned forward, her brows pulled down over her nose. "That is Guy de Lusignan," she said. "Where is my cousin? I know Richard sent Rouquin on this quest."

Edythe went to her and took the cup before she spilled it; the other women were also canted forward to see the men pass. As he rode by them, the red-plumed knight raised his arm and shouted, "God wills it!" and all the women cheered and the people on either side whooped and yelled, happy enough to see them leave.

Johanna said, "He had better have Rouquin with him, or he'll get tossed in a bramble." Now ranks of men on foot tramped by, iron-tipped sticks tilted against their shoulders, bows strapped to their backs. Edythe sat next to the Queen with the cup, her eyes follow- ing the marching men; did any of them think he might die? Many of them would likely die. She reminded herself this was the Cru- sade; they would go straight to heaven.

Lilia cried, "There he is!" She lifted her scarf and waved it. "Rou- quin! My lord Rouquin!"

In a loud clopping of hooves more knights were passing, among them the Queen's cousin, his head turned to talk to the swarthy man riding beside him. Johanna sipped from the cup, gave it back to Edythe, and pointed. "That's his officer, Mercadier." Rouquin paid no heed to the women, although Lilia screamed his name again and fluttered her scarf above her head.

Johanna said, amused, "She shouldn't set her lures for him; he's light with women, he'll give her nothing but a lot of trouble." She took the cup and drained it. "Well, I think we're done here. Let's go back to the palace."

．　．　．

Johanna was receiving the important local men as one by one they came in to submit to Richard's rule. She wore a gown of blue silk stitched with gold and a gold crown on her head. Under the full skirt she slipped off the shoes, which pinched her feet. When she had seen a few of the Cypriots, accepted their tribute, and proclaimed them under Richard's protection, she called for a moment to herself, the steward shut the doors, and the pages brought out dishes of dates and bread and wine. Her women sat around her and they ate.

Lilia said, "These people have such lovely clothes."

Johanna had been thinking much the same thing, that the ordinary merchants of this little island were more richly arrayed than even she, the Queen of Sicily. "It's all the fabrics, which are very fine. I hear the Emperor himself oversees the weaving of it in Constantinople."

Berengaria came in with her women, and they made room so she could sit beside Johanna. They had not yet decided the issue of precedence, but Johanna meant to keep a strong hand on this and watched for her chance. Gracia said, "My lady, I have heard there is a market now, in the town, down by the beach."

"Oh," Johanna said, clapping her hands, "we should go." She turned to Edythe; the doctor had found a book somewhere and was reading it in her lap. "You'll come. You said you needed honey."

Edythe straightened up, her eyes wide. "Yes. I will. Thank you, my lady." She closed the book, but Johanna marked that she kept a finger between the pages, holding her place.

Johanna turned toward her brother's wife. "Will you join us, my lady Berengaria?"

The little Queen straightened, blinking. The blue veins showed at her temples; she seemed frail enough to break. She said, "Go out, to street?" as if Johanna were proposing she fly.

"To the market," Johanna said. "We'll buy everything they have. Hear all the news."

Berengaria lowered her eyes. "I stay, lady. My place here."

Johanna glanced meaningfully at her own women. "Very well." They all turned pitying looks on Berengaria, except Edythe, who was staring down at the book in her lap. Johanna laughed, and when the woman twitched upright, looking guilty, she nudged her.

"Oh, read it, my dear, go on. I shall see you happy." She clapped her hands together. "We shall be a merry band in the Holy Land, I promise you." She turned her gaze on Lilia. "You know, King Philip Augustus is there." She put much into her voice as she said the name.

Even without looking at her, she felt Edythe startle at that. But when she glanced over, Edythe was looking down at her book again.

Gracia said, "Yes, he is supposed to be." Lilia giggled, her hand to her mouth.

Johanna turned to Berengaria. "The King of France was in Palermo before we left, and he wooed me so ardently my brother sent me away." She and Lilia traded another meaningful look; Lilia had been much involved in that trysting.

Berengaria tipped her head to one side. "My King want not you Queen of France?"

"You don't understand." Johanna gave her a sideways, disdainful look. "They are enemies, Philip and my brother. Philip wants my brother's lands. Richard wouldn't take the cross at all unless Philip did, too, so he couldn't meddle behind his back." She wagged her head. Let Berengaria know how little she understood, and how much Johanna herself was part of it.

Berengaria seemed not to be noticing that. Her pale eyes were thoughtful. "You did not be Queen of France."

Johanna said, "When you see him, you'll know why I'm not."

Berengaria murmured. She had brought in some handwork and turned to it now, one maid holding out a threaded needle, the other a band of cloth. Johanna felt that this had slipped away from her, but she couldn't say how. She turned back to Edythe.

"What is that, some scripture?"

Edythe straightened, lifting the book so that Johanna could see it: a plain board-bound book with a Latin name. "It's an herbal, my lady. I found it in the chapel library."

"Oh. Well, excellent. There's a library? These Greeks. Come, now, take all this away, I must open my court again."

*   *   *

Edythe bowed in the doorway. "My lady, you sent for me?"

Berengaria stood up, dumping a heap of cloth off her lap. She had cast off her shawls, at least, and wore a plain, light gown. She chewed at her lower lip, her eyes fretful. "Yes. Lady Edyt'. Come in."

Edythe hovered in the doorway. "My lady, I—"

"Please." The girl put out her hands toward her. "Help me. Help me."

Edythe went to her and took her hands. "Tell me, my lady."

"I hear—someone say when all here is well—" Berengaria blinked at the effort of finding the words. "We go again on the ship. I—I—"

Edythe took the small, damp, fine-boned hands. "My lady, it's true. When the King has taken Cyprus, we will all sail to the Holy Land. But—"

"No ship. I stay here. No ship." The sleek, terrified eyes searched her face. "Please."

Edythe wanted suddenly to gather her into her arms, to shelter her like a child. Instead she led her back to the chair. She said, "My lady, it will only take one day. Just across the sea to Tyre. There won't be a storm this time. We will spend the night on land."

Berengaria clung to her forearms. Her blinking lashes were full of tears. "I hate Johanna. She hate me. I alone. All alone."

Gently Edythe pressed the little Queen down into the chair. She understood this, after the terrible sea journey here; sometimes the idea of getting on a ship again made her heart gallop. But there was no use for it. They would take Berengaria along like baggage, if she wanted or not. Some anger stirred in Edythe at this, but she forced it away. The thing was to help Berengaria.

Berengaria said, "Help me."

"My lady, you aren't alone. And Johanna doesn't hate you, she's only high-spirited. I—I will find a potion." The herbal she had found here was full of recipes.

The little Queen chewed her lip; the tears spilled down her cheeks. "Something against seasickness. And—and—to make you easier of mind." She knew nothing that did that, not without terrible consequences.

"Please," Berengaria said. Her hands still lay on Edythe's forearms.

"I will," Edythe said. "I promise. I will."

·   ·   ·

The market stretched under its awnings all along the top of the beach, rows of open stalls stacked with bread and jars of oil and heaps of onions, chickens squawking helplessly from cages, folded stacks of cloth. Edythe had brought the herbal; she trailed after Johanna, looking for the right vendor.

Johanna was buying something everywhere she stopped, and the merchants crowded toward her; the two men-at-arms with her stood forward with their pikes to hold them away. Johanna lifted an embroidered shawl from a pile on a little crowded counter. The man behind it bobbed and bowed to her, grinning.

"Lady—" He spoke some French; they all spoke a little French now. "Lady like? More here. Many many."

Johanna haggled with him, using her fingers, her hands, nods and wags of her head more than words. Edythe found a little stall heaped with bunches and sprigs of herbs and turned and beckoned to Gracia, with the basket.

Gracia came over; Edythe bought a jar of honey, some green maid's-apron, thyme leaves. When she had put these in the basket, she held out the herbal to the vendor.

"Zingiber? Where can I find this?"

His brown finger poked at the drawing, the leaves and stems. "Zingiber."

"Yes! Where can I find some?"

He shrugged, his whole body seeming to rise up and then down, shoulders, eyebrows, hairline. She paid him and went on after Johanna.

Beside her, Gracia nudged her and nodded toward Lilia, who was dawdling along, trying to catch the eye of one of the men-at-arms. Edythe laughed and exchanged a look with Gracia, who shook her head, her lips pursed.

Onward, at a stall selling scents and unguents, the Queen had found someone who spoke better French; he uncorked a bottle and held it under her nose and said, "King Richard glorious. Make—" He swept his hand into the air. "All Cyprus him."

"Good. Then we will be leaving soon. Have you heard anything about Isaac?"

"Isaac," the man said. He was offering her another bottle, withdrawing the glass stopper with flourish. "Isaac noplaces." He spoke with force. "Richard glorious. Richard lord now. No Isaac. No matter Isaac." His voice was edged. "All taxes Richard."

Johanna said, "Good." She pointed to the bottle in his hand. "I want that." She opened her purse and began to count out the silver.

Edythe leaned across the counter with the herbal. "Zingiber? Where can I find this?"

The man stared at the drawing, looked at her, and rubbed his belly. "Zingiber."

"Yes! Yes. For stomach ills."

He pointed, not into the market, but up to the town. "*Iatros*. Sick house. *Hospil*."

"A hospital," she said, relieved, and straightened. Johanna gave her new bottle to Gracia to tuck into the basket.

Beside them, Lilia said, with a sigh, "I can't wait for the men to come back."

Johanna snorted at her. "Yes, my dear, we know that."

· · ·

The King of England, now master also of Cyprus, sat on a balcony in Famagusta; the sun had just set. He had taken Cyprus with no trouble, and he expected to have Acre and then Jerusalem soon as well. That would require some planning and force, but he foresaw nothing that would stop him. He looked at the man on the other couch, who was part of the planning.

"Conrad did hold Tyre against Saladin, after Hattin, when everywhere else in the kingdom went down. He must have some wits."

"A child could hold Tyre," Humphrey de Toron said. He lounged on the divan, his legs stretched out, his long hands still. "It's on a rock just off the coast, with a connecting mole no wider than a wagon axle. After Hattin, the kingdom was in chaos. Conrad took the opportunity to make himself great. He cares nothing for the Crusade; he works always in his own interest. He refused to let Queen Sibylla and King Guy into the city, back when Sibylla was certainly the rightful Queen, and he would not help them against Acre. It's said he treats with Saladin."

Richard had a lute in his lap, his legs propped on a stool in front of him. He plucked a run of notes from it. "Yet he's got some powerful support, those northern barons, the Church. You've known Saladin awhile."

"Some years. He's a man of broad tastes. He loves poetry and music as much as war. I've always enjoyed talking to him. He's a Kurd, also, not an Arab, not a Turk. These are important distinctions."

"Then how did he become Sultan?"

"Quick thinking, loyalty in the right places, and a few well-chosen murders. A point of some interest to you: He prefers to fight on Fridays."

"You were his hostage?"

"Briefly. It was not unpleasant."

"You speak to him in Arabic."

"Yes. He doesn't speak French."

A page stepped just inside the curtain and bowed. "My lord Philip de Rançun."

Humphrey stood and backed to the wall, deferring to the King's cousin. Rouquin walked in, glanced once at Humphrey, and faced Richard. He had obviously just gotten off his horse. He still wore his mail, but the hood hung down his back and his short hair stood on end. Richard laid the lute down beside him and put his feet on the floor. They had not talked much since Richard forced him into the army with Guy de Lusignan, and the King was a little unsure of Rouquin's temper.

His cousin did not bow. "I've got Isaac trapped in a monastery out on the northeastern cape. He was trying to run to the mainland, but now he's asking to talk. If you want Guy to do that, you'll have to send to him; he's in the west somewhere chasing his tail."

"Good work," Richard said, mildly. He sat down again, set one foot on the stool, and picked up the lute. "I knew you'd get him."

"It wasn't easy."

Richard smiled wider and thumbed a laughing note out of the lute. His left hand moved on the frets. "That's why I sent you."

Rouquin grunted at him. Richard flicked a glance at Humphrey and back to his cousin. He said, "Guy was useless?"

"Worse," Rouquin said. "He cannot make his mind up. I rode out on him."

Richard shrugged. There was another rumor, but this sounded more like the truth. "Still. We need him to have some respect again, when we get to the Holy Land. Where there will be honor enough even for you, Rouq'. Be patient. You are my right arm; I can't do anything without you."

"God, you talk," Rouquin said. He scratched in his beard; he was frowning, but Richard could see that he understood the purpose now. He had used up his fury on Isaac anyway. He said, "What do you want me to do now?"

"Go down to Akrotiri and fetch the women back here. We sail as soon as Isaac's secured."

"Why do you have me herding women?"

"Maybe they'll teach you better manners," Richard said.

Rouquin snorted at him again and left, brushing through the curtain. Richard studied the empty doorway a moment. "But probably not," he said.

Humphrey de Toron came back to the divan across from his. "No, I think he is rough by trade."

Richard laughed. His vow of chastity was already wearing on him. But he meant it, even with the familiar lust rising in him, and he lowered his gaze from the young man opposite him and studied his hands on the lute. A vow was something serious, and God would not yield if he broke his. He could keep his hands off Humphrey. Meanwhile it was pleasant enough to talk, and useful besides. He watched his fingers move on the throat of the lute, up and down.

"Tell me more about Saladin."

Three

SAILING TO TYRE

Edythe bit off a little of the pale brown root she had bought from the Greek hospital, and it burned her tongue. From that and the strong taste she guessed its power, but she knew Berengaria would never take it plain. Finally she mashed it up and steeped it in a flask of oxymel, the tonic of honey and vinegar she gave Johanna when she felt gloomy, and Gracia for her cough. That tasted awful, and Berengaria would only swallow a few sips.

But it was enough. Now they were gliding over the sea, halfway to Tyre. Under the awning by the mainmast, Berengaria sat placidly in the midst of her women; being married, she could wear her hair in a different way, and she had her servants combing and braiding it and arranging it in loops around her head, pinned in place with ebony combs and big silver clips.

Edythe and Johanna and Johanna's other women sat on the foredeck, where there was a little breeze. The wide triangular sails of the galley spread above them, billowing and shaking in the light wind, and the oars swung on either side with their steady creak. Edythe loved the sway of all the oars together, the power and grace that seemed to lift the long ship across the tops of the waves.

Johanna said, "Whatever you gave her, it seems to have worked."

"It's been calm, though," Edythe said.

In truth the sea around them was mild in the sunlight. The rest of the ships stroked along around them, scores of galleys big and small, stretching to the horizon. Richard's fleet filled the sea; with all their prows aimed in the same direction, all the oars swinging at once, they seemed unstoppable, as if when they reached the land, they would just go on over it, striding on their wooden legs.

Johanna said, "Edythe, I've meant to tell you this. You have been an excellent servant to me, to us all, and the Crusade hardly begun."

"My lady," Edythe said. "The Queen Mother bade me do it."

"My mother is very wise." Johanna lowered her voice. "Tell me—I want to know—there is a story of how you came to be with her."

Edythe went stiff all over, her mouth dry. She did not want to rehearse this; every time she said it, every new ear that heard it, made the story more real. Johanna watched her steadily. She could not look away. She said, "I—I was in a nunnery, in England. There was—there was a man—I ran away." Her ears and throat felt red. She was blushing all over. She hated this. "The Queen took me in. So I—" Now at least she was climbing up again onto a solid shore of truth. "I owe the Queen my life."

Johanna nodded and put her hand on Edythe's arm. "This agrees with what I have been told. I understand. A young girl can be misled. As I said, you have made yourself dear to me. So when this is over, when we are home again, I will find you a noble husband, and we will dower you. Whatever happened before, I shall make you a fine marriage. I promise you."

Edythe lifted Johanna's hand and kissed it, more to hide her face than in homage. She struggled to school her expression. She should look happy. Grateful. "My lady, you are most kind, I hardly deserve . . ." That came out as a whisper. She looked out over the sea.

She should want this. The weight was the weight of belonging. A well-born husband would bring her a title, a home of her own. Children, with names.

But then the bad story was true. The wrong name became right. She was losing something. She wasn't even sure what it was. She would have to be happy with it. She said, again, "Thank you, my lady," and heard her own voice croak out like a raven.

Behind her, Gracia coughed again. Glad of the distraction, Edythe turned and frowned at the other woman, and the plump face creased in a smile.

"Don't worry," Gracia said. "It's only the same old thing."

. . .

Johanna, with Edythe at her side, went swiftly across the beach; the great galleys were already drawing up in the shallows. The resounding crash of a ramp falling made Johanna start and look around. On the ships men shouted to the shore, and the others there answered. The neighing of horses mixed with the frantic trampling beats of their hoofs on the ramps. She urged Edythe up the beach ahead of her, toward safety.

On their left, on its rock in the sea, the great walled city of Tyre stood, black against the fading sunset. Pennants flapped from its peaked towers. It seemed a single impenetrable mass, a dark hulk in the gloom.

Shouting, a man at a dead run led a string of horses by, and Johanna stopped, one hand on Edythe's arm, waiting until the way was clear. The porters were hauling baggage off a beached skiff and piling it in the stalky grass above the tide line.

Beyond the windblown sand, palm trees sprouted up in their

elegant arcs, a dozen square stone houses around them. Out of these houses several women were hurrying, bundles over their shoulders. Johanna saw her brother standing under the closest palm tree and turned that way, and then Rouquin strode up to her, trailing some other lords.

"We've ordered a tent for you, Jo, you and the rest of your gaggle. Stay here, Richard's busy."

"A tent," she said, startled, and turned her gaze on the city with its jagged spires looming on its rock at the end of the beach. "Aren't we going into Tyre?"

"They won't let us in," Rouquin said, and behind him, among the other men, there was a chatter of rage.

"What?" she said.

"Conrad of Montferrat and King Philip have refused to let us enter Tyre."

The Grand Master of the Templars pushed forward. "It's an insult, to us—to the King especially." He gripped Rouquin's arm and bawled into his ear. "You must call for an attack. He'll heed you." Rouquin shook him off with a hard look.

"Attack?" Johanna said, alarmed.

"We can storm the city," said another of the men behind Rouquin. "Conrad is unlikely to have more than his personal guard. We'll crush him like a worm."

Johanna said, "I won't hear this. Rouquin, show me our tent."

He gave the barest glance at the other men. "The King will hold a council tonight, talk there." He led the women off down the beach.

Johanna glanced at him; she could see he was angry. She said, "They would attack Christians! It's all mad."

He gave her a hard look. "Stay out of this, Jo. Don't make trouble."

"I'm not making trouble, I'm telling the truth. Wait." Her eye caught on the row of village women who had spread out their bundles under the next palm tree, offering fruit and bread, cheese and fish for sale. "Let's get food first."

.   .   .

Berengaria said, "I want good place, bed, room, city. Up there. Why we have no hall?"

Busy with the work of making the room ready, Edythe pretended not to hear her. Berengaria was sitting on a fringed cushion at the back of the tent; when Edythe made no response, she looked away and her hand clenched into a fist. Edythe stacked the linen on Johanna's bed. Outside, nearby, a yell went up from the crowd of men around the King, down by the palm trees; they were holding their council. In here, the pages were going around the space lighting lamps, and in a moment the tent would be hot and smoky.

But the warm light sweetened everything. The work done, for the moment, Edythe went back to the corner, where Gracia was sitting on a cot, and said, "Are you all right?"

The elder maid's eyes were hollow and her skin flaky. She had been coughing all day. She looked haggard. She said, "Oh, I'm just tired." Edythe put one hand to her cheek and felt a flush of heat. Then Gracia started to cough and did not stop for a while and finally hacked out a thick green glob.

Alarmed, Edythe said, "You must lie down. I'll get you some wine." She stood up; she had some feverfew and rosemary to put in the wine, but this was getting past what she could do. Gracia's body was wracked with an excess of humors, the cold and moist phlegm, the hot and dry fever of the choler. Soon the other humors might swell out of balance too and find their own escape, and ruin Gracia as they went.

The tent was crowded with people and chests, and nobody knew where anything was. Finally she got a cup of wine and mixed the

herbs in, but no one had lit a brazier—it was hot, maybe there would
be no brazier—and she took the wine back to Gracia without warming it.

Lilia and the Navarrese women were fluttering around Berengaria. Johanna stood alone in the middle of the room, listening to
the men yelling in the distance, a frown on her face.

A page came in the door.

"The Queen of Jerusalem!"

There went up a collective gasp. Falling silent, everybody in the
tent tuned to face the opening, even Berengaria. Three women came
in through the drawn back flap, maids in their dark rich dress and
bowed coifed heads, and then a lovely girl.

At the sight of her, they all gasped. She was as beautiful as an
icon. Her skin was smooth and white, her blue eyes wide under the
plucked arches of her brows. The layered blue satin of her gown was
trimmed with clusters of little white pearls and silver lace ribbons,
so that as she moved the cloth whispered and winked around her.
Her coif was of white silk and over it there fit a simple gold circlet
of a crown.

As she came farther into the tent everyone bowed, except Johanna,
so the newcomer knew at once who she was. She came to Johanna
with her hands out.

"My sister—for so I feel you are my sister—"

Johanna said, "Isabella, we are sisters all." She drew the girl into
her embrace, and Edythe, behind them, saw the tears in the eyes of
the Queen of Jerusalem.

Isabella drew back, her hands on Johanna's sleeves. "Lionheart's
sister," she said. "I should have guessed you would be a lioness." She
blinked, her eyes sleek; she looked sad, even in her youth and beauty.
"I only could get away because all the men are in council. I can't stay
long."

Johanna said, surprised, "Your lord came down here—"

"No, no." The girl's voice was uneven. Her white hands were clasped at her waist. "They are holding council in Tyre, also, do you doubt that? My—Conrad is there, scheming. But I came to tell you—to warn you—"

Johanna said, "Come sit. The rest of you, go. Edythe, bring us wine to drink. The rest, go!" She led Isabella into a close side of the tent where they could talk unheard. The rest of the women stood back, and Edythe went for wine.

When she returned, the two Queens sat with their heads tilted together. Isabella was saying, "Don't believe what they tell you. What anybody tells you. I love Humphrey. I hate Conrad. Conrad hates everybody else."

Johanna took a cup from Edythe. "We'll restore your rightful husband to you, my lady." She handed one cup to Isabella and took the other from Edythe. With her eyes she sent Edythe off also.

Isabella was saying, "No. Humphrey and I will never be together again. But it is Conrad I warn you against. Conrad is double-hearted. Black-minded, and wicked."

Edythe moved away from all of them; she went to Gracia, now lying on a pallet at the far side of the tent. All the other people in here had their backs to her, rapt, watching the two Queens whispering gossip over their wine, while ignored in their shadow Gracia sank into disease.

Edythe gave the older woman wine and oxymel to drink and held her up while she coughed. The fever was steadily mounting, Gracia's skin dry and harsh, her eyes dull as stones. Edythe wiped her mouth, and putting her ear flat against Gracia's back she heard the squeaks and gurgles and rasps of the humors corrupted. She thumped Gracia's back to get her to cough again. If Gracia could rid her body of enough of the cold, moist humor, the rest might come back into balance.

Edythe's heart knocked in her chest. She felt helpless against this. Although her arm was tight around the maid, she felt as if Gracia were miles away, and drifting farther every moment.

Now Isabella was leaving, as swiftly as she had come, with a kiss for Johanna and an embrace, and then with her women out the door. Lilia came at once across the tent to Gracia.

"Is she all right?"

"No," Edythe said.

Lilia wrung her hands. "It's this terrible place. It's this terrible place." She looked around the tent as at a cave hung with bats.

Johanna was pacing nervously around the room. When she heard that, she came toward them.

"What is it?"

"The cough," Edythe said, and put a hand on Gracia's shoulder. "She's not well."

"She always coughs," Johanna said. She wound her hands together. Outside, the men's voices rose again in a thunderous howl. Johanna said, "Mother was right, the whole Crusade is cursed. They call this the Holy Land, but it turns them into devils. The first thing they want to do is kill each other."

Berengaria came forward, her gaze on the sick maid. To Edythe, she said, "I help. I pray. I pray for Gracia."

Edythe smiled at her and touched her arm. Johanna flung her arms up.

"As if that will do any good." Her gaze was steadily on Edythe. "Come with me."

"My lady—Gracia—"

"Let Lilia care for her awhile. I—" Johanna's tongue slipped over her lips. "I must talk to my brother. Come." She got a page and sent him on ahead, and took Edythe by the hand.

Edythe gave Lilia a single, pleading look and followed Johanna out of the tent. She guessed Johanna needed to tell Richard what had just happened, that the Queen of Jerusalem had suddenly appeared. A great crowd stood all around the center of the camp. Night had fallen; the dim glow of lamps showed through the cloth of the three other tents near theirs. Johanna slid her arm through Edythe's and held her close to her, and led her toward the King's tent.

Packs of armed men surrounded it, and now more men, shouting, streamed out of the tent, arms shaking in the air and feet stamping. The council was over. Moving through the crowd felt like being in the midst of a great jumble of moving rocks, the men stirring around them in their mail and shouting in their ears. The page went ahead, his voice unheard, and the women had to sidle and creep and edge their way forward to the tent door.

There the page went in before them, but Johanna followed before she was announced, with Edythe on her heels.

The tent was all but empty. Heaps of gear stood around in it, saddles and lances, lumpy sacks and barrels and the treasure chest, a bed back by the far wall, the middle ground trampled to dust, one lamp burning. Richard stood in the light. Johanna flew through the room toward him.

"What are you doing? Is it true? Are you going to attack Tyre? This is folly, Richard—you must see—"

He said, "We are not attacking Tyre. We are going to Acre in the morning."

That took some of the wind out of Johanna, but she pushed ahead, her voice swelling. "You must call off the Crusade. This is evil—what is happening is evil—"

"Call it off," he said, with a laugh. "We just started." He turned to Edythe. "You can go."

She bowed and went back, as Johanna turned and watched her

with a pleading look on her face. There was no way to refuse the King, and Edythe slipped out the tent door. Behind her, Johanna's voice rose again, less certain.

Edythe lingered outside the doorway. She had expected Johanna to tell her brother about the sudden appearance of the Queen of Jerusalem, and it bothered her that she had not. The crowd was thinning, the men, still shouting, still angry, going off by twos and threes toward their camps. She looked toward Johanna's tent; she should go back to Gracia. But the idea revolted her: the close, dirty, sweltering space, the moaning women, the helplessness. Her mind seethed, too full, and every thought a question. She wiped her hand over her face. She could not help Gracia; she needed to calm down. The long rolling of the surf drew her, and she went down toward the shore, drawn toward the sea, away from the other people, searching for some dark and quiet place where she could think.

·   ·   ·

Rouquin walked down along the shore, past the curved prows of the galleys beached there, his back to the city on its rock. His gut was churning. The unruly council screaming to attack had heated his blood. He longed to storm the city that refused him. Richard had cut this idea off from the beginning. They were going to Acre. They were going to Acre in the morning. The other men roared and screeched about honor and respect and the small garrison at Tyre, and Richard stood there utterly unmoved.

Rouquin had said nothing. On his own he would have seized Tyre, but he was Richard's man and so he had to swallow the King's decision. This tore at him and he walked past the high sterns of the galleys, along the white slop of the surf. The moon hung in the west like a sleepy old eye. The night air was cool on his face and his temper ebbed a little. Taking Tyre might not be so easy, anyway; the Saracens had failed.

In the shadow of one of the ships, something moved.

He wheeled, his hand on his sword hilt. "Who's there?"

The dark prow rose up over him; in the distance, they were shouting again. Someone was standing in the shadow under the prow. He went in closer, drawing his sword. "Come out! Let me see you!"

"My lord." Johanna's woman came forward, the doctor, her hands at her sides. The moonlight washed over her. "It's only me."

He relaxed, pushing the sword back into its sheath. "What are you doing here?" He remembered from Cyprus how she went around by herself, and he was minded to show her why that was a risk. He felt a stir of excitement in his gut. Richard did not allow whores with the army, and in Cyprus he had been fighting all the time.

She did not seem frightened; she stood straight and high headed, her eyes direct. She said, "I wanted to think. It's so loud. What happened in the council?"

He said, "Nothing much." The bad feeling it had given him came back to him and his temper seethed up, crowding out his other interest. "I don't see how we can turn meekly away from this. This is an insult to everybody, to the whole Crusade."

She said, "Do you know that the Queen of Jerusalem came to see Johanna?"

That jarred him. "Really. Isabella? Alone? What did she want?"

"I didn't hear." The wind blew wisps of her hair loose round the edge of her coif.

"Why are you telling me this?"

"Because it bothers me." She gave him a startled look. "If they won't let us in, how could she get out? Could this be a trick?" She frowned a little. "Why should it be a secret? I have to go back; Johanna will miss me."

He grunted at her. She was quick, he thought, and probably right, or at least right to be suspicious. He felt the churning around them of cross purposes. He longed to get to Acre at last, where there would be honest fighting, where he would know who the enemy was, no more of all this boiling undercurrent. "Go back," he said. "Probably it's nothing. They're women, they like to cluck together. She could know a lot of ways to get around Conrad."

She muttered something. Turning, she crossed the beach toward the Queens' tent. As she went she poked the stray hairs back under her coif. He watched her go until she was out of sight among the tents, wondering what was going on.

* * *

In the morning Gracia could scarcely open her eyes, and when she coughed, the green stuff that came up was streaked with red. Edythe gave Berengaria more of the zingiber root in a lot of wine. They got back onto a galley and joined the fleet moving south along the coast. Richard as usual was on another ship, and the Queens' galley went along well behind the leaders. Edythe took Gracia up onto the foredeck, away from Berengaria under the awning, and sat helplessly beside her.

Johanna and her other maid, Lilia, joined them. The Queen had at last realized what was happening to her dear old woman, and sat there holding Gracia's hand and moistening her lips with a cloth dipped in wine. Lilia prayed. Edythe thought either one as useful as anything she could think of.

"Here," she said, after a while, "we have to turn her over. Help me."

When they turned Gracia onto her side, she threw up. That at least kept them busy for a while. The sun was rising into the bleached white arch of the sky; Johanna ordered a shade rigged for them, and two of the oarsmen off duty suspended a cloak from the mast stay. Edythe looked out at the long low coast they followed: brown, featureless except for some palm trees, here and there a cluster of little square huts and some boats. In the distance blue hillsides rose, the tallest capped with snow.

She thought, *This is the land where Jesus walked.* If she were a true Christian, that would move her. She helped Johanna slide a cushion under Gracia's head; the Queen was weeping. Johanna looked up once and said, "Why did we come? Why did we do this mad thing?"

Beneath them, Gracia stirred. Edythe put her hand on her, amazed at this; she had thought the woman in a death sleep. She did not open her eyes. She whispered, "Here. Die here." Her lips moved, but nothing came out. Her cheeks were sunken. She whispered, "Go to heaven."

"Oh, Gracia—" Johanna bent over her, sobbing, and daubed her lips with the wine-soaked cloth. Edythe turned away, heart-stricken. That was the faith she did not have, the fulfillment where she was empty. Lilia crossed herself, and she did also, but it gave her nothing.

In Jerusalem, maybe she would know.

Somewhere ahead, a trumpet sounded, faint in the wind. Sunk in her grief, she paid no heed at first, but then from the front of the fleet more horns blared, and a great shout went up.

She lifted her head. "Did you hear that?"

Johanna, overcome with weeping, lay down beside Gracia with her arms around her, their heads side by side. Edythe went up into the V of the prow.

Ahead of her dozens of ships, their great sails furled up on the tilted yards, rowed through the flat blue sea. The horn sounded again, far down there. She squinted, shaded her eyes with her hand, trying to make out what was going on.

A confusion of wooden castles, masts, and oars. Out there ahead of them a galley bigger than any of theirs was moving broadside to their course. Their passage lay athwart the wind, but the strange galley plowed forward under a great round-bellied mass of canvas. Edythe looked toward the coast, curving out ahead of them into a jutting headland.

On this headland, yellow walls rose above the sea, and behind them, buildings, roofs, the narrow spikes of towers. The fleet cruised steadily past, a league of sea between, but the big galley was going toward the headland city. In the front of the fleet, where Richard's ships met the strange galley, they were shouting, and down in the stern of the women's ship, somebody was calling orders.

She stood back, tired of looking. By her feet anyway lay the greater mystery. She went back to sit down next to the dying woman and took her hand.

Gracia's fingers tightened a little around hers. Edythe felt her living strength, the response of her touch. In the distance the shrieks and horns grew louder, but the air around her seemed to grow still. Slowly the fingers in her grasp slackened, and as much as she held tight they lay loose, and then she knew Gracia's soul was gone.

·   ·   ·

Richard said, under his breath, "French. Not likely."

His eyes were on the big galley sailing across their path; the strange ship had just suddenly unspooled a long blue banner from its mast, its tail slit into three spikes and a white cross on its belly. Rouquin gave a snort. "If it is, they don't know their own flags."

"Just so." Richard swung toward him. "We're going to take her. Get some archers up in that castle." He reached out and grabbed the page with the horn. "Sound the alert."

Rouquin strode back amidships, where Mercadier was already coming toward him. The Brabanter cried, "Should we put on mail?"

"There's a chance we'll wind up in the water," Rouquin said, and went by him without pausing, toward the sterncastle where the weapons were. "I'd rather not do that wearing twenty pounds of iron." He threw open the sterncastle hatch and began dragging out bows. All around the horns were shrieking, and on the crowded deck the hands were lowering a small boat over the side; men swarmed around him, grabbing weapons.

A crossbow in one hand and a small round shield in the other, he sprinted back to the amidships castle, taller and more rickety than the one in the stern. Slinging the shield on his back, he climbed one-handed up the crossbeams to the top level. Six of his men swarmed after.

Their galley was stroking down hard on the galley with the fake French flag, and all around them small boats from the fleet were scooting forward through the waves. The pitch and roll of the ship was worse on top of the castle. Rouquin braced himself against the mainmast, got his foot into the stirrup of the bow, slid a bolt into the box, and cocked it. He threw a quick glance down toward the foredeck, where Richard stood pointing ahead.

Then the ship began to heel over, and Rouquin grabbed for the mast as the galley swung broadside to the fake French ship.

On the enemy's raised afterdeck he could see men running up a little catapult. Around him his men were lifting their bows; three knelt and the other three stood up behind them. Two of the small boats bouncing over the waves had almost reached the big galley.

The catapult shot a hail of objects into the air, and on the small boats men thrust their arms up and cowered. Rouquin aimed his bow and pulled the trigger. The string twanged. His men fired with him; their bolts disappeared into the next volley from the catapult, which pelted the small boats below. One of the little boats turned turtle.

For a moment the two galleys slid along side by side, moving in opposite directions, bow to stern. He loaded the crossbow again. On the other ship a man in a fancy hat stood on the afterdeck and, deciding this was the captain, Rouquin swung the crossbow toward him, and then another spray of missiles hurtled through the air at him.

He ducked, trying to get as much of himself as possible behind the shield, which now seemed smaller than a button. Stones and arrows clattered down around him, a jar that broke and splattered oil, a pronged iron caltrop. Something hit his shoulder, hard. The other men yelled, and two crumpled and fell over the side of the castle to the deck below. Rouquin swung up again, leveled the crossbow, and shot at the other galley's captain, gliding away from him.

The oily deck under him rocked and yawed, and he slid toward the edge. For a moment there was nothing between him and the water, twenty feet down. The other men were clinging to the high side of the castle deck; the ship rolled the other way and, with a scream, one man dove headlong. Skating on the oil, Rouquin lunged for the mast and fell flat. The blaring of the horns and the shouts of the men below him suddenly doubled. He twisted to look toward the enemy galley. Small boats surrounded her, closing in. They had her now, and he let out a yell, exuberant.

But a plume of dark smoke was rising from her open hatch. His ship was trying to turn, to cross the bigger vessel's stern. Rouquin shouted, got to his knees, still holding the crossbow; he had lost the shield. The other three men staggered up around him. He fumbled for a bolt. The smoke rising from the enemy galley flattened on the wind, flowing east. Under the dark plume, men were streaming up through the hatches, running across the deck, and diving over the rails. Rouquin realized at once what this meant, even before the big galley began to list.

"They're scuttling her!" He scampered down the side of the castle again, nearly losing the crossbow, and went toward the prow.

Richard stood there with his hands at his sides, watching the big galley sink. The small boats were clawing frantically away from her. Her prow rose into the air and her stern disappeared into the sea; for an instant she hung there half in and half out of the water. The surface around her was dotted with heads and pieces of cargo. Then the ship slid down and away, taking some of the closer swimmers with her. The sea boiled over her grave.

Richard said, "I guess we took care of that."

Rouquin felt the wave from the sinking ship roll away under their keel. "I guess so." He uncocked the bow and took the bolt out.

.   .   .

Johanna said, "I never thought . . . you never think, do you. That in the end everybody dies." She wiped her eyes. "A thousand things I should have said to her, now I'll never say." She wiped her eyes again.

Edythe's arm was around her shoulders. She had covered Gracia up in a blanket; they would bury her in a churchyard in Acre. The Queens' ship had turned, was holding its place with the oars set in the water. Looking out across the railing, she could see ahead of them, where they were fighting again.

The first rank of Richard's fleet had surrounded the strange galley; horns were blowing, and she thought she saw things flying through the air. Arrows, rocks. Smoke rose in a thick black plume from the strange ship. The trumpet blew again. People were screaming. It looked as if the big galley were sinking. She leaned on Johanna, wondering what was going on.

•   •   •

All around the fleet, the small boats of the Crusaders were hauling the sunken galley's floating cargo up out of the sea. With oars they thrust off the Saracen sailors trying to climb on board. Rouquin stood by the rail, and Richard slung one arm over his shoulders.

"Look!" With his free hand Richard pointed across the galley, out over the rail. "Look!"

Rouquin thrust the crossbow into a squire's hands and turned to see. Their galley was coming around to due east, standing well wide of the headland there. They had reached Acre, the city they had sworn to save.

Reefs and rocks cluttered the shallows along the headland and made a foamy crease out into the sea, and they were sailing well wide of it. As their angle changed, so the sun-gilded city on its headland swung past them. Now they were thrashing into a broad bay, cradled on the north in the arm of the headland. The far shore stretched straight south into the haze. The city on the headland stood silent, like cliffs against the sky, but from the shore across the bay a distant yelling rose.

The open beach there was packed with a solid mass of cheering people. They waved banners, they held up crosses. Those were his people, the Crusade. He flung one arm up, saluting them. And all along the beach, in a vast teeming motion, they threw their arms up in answer.

They were cheering for him. For him and Richard, for sinking the Saracen ship, for coming to save Acre. Richard's arm hung over his shoulder. They swept on, at the head of the fleet, toward the welcoming mob before them.

. . .

Johanna said, "This is what he did at Messina; he had trumpeters and drums and lots of flags, and him up there by himself on the prow of his ship, like an old statue. There were mobs of people. Nobody could hear anything, it was so loud."

Edythe had met Johanna in Messina, long after Richard's famous entry into the conquered city. Now, in the dying afternoon light, as the women got off the skiff onto the sand, the bang of the drums and the shrill shriek of horns sounded far away. They had come to land well up the beach from Richard's entry. Several porters were waiting for them, and a tall young lord in a broad-brimmed hat.

"Henry!" Johanna cried, and rushed to him. "You've grown so."

The young man swept off his hat. He bowed to her properly, his face wide with his smile, and then embraced her. "Aunt Jo. Richard sent me; I'm here to take you to your quarters." He turned and spoke rapidly to the other men, who went onto the skiff, muttering to each other. Edythe herded the other women to one side while they carried out Gracia's body, crossing themselves with every other step.

Seeing her maid, stiff now in her wraps of cloaks, Johanna burst into weeping again, her hands pressed together. The young man, Henry, said, "Oh, Jo, just a maid," and, taking her arm, led them off up a trail.

Edythe put her hands together. The death still worked on her, as if Gracia's passing had torn a hole through a necessary wall in her mind. Among the other women, she plodded after Johanna. They were not part of the joyous entry over on the beach, where now the cheers doubled, and doubled again.

That must be Richard coming ashore, that sudden piercing intensity of yells. She stumbled along the sand after this Henry, who was getting Johanna to talk, to smile even, with Gracia's body not ten feet in front of them. Henry cast a lingering glance toward the swelling uproar to the south. Clearly he wished he were there and not here.

"That was very brave, sinking that ship. She was bringing supplies to the Saracens."

Johanna said, "The Saracens did it, not him."

"Now that Richard is here, everything is going to change."

"Oh, you think so. Well, let's pray for that."

Henry was leading them into the camp by a back way. The porters came groaning after, and they climbed a long flat rise, well inland of the city. The path wound through mounds of rotted garbage, bits of gnawed bone, shredded cloth, piles of shit. The rain had pounded everything into a stinking mush. The smell of urine made the air sick. Lilia crossed herself, tears sliding down her face. Johanna's shoulders were hunched again, and now Henry did not try to jolly her out of it. Every few yards they passed an abandoned cesspit. Up on the top of the ridge was the first line of the camp, a row of wretched little hovels, dug halfway into the ground and cobbled together of scraps of wood and stones and cloth. Gritty wood smoke hung over everything.

They passed through these clots of huts, fire rings, and heaps of garbage toward the long ridge of the hill. There on the only flat high ground, a dozen tents had been pitched in a circle. Henry said, "This is the royal compound," as if it were a palace. They carried Gracia into one of the smaller tents, and the other women followed, praying and moaning.

Edythe drew back, unwilling to go inside. A vague horror tingled on the back of her neck. She stopped outside the door and turned toward the city. From this height she could see what lay before them. She went out past the next tent, to the top of the slope.

The smoke from the nearby fires drifted in the air, but she could see all the way to the far wall of the enormous city, larger than any city she had ever seen before, Troyes or Rome or Messina. Curved around the top of the bay, the headland itself was low and flat, but on every inch of it was a house or a wall or a street, many piled on other houses and walls, all made of yellow stone, or maybe the smoke made it yellow.

Much of it lay in ruins. The whole city seemed knocked to earth, to rubble. The great walls along the water stood untouched. On the narrow neck of land where the headland connected to the coast there had once been a wall, but now it was a crumbled mass of rock, the tower blasted, the gate broken down.

The whole sweeping view was quiet now. At first she saw no people there at all. In the litter of rock, bits of wood stuck up, scaffolds, wheels. Down toward the beach some giant siege engine stood half-burned, its base whole but the uprights only charred and broken stubs, like grotesque fingers. Closer to her, she saw signs of a great fire, which had blackened even the stone.

Not a green thing grew on this place, not a stem or a leaf. Here and there a bent figure crept hunched among the rocks, feeling around the ground and picking things up. A haze of smoke and yellow dust hung over everything.

As she watched, Richard's grand entry was passing the far side of this ruin from her, along the crumpled wall. On the barricades behind the rubble, a few defenders appeared, but they made no sound and skulked along like wolves from cover to cover. Outside, the Christians had gathered all along the way to whoop and cheer. The wind tore their voices away, inhuman howls that swelled and fell to a mutter.

The serpentine parade of armed men would be gone in a moment. The Christians would come back to the hovels and shanties

cluttering the slope before her like the dens of animals. The sprawl-
ing wretched wreckage of the city, the stench from the pits behind
her, and Gracia's death all weighed down on her. She struggled to
see the hand of God in this. To fit that image over this truth like a
magic shield that would ward away all the evil. She could not master it and she went on into the tent, grateful for once for its closeness
and dark.

Four

ACRE

Berengaria said, "I tell you stay in Cyprus."

Johanna said, briskly, "Oh, I think this is much better."

Edythe and the other waiting women led in the porters, and Lilia pointed out where they should put the trunks and chests. After the cramped deck of the galley the tent seemed huge, and Edythe felt like leaping and dancing in and out of the poles that braced up the canvas. The last sunlight streamed in through the cloth, veiled, mysterious. The wind puffed up the fabric in a constant ruffling. The floors were covered with thick woven stuff, rapidly becoming filthy under the trampling feet. Another train of men hauled in more trunks.

Outside, the raucous crowd still shouted; Richard had issued them all huge rations of wine and they were roaring around bonfires and yelling fight songs and Te Deums and pledges to die for God. Inside the tent, Berengaria, flanked by her women, went to one side and plunked down on a stool. Her sunburned face was thin with fatigue, her long gown dirty. She crossed herself, which she did a dozen times an hour. Johanna glared at her. The air between them crackled with dislike. Berengaria turned her face away.

Night had fallen. Edythe drifted to the door of the tent, her hand over her face; the stench of the camp made her nose burn. A man passed her, hunched over under a sack half full of bits of wood, cloth, metal, his gaze on the ground, picking up anything he saw. In the big tent just down the slope, a number of men were cheering and shouting. They were having another of their endless councils. She turned back into the tent, where they had laid Gracia's body beside the wall.

Johanna was kneeling there, her head bent, praying and crying. Berengaria had withdrawn with her two women into a corner. Edythe circled the place lighting the candles. Slowly their light swelled up into the room. Outside, the shouting and cheering suddenly doubled, but it was far away. The Queen rose, crossing herself again.

"Where is Lilia?"

"I haven't seen her, my lady."

"Oh, she's got a new flirt."

Edythe thought briefly of Rouquin, her old flirt. She wondered why that mattered to her. She could hear voices yelling, in the biggest tent across the way, where soldiers were gathered also outside the canvas walls, listening, passing the word around of the Kings' deliberations. Suddenly Johanna came up beside her.

"You must go with me," she said to Edythe. "I have a task to do." She favored Edythe with a candid look. "None other would I trust than you in this."

"My lady," Edythe said, warned by the edge in Johanna's voice. She went to fetch her cloak.

•   •   •

Rouquin drifted to the back of the council, toward the tent flap, where he could see out to the city. The council did not interest him much. All the great lords had come in to shout and complain and threaten and ultimately to hear what their leaders decided. Those leaders were in the center of the tent, on a quick-made wooden floor. Richard had finally caught up with Philip Augustus, the French King, small, one shoulder lower than the other, as if his crooked mind had warped his body. A German duke had come up to sit beside them.

The other men crowding around them were the lesser lords who had answered the Crusading call a lot sooner than either King: local men, some Germans, a lot of northern French, Burgundians, Lor-rainers. A cup went around among them, and a squire took it to fill it again.

Rouquin turned his back on this, his eyes aimed out the tent flap toward Acre. The late sun shone on its honey-colored walls and made even the rubble look beautiful: a golden city. That was what mattered: the prize.

He had looked over the ground when they came in. Since then, talking to a couple of people, he had formed a picture of it in his head—Saladin's camp was just to the east of this hill, and numbered less than the Crusaders, with Richard's army come.

They were not equal man to man, either, he guessed, the Saracens mostly mounted archers, lightly armed and armored. They couldn't stand against mailed knights. Even Guy de Lusignan had had some early victory over them, before, typically, he had thrown it back. But with a shrewd general who knew how to pick the right fights, the Saracens camped just inland would attack the Christian camp whenever the Crusaders attacked the city, so that the Christians had to fall back to defend themselves, and Acre could recover. By all ac-counts the Sultan Saladin was such a general.

This strategy would work for the Saracens as long as they could keep the defenders of Acre supplied. The Crusaders had never been able to block the city completely from the sea; that was why sinking the big galley when they arrived was such a triumph. As for the land side, Richard's war machines, catapults, a belfry forty feet high, could roll right up to what was left of the wall and drop a bridge onto the top of it.

Then, he thought, with the numbers they had now, they could throw a lot of force against the gate while part of the army waited, ready to meet Saladin's counterattack, and drive the gate and hold the city in a week. It wouldn't matter what Saladin did after that.

Rouquin turned toward the council again, where a gaunt man in a dirty surcoat had come up through the general yells and snarls to stand in front of Richard.

"I am Baldwin of Alsace," he said. His voice cut through the noise, and everybody hushed. He went on, "I have come here to ask you one question. I have been here over a year. In that time I have drunk mud and eaten wormy dog meat, and gone days without eating anything. My men and I have burned in the summer sun and slogged around barefoot in the winter in the pouring rain looking for dry wood; we have battled the assaults of the Saracens and dug tunnels and burrowed into the walls of the city only to meet Saracens burrowing toward us. And we have died. We have died by the one and the two, and by the dozen. We have died of Saracen arrows and rock barrages from the city and tunnels collapsing, of hunger and of plague. Now"—he folded his arms—"tell me why we should pay any heed to you at all."

Rouquin knew Baldwin somewhat, Count of somewhere, who held important lands north of Normandy and France. He was in fact a close counselor of the King of France, which was probably what was going on here: a challenge to Richard. Everybody in the place was watching, intent.

"Have I asked you to bow down to me?" Richard said. "We own the same liege lord." His head moved a little, toward Philip Augustus, as much acknowledgment as he would ever give the little French King.

Baldwin said, "Yet you dare come in among us with banners and trumpets and a grand display, as if Acre is yours now, and we should step aside."

Rouquin saw a smile tilt the French King's mouth. This, then, was going his way. Richard got up from his stool and came forward to face Baldwin.

"My lord Baldwin, as a Crusader, I should bow down to no one but Christ, and I expect that you would agree; this is not the matter. I am not here to disparage any man, but to take this city. You have been here two years, true, some of you"—he looked around for Guy de Lusignan, who had begun the siege, and tilted his head slightly toward Philip Augustus, who had arrived only weeks before—"but you are still on the outside."

The crowd let out a howl of wrath. Rouquin grinned; he stepped back into the open tent door, where the air was better.

Baldwin cried, "We have suffered—"

Richard thrust his hand up, pointing, as if he could see the sky through the canvas. "You can suffer, or you can win. Which is it? Listen to me. In twelve days the moon is full. Mark that. I want forty days. In forty days, that moon will be full again, and I will have this city. Are you going to be with me or not?"

A roar went up from them all. The scraggly Baldwin, who did look as if he had been sick, flung a glance from side to side. "Who made you lord here?"

Richard had stopped talking to him. He lifted his gaze and took them all in, and under his gaze the whole place gradually fell still. Richard spoke to them all. "I am not lord. Christ is lord. I serve Christ. Do you?" He looked from side to side, meeting all their eyes, one at a time. "I need every man with me. I promise you Acre, but you must follow me, and give me everything you have."

The crowd's mutter rose steadily, for and against. Somebody yelled, "We don't need him—" Someone else called, "Lead us, Lionheart!" On his stool Philip Augustus was hunched over in a coil of bad temper.

Richard's voice rang out over all the others. "And to every man who follows me I will pay four bezants a month as long as the war goes on."

For an instant the tent was utterly still, as if the whole crowd had lost its breath. Then they bellowed, full-throated, beating each other on the shoulders. Suddenly they all agreed. The wordless yell became a score of voices screaming Richard's name. Two men dashed out the tent flap with the news, and outside the cheering began also.

Philip Augustus stood. Rouquin could just see him through the weaving bodies between them. The King of France was talking, his voice lost in the yelling, but the meaning was written on his face: Richard had done it again, Richard had undercut him again. He got up and rushed out of the tent by a back way. Rouquin laughed. The German was still sitting there as if somebody soon would tell him what had just happened. Richard stood in the middle, looking nowhere, silent in the uproar. He looked tired suddenly. Rouquin turned back to the city of Acre, which he would begin to attack in the morning.

· · ·

Edythe thought: *This is why she promised me a husband.*

They had not come far, she and Johanna, only two doors along the hilltop ring of tents that housed the great men of the Crusade, to the one where the French King's banner hung. Johanna had sent a page ahead, so they got in with no fuss. Now Edythe kept to the shadows at the back of the tent, stacked with crates and gear; up in the lighted part, Johanna walked restlessly around. The floor was spread with a carpet, but there wasn't much space and she walked two steps one way and two back.

Through the cloth walls of the tent, the sounds came from the nearby council: an uproar, a cry, a sudden cheer. Edythe, in the shadows, shivered even in the warm summer night. Her stomach hurt.

She was sitting in the tent of the King of France, where she should not be. Johanna should not be here. The Queen of Jerusalem should not have been where she had been, last night at Tyre. What Johanna had promised on the ship—the husband, the dowry—that had been a bribe, not a reward, for just such a moment as this, to keep her quiet. She wondered what she ought to do. She wondered how she could be sitting in the tent of the King of France and not bay like a wolf in rage.

She had had the dream again. It was almost every night now. Not all night, just toward morning, and nothing but a voice. *Awake,* it said. *Awake, awake.*

· · ·

After a while, Johanna thought, *This is folly, now, I should go,* and just then, in a burst of noise, several men came through the tent door.

The first, so angry his lopsided face shone, came three steps inside and saw her and stopped cold. His face softened like warm wax. At once he waved at the others. "Go. Leave me." His eyes never left her, and Johanna smiled, seeing she had the same grip on him as ever. She bent her knee to him, a sovereign lord, and bowed her head a little.

"Johanna," he said, and came toward her, his hands out.

"My lord Philip." She took his hands, held them away from her, and pressed her cheek to his. "I am glad to see you."

"I am overjoyed to see you," said the King of France. He sat down on the nearest stool. He had a pointed chin under a sparse beard, a wide forehead, pale deepset eyes; the left half of his face was smaller than the right, so he seemed always tilted. "Johanna, your brother is a devil."

She sat, too, inclined toward him, earnest. "Philip, it isn't Richard, it's the Crusade. It's evil. I'm convinced of it. You must unsnare yourself."

His gaze traveled over her face, from eyes to lips to eyes again, and he said, "I would make you my Queen, if he would let me." He shook his fists, his face twisting. "Who does he think he is—he is my vassal! Mine! I have had his hands between mine—but he won't marry my sister and he won't let me marry his!" His face had turned the color of a holly berry.

She murmured, consoling. For years everybody had known that Richard would never marry Philip's scandalous older sister, in spite of their long betrothal, and now of course he had married Berengaria. Johanna certainly had no wish to marry Philip. The French King rubbed his hand over his face. He looked worn, unsteady. He was younger than Richard and had always been sickly, reptilian, given to bursts of rage. But he was wily also, with a fearsome grasp of his kingdom's interests, a better King than his father had ever been. Suddenly he glared at her.

"I am his liege lord. Yet he comes in here and overstands me as if I were a peasant."

"My lord," she said, "it is the Crusade that poisons minds. You must go back where you belong. I plead with you, as a woman, as a Queen, as one who—loves you."

His eyes blazed. "Love," he said. Then he settled back, blinking. "What can love mean to a Plantagenet?"

Johanna glared at him, affronted. A furious response came to her, but angering him countered her purpose. This was the moment to leave, anyway. She rose to her feet. "Yet consider what I've said. I am glad to see you, sir; I have often thought on those days in Sicily, in the garden."

"Johanna," he said. "I didn't mean what I said. Stay."

She went to the door; Edythe came quietly up and followed her out. In the darkness outside, Edythe gave her a single sharp look. But she would keep faith, Johanna thought. Edythe was her mother's woman, and Eleanor abhorred the war, too.

Johanna did not know what else she could do to destroy the Crusade, except to prize out the French King and send him home. Losing the French army, which was much smaller than Richard's, would not stop the war; if Philip went back to France, Richard would have the whole command in his hands, with no rival. But back in France, Philip would certainly be tempted to meddle in Richard's lands, left defenseless without their lord, and plenty of people would help him. At the right moment she would remind Richard how likely that was to happen, and he would go home.

Then she could marry whom she wanted. Her mother had promised that. She would have more babies. Her life would go again as it should. In the door of her own tent, across the way, she saw Lilia watching for her, and she led Edythe back to their own candles.

·   ·   ·

Edythe lay rigid on the pallet, listening to the other women breathe and snore around her. It was hot in the tent, too hot to sleep, and her mind too unquiet.

She could not keep the memories away anymore. Eleanor had

told her, "Forget everything. You must not think of it. It will go away if you forget." And she had managed not to think of it, for so long.

The unspoken reasoning: *If they know, no one will want you. You will be cast out, lost and alone. I love you, I will save you, but you must do as I say. So forget.*

Seeing the King of France had brought it all up again, like a drowned body rising to the surface: this weasel King, whom Johanna tried basely to seduce. This King, who had brought Edythe's family to their deaths.

Then her name had not been Edythe. She had been only thirteen. She had not been home; when the decree came she was in Rouen, far to the west, with her aunt and uncle, at some family festival. She still remembered the white dress, the pretty slippers that were too tight, the sound of a glass breaking. Her mother and father had stayed behind in Troyes because her mother was so near her time. Then the decree was published. Her aunt and uncle made ready to flee, and her aunt bundled Edythe off to England, with a letter to the imprisoned Queen.

It was only later that Eleanor told her what had happened to her family. "It is terrible. You must forget. Forget it all. Begin again, now, be Edythe and Christian, from now."

She groaned, her fist pressed to her stomach. She knew the bitter wisdom in the Queen's words. There was nothing she could do, anyway. She had no power of revenge. She had no will to revenge. But she hated him, that weasel King. And now she could not push it down below the top of her mind. Johanna had made her somehow complicit with him. In the dark of night, among the other sleeping women, she thought over and over of her mother and father, her tiny brother, burning.

*   *   *

In the gray dawn, the women buried Gracia behind the camp, in a graveyard already full, the mounded earth patchy with weeds. Most of the graves were marked only with rings of stones. Dogs had been digging at them. Johanna and Lilia both wept, and Edythe kept her head down and thought with an ache in her throat that Gracia would be alive if she had known what to do. She thought again about Jerusalem, where all of this would make sense. When she looked up, she saw Berengaria and her attendants there, a little apart from Johanna. After the priest was done, the little Queen went up to him and knelt for a blessing. Tears streaming down her face, Johanna trudged back up the slope, Edythe and Lilia behind her.

Johanna had brought only a few chests and a bed, which they had put in the back of the tent, well separate from Berengaria's corner. The two maids slept on a pallet, which they folded away every morning. A page came in with a basket of bread and cheese and some wine and they ate. The bread was bad and not much of it. Johanna lay down on the bed and buried her head in the cushions; Berengaria had brought the priest back with her to pray and, with Lilia, Edythe went about their small daily chores.

The ordinary work settled her, the pattern of what she knew, what she was supposed to do. Lilia's eyes were red. They went out to shake the bedclothes; the day was blooming with the summer heat. The city lay still as a graveyard, nothing moving beyond the crumbled wall or on this side of it, except for a row of men who stood on the slope looking the place over. Already it seemed familiar, as if they had been here for years. But it wasn't, she knew; everything was different here, everything had changed. Lilia lifted her apron to wipe her eyes and plodded back into the tent, and Edythe followed her to bring out the chamber pots.

· · ·

The men worked along the walls, dragging in the pieces of the great war machines from the ships and putting them together. The heat was terrific. Rouquin shaded his eyes, looking toward the city. The battering that destroyed the wall had left in its place a broad, almost impassable barrier of rubble. Ahead of him among the enormous stones, six men—naked but for their hose—were digging a tunnel. On the broken stones of the wall a darker shape moved, a sniper with his bow.

Richard was riding toward them, a dozen other men behind him. Rouquin picked up his shirt and wiped his face with it, and took off his hat.

"Mind the archer," he said, when his cousin reined his big black horse around beside him.

Richard looked toward Acre. "They're all over. They can't hit anything at this reach; they're just wasting arrows."

Among the men behind him, someone said, "Word is at night they sneak out here and pick them up again. It's worth your life to come down here at night, my lord."

Richard leaned on his saddlebows. There were lines around the corners of his mouth, and his eyes had a dark sheen. Rouquin thought he was beginning to regret the promise he had made the night before, to take Acre within the biblical forty days. The King's gaze traveled over the men trying to clear a ground for the belfry. "This is slow work," he said.

Somebody shouted, "Watch out!"

From the city came the whine and thunk of a catapult, and then a high arching shower of junk, arrows, pebbles, and jars of burning oil began to pelt down just short of the Crusaders. The oil stank. A stone bounced past Rouquin's shoe. He turned to Mercadier.

"Get somebody to collect all those arrows." He turned back to Richard. "You were saying?"

Richard rubbed his hand over the pommel of his saddle. "I've had an offer from Saladin to talk."

"You know what I think of that."

The King laughed. He looked tired. He said, "Well, come up to Johanna's tent, and we'll discuss it." Which meant he would accept the Sultan's offer and order Rouquin to go along. Rouquin turned his eyes to the war machine. A truce might give him the chance to build it much closer to the walls. He shouted at Mercadier to bring up the next crosspiece of the frame.

Five

ACRE

Berengaria and her women now spent most of their time with the priest, who kept church in a separate tent, so Johanna and her women had more room in theirs. They brought in new reed mats for the floor and kept the door flaps folded back, to let in the air and light. The dust from the camp drifted everywhere. In the evening, while Lilia and Edythe shook out the Queen's linen and made her bed ready, Lilia said, under her breath, "You will never guess who loves me now."

Edythe glanced at her. "Who?"

The girl had shed her gloom about Gracia. She smiled; she had dimples at either corner of her mouth. Her dark eyes flashed. "You will never guess." She flipped her hips back and forth and put a finger to her lips.

Edythe shut her mouth tight, ashamed of even caring. Lilia would get nothing for this but a few baubles, maybe worse. But the girl was happy, glowing. Someone loved her. Edythe felt a low roil of envy, herself old and juiceless.

She bent over the pallet bed, tucking down the corner. "Then I won't try. We should bring her some bread and wine; it's getting late."

"The King is coming," Lilia said.

"Well, then definitely we should get some wine."

Johanna came in, a train of pages after her, carrying a table, and some ewers. Right behind them another page appeared, stood to one side, and piped out, "The King!" Johanna fussed over the placement of the table, and Richard sauntered in, trailing Rouquin and King Guy and Guy's brother Hugh and the Templar Grand Master. They crowded the place. Edythe drew back almost to the bedside, the sharp smell of sweat in her nostrils. Johanna called Lilia to light the candles.

Richard came up to his sister. "Not getting on so well with my dear bride?" He kissed her cheek. "God, what a shrew." He left the ambiguities of this hanging in the air. Edythe, watching, was startled at how pale he looked, his face gray beneath the brown of the sun. While Johanna bustled around she stood quietly watching them all.

Guy was saying, "Everybody is lining up to take the four bezants. Even the Germans." He drank from a cup and handed it off to a page. Rouquin, a few feet away, kept his back to him; watching from the back of the tent, Edythe had seen before that Rouquin hated Guy.

"Nonetheless," said Guy's brother Hugh. "One month. That's close."

Humphrey de Toron walked in among them, trailing three of his pages. He made his bow to Guy, his overlord, and Guy spoke and shook his hand, smiling. Guy played a perfect King; Edythe wondered, briefly, why that wasn't good enough for a nonexistent kingdom. Her gaze lay on Humphrey, whose puzzling elegant manners fascinated her. If she had such a grace, she thought, she would have more than one to love her. Humphrey's page brought him a cup of the wine. He said nothing, but Edythe saw his attention slide across the room, as if against his will, toward Richard. The look on his face reminded her suddenly of Lilia.

"What about the fleet?" Richard said. He was at the center of the flaming lamps, under the peak of the tent. When he spoke, all the rest of them fell silent and faced him, a ring of moons. The Templar stepped forward. He wore the silver medal of his order on a chain around his neck. The red cross was like a bloodstain on his snowy white surcoat.

"A lot of the shipmasters who brought us here want to go back to Sicily, but there's a Genoese captain who came with the King of France who can take charge of that. Simon Doro."

"No," Richard said. "No Genoese. They're all French under the skin."

The Grand Master's voice was measured. "We have to seal off the city completely, that's the key to it. For that we need a fleet."

Richard put his hand to his head. Maybe he had a headache. His voice was mild. The Grand Master might have no overlord but the Pope, but he only advised, and Richard disposed. "The Pisans will do it. The fleet that came with me. If we offer them enough. Rouq', did you scout Saladin's camp?" The Templar backed off, frowning.

"Mercadier and I did, this afternoon," said his cousin. "It's a clever setup, several rings deep; it would be hard to storm. Still, from all the signs, they used to have a lot more people, so they're losing men. I think we outnumber them two to one, maybe. Mercadier has heard they send swimmers back and forth across the bay with messages, so we should have the fleet on the watch."

Johanna walked up to her brother and put her hand on his arm. "If you must talk of war, get out of here. I want this for a place of peace, a woman's place, so if you want to stay, talk more gently."

Richard said, "Go, then. Humphrey—my lord de Toron, stay."

He sat down on a stool in the middle of the tent and asked for some wine. Humphrey de Toron lingered, waiting to be called on. Richard turned to Johanna, who was bustling around him, directing Lilia with the wine; Edythe came up quietly and put another stool beside the King's.

Johanna's brother said, "So where is the lady Berengaria?"

"At church," Johanna said, and gave an imperious sniff. "Or what passes for a church here."

"What's wrong between you? I thought you women clung together like brambles and sheep."

Johanna sat down on the stool. "She prefers the company of God. No, believe me, I am much happier without her. It's men who are the brambles and the sheep; men can't endure life without another man around to be better than, or in liege to." Nearby, Humphrey de Toron smiled.

Richard took the cup of wine. This, Edythe knew, was an old game with them. She frowned; his eyes seemed unnaturally bright, and his face shone with sweat. "Women," he said. "You're just like Mother. You love circles, everything's got to web together for you, which is why you can't decide anything."

Johanna began a sharp reply. Richard swayed, as if his head were suddenly heavy; the cup slipped out of his hands, and he pitched forward onto the floor.

Lilia screamed. Humphrey de Toron started toward him, and Edythe leaped up from her place by the bed. With a cry, Johanna had dropped to her knees beside her brother. She swung toward Humphrey.

"Please go, sir." Her eyes came pleading to Edythe. "Help me."

Humphrey left, with his pages. Edythe sank down beside the King. He was alive, still, she saw at once with a ridiculous gratitude, and struggling a little, as if to get up. Or just twitching. His eyes were only half-open. She laid her hands on him. He was shivering in long furious spasms, his muscles knotting under her touch.

"What is it?" Johanna said. She wrung her hands together, leaning over him. "Is it poison?"

Edythe said, "I don't know." She looked around them. "My lady—we must cover him. We could put him in your bed."

"Yes," Johanna said. "I'll bring Rouquin."

Edythe knelt by the King, struggling to understand this. He was breathing well enough. Now his eyes opened; he put one hand on the mat beneath him and tried to get up, but he was too weak even to lift his head off the ground, and he lay flat again. Sweat trickled down his cheek. Rouquin came in, swearing under his breath, and lifted Richard in his arms. Edythe, standing back, remembered how strong he was; he lifted his tall cousin like a child in his arms and took him to the Queen's pallet.

Johanna said, "Let no one in." She turned to Edythe. "You must help him. You must save him, Edythe."

A plea. Or a command. Edythe licked her lips, trying to think what to do. She had lost Gracia. *Help me*, she thought. *Please help me.* But she could not think to whom she prayed.

·   ·   ·

Edythe got Lilia to heating wine, the last of the zingiber potion and a good dose of oxymel, and with Johanna she wrapped the King in the bedclothes; before they were done, he thrashed and retched and his knees jerked up and he spewed vomit. Johanna began to weep, her hands to her face, sobbing helplessly. Edythe mopped up the mess, pulling the dirty blankets into a heap on the floor. She unwrapped her coif and wiped his face with it and tossed the soiled cloth after the blankets. He was still shivering and he was unconscious. His clothes were filthy and she began to undress him; she pulled his belt out from under his body and cut the lacings of his shirt with a knife. Johanna brought more blankets and helped her peel his shirt off. They covered his chest with fresh blankets and pulled off his boots and hose. He had fouled himself. Johanna turned her eyes from his nakedness, put her hand on Edythe's shoulder, and stared steadily away while Edythe cleaned him up and then covered him.

Edythe's heart was pounding. She had never touched a naked man before. Of course she had seen them, and drawings and descriptions, but this was different. His efflorescence amazed her. He was beautiful; she could not let him die.

When he was clean and covered snugly, she got the potion from Lilia and pointed to the heap of filthy clothes and blankets on the floor.

"Take that. Have it burned. See to it yourself." The cup in her hand, she turned to Johanna. "Help me."

They could not budge Richard, lying cramped on his side with his knees drawn to his chest, shivering and sweating at the same time. Berengaria came back, saw her lord husband bundled on the bed, and fled away again to the makeshift church. Johanna sent again for Rouquin.

The big man came in. Edythe had thought him always a little angry, but there was no anger in him now. He went down on one knee beside the low pallet and put his hand on Richard's cheek.

Johanna said, "We need to get him to drink. He has to be up—" She looked at Edythe.

"He must sit up," Edythe said.

Rouquin went behind the pallet, squatted down, and laid his arm under the King's shoulders. His voice sank almost to a whisper.

"Sit up, Richard. Sit up, boy."

The King's head moved, and his lips parted. Johanna gave a long sigh. Rouquin raised him effortlessly against his chest, supporting his head, and Edythe held the full cup to his lips. She stroked his throat, to make him swallow. Rouquin said, "Come on, sonny, drink it, drink," in that same crooning, tender voice.

Richard's eyes fluttered. His lips touched the wine, and he lifted his hands unsteadily, but he had no strength even for that. Under Edythe's fingers his throat worked in a swallow, and then another.

His eyes closed. His head rolled back against Rouquin's shoulder; the big man looked at Edythe.

"Let him down," she said. "Let him sleep." She could tell they had used all the strength Richard had left. The moon was old and weak, which was in his favor. She would have to see where Mars was. She hoped the potion warmed him; she could think of nothing else to do.

Rouquin stayed in the tent, near the door; Lilia came back, carrying a bundle of fresh blankets, and made another bed on the far side. At the prie-dieu in the back, Johanna was crying and praying.

Rouquin said, "Is it poison?"

Edythe sat on the side of the pallet, one hand on the King's chest over the blankets. "I don't think so." She would look in her herbal, where there was a section on poisons and their effects. She slid her hand under the blankets, to the King's bare chest, to feel his heart's pulse.

Against her palm the pounding of his heart was another sign that his humors were swelling out of balance. Sweat covered his skin, his knotted muscles shivered; she imagined the black bile seething in his gut, the yellow pooling in his belly. She wondered if they were right about the poison, or if it could be magic, an evil spell.

By midnight Richard was scorching with fever. Maybe she had given him too much zingiber. Nonetheless, the fever proved that it was not a poison. She boiled some lemons with their cooling properties in a lot of wine and water, let this potion stand awhile, and then called Rouquin to help her; Johanna and Lilia were asleep, spooned together, on the pallet across the tent. Berengaria was still in the church.

Rouquin gathered the King in his arms, whispering to him, and sip by sip she fed Richard the new drink. As she did she looked him over for swelling, lumps, or bruises that would show where the rioting humors were collecting in dangerous masses. Foul stuff matted his hair and beard.

Rouquin said, "Will he die?"

"No," she said, without thinking about it much. She would not let him die. He had drunk nearly all the potion, and she nodded that Rouquin could lay him down again on his back. She went and found a comb among Johanna's things and came back and began to comb out Richard's hair. Rouquin stayed where he was, hunkered down behind the pallet.

She groomed Richard's beard and hair, stretching the long curls across the pillow; glinting clumps of hair clogged the comb, and she pulled them off into a little ball. She would have to burn that, lest someone plotting against him find it. Rouquin sat on his heels, watching, his hands together. He looked tired; she knew he had spent most of the day fighting.

She got a basin and a ewer of water, poured the water into the basin, and cast around for some cloth. There was nothing obvious to hand and she stood up, pulled up her skirt, and ripped off the front of her underskirt. She wrung this big sheet of cloth out in the basin of water and began to wash Richard's face.

The King sighed, although he did not waken, and turned his face into the cool cloth. She washed his throat and behind his ears. She folded the blanket down to bathe his chest, and he murmured again at the touch. She said, "Will you roll him over?"

Rouquin got up and moved closer; he slipped his arms under Richard and effortlessly turned him. "The fever's gone down," he said, and sat back on his heels again.

"I think so. A little." She would have to go look at the stars. Maybe the planets had shifted. She was very bad at the whole matter of stars. She began to wash Richard's back. She glanced at the big man, sitting there beside him on his heels. Rouquin was watching Richard, his face slack; he looked a little lost.

The King had a lot of cousins, even some others here in Acre. Only Rouquin was so faithful, so useful. She wanted to reach across the space between them, somehow, and honor him for this. She said, "You grew up with them, didn't you?"

His head bobbed. "In Poitiers. Winchester." His head swayed, as if he were avoiding some memory, his gaze turning elsewhere. "Eleanor took me, when my mother died. I got there just after they lost William, their first. Henry was only a baby, so she paid a lot of attention to me for a while. But then she started setting them like a clutch."

He shut his mouth tight, as if he had said too much. She said, "How old were you then?" She knew his mother had been Eleanor's sister, and he looked much like her.

"Three, I think."

Under her hands the King's muscles were kinked and cramped, and as she came upon each knot she rubbed it with her fingers until it went away. His right arm was a great stack of muscle, his left arm much thinner. The groove down his back was two fingers deep, straight and clean.

She said, "Her children came late to her, and she loves them all." She wanted to keep this bridge of words open between them. Also she was grateful that Eleanor's passion for her children had spread somehow to her, Edythe.

He said, "She is a fierce, noble woman, my aunt. It's for good reason they call her the Eagle."

"God bless her. God be with her."

He said nothing. She worked her way from Richard's shoulders to the small of his back. Her arms began to ache, and she could hardly keep her eyes open. She pulled the blanket up over him and tucked it around him, and the effort left her exhausted.

"Go to sleep," Rouquin told her. "I'll keep watch."

"There's nowhere," she said, but she sank down beside the pallet and put her head on it, down by Richard's feet, and was asleep at once.

•   •   •

Rouquin rubbed his hands together. He felt weak and stupid, unable to do anything, while Richard whom he loved lay suffering before him. Richard whimpered in his sleep, and Rouquin jumped as if at a shout. He drew the blanket higher to the King's chin. At that, the woman at the foot of the bed stirred and turned her head and was asleep again.

She knew what to do; he had watched her hands tending the sick King, her actions swift without haste, precise, assured. Like a man fighting. Except she could not see the enemy, nor slay it with a sword, so what she did was harder. Her touch alone seemed to heal.

She had thrown off her coif at some point, her dark hair loose across the bed. She had an interesting face: big eyes with heavy prominent lids, a wide mouth, a long thin nose. Not pretty. He liked how she looked. He remembered how she had pulled up her skirt right in front of him, heedless how much long leg she showed him, to get a useful piece of cloth. This somehow stirred him more than an intentional flirt.

What he had told her came back to his mind, and that led him into the thickets around it, the wilderness of his childhood. Older cousin of the princes. The splendid courts, the great feast days. Always, he sat below them, he went last, the mere cousin.

But they were always together, and as he was the oldest, when they were boys he beat them at everything. As they grew up he kept it that way. He could ride wilder horses, pull stronger bows, jump onto the table in full mail when Henry and Richard were still struggling to stand upright under the weight. So when they were young, he was their king. He defended Richard and Geoffrey from Henry, and Henry from Richard and Geoffrey. He picked on all of them, save John, who was much younger and in a monastery half the time anyway.

The other boys matched themselves against him. "I'm as good as Rouq' at that." As they grew it seemed natural for them to take sides, Rouquin and Richard against Henry and Geoffrey, in wrestling and swimming and running and horse racing, playing the lute, hawking and tilting and hunting. Rouquin was the first one knighted, by the King's own hand. Unlike the others, he would not go to tournaments; there was real fighting doing the King's work. Anyway, he had no money.

But the old King, in all their view, constrained them. He got along with none of his sons, still less with Rouquin. There was the bad Becket incident, young Henry's debts, old Henry taking Richard's betrothed to bed, a lot of threatening, cajoling, spiteful talk. Eleanor, who had come to hate the old man, talked the boys into rising against him, a sputtering, grievous rebellion that ended in failure and humiliation for them all and in Eleanor's imprisonment.

The Eagle. "Mine to make," she had told him once, just before she was captured, "mine to break." He had known then that Henry's ambitions were small compared to hers.

Even from a dismal tower the great Queen had her reach; when after a nasty screaming match the old King exiled Rouquin to wander, she arranged to have him wander to Johanna in Palermo.

A year later the old King let him come home and forgave him with a kiss. But in the family there was no peace. Eleanor was still locked up. The King let none of them anywhere near her. John had wheedled his way into the old man's favor and demanded land of his own, although old Henry had already parceled it all out to the others. So John wanted a little of everybody else's. Then young Henry died, the young King, the eldest, the crowned heir, and suddenly also Geoffrey, in a tilting accident in Paris. Then the old man himself was dead, and Richard was King, and master of everything.

Rouquin had nothing. A place at the table, the King's favor, nothing of his own.

He had made a company of mercenaries, because Henry and then Richard always needed soldiers and the pay was very good. He liked to fight anyway. Richard promised him a castle someday, an heiress, a title, but there was always another call to arms. This time, the Crusade.

"We have to do this," Richard had said. "Don't you see? We have to do this, or we aren't men."

Now he sat in a tent outside Acre, always hungry, always nervy, and Richard was trembling again. Rouquin laid one hand on him, but he could do nothing. He said, "Edythe."

She turned her head but did not waken. He liked saying her name, this old-fashioned, Saxon name, not fitting her somehow. He reached out and touched her. "Edythe."

Now she did wake up, with a start, and her gaze went at once to Richard. She crept up beside him, put her hands on him, and then suddenly pulled back the blankets and laid the whole side of her head to his chest. Rouquin muttered an oath. After a moment she sat up and folded the cover around Richard again.

She looked straight at Rouquin for the first time. "Has this kind of thing happened before?"

Rouquin said, "He was sick for a while in Italy. He threw up then, and shivered."

She made an unfeminine grunt in her chest. She got up, raked her fingers through her hair and coiled it up in a knot at the nape of her neck, and went off out of the tent. In a few moments she was back, and she lay down on the floor by the bed and slept there. More than anything else that reassured him, that she went back to sleep. He settled down to wait out the night.

． ． ．

In the morning, swarms of men had gathered outside the tent to attend on the King. Rumors swept through the camp: He was dead, he was raving, devils had issued from his throat. Johanna went out several times and ordered the crowd away, but they would not go. She was constantly on the edge of crying, but she dared not leak a single drop. Everybody was watching her. Whenever they saw her, men shouted questions at her.

The King was well enough, she said, but sleeping. Now they should all go. They did not leave. Guy de Lusignan pushed through the crowd—or his men came first, pushing, to make way for him— and she had to let him in. Her page pulled the tent flap firmly closed on the gawkers outside.

Guy went toward the bed, where Richard lay, his eyes closed and his mouth open. Rouquin was gone and Edythe was sleeping in Johanna's bed; Lilia sat by the King's shoulder. Guy crossed himself.

"Is it the fever?"

Johanna pressed her palms together. She had a confused feeling this was her fault, that talking to the King of France behind Richard's back had sickened her brother, like the hole in the thatch that let in devils. "His doctor believes he will be well soon." This was not exactly what Edythe had said. Guy, she remembered, had seen his wife and children die of a camp fever.

"He will be well," she said, again. Her voice rang harsh in her own ears. "He is getting well."

"This is not a good time for him to be sick." Guy faced her. "Conrad is coming."

"The other King," Johanna said, and wished she had put it more gracefully. She half-turned away from him. She did not want to heed anything outside this tent, but she had to. "Aren't the Crusaders supposed to hold a council? To determine the true King of Jerusalem?"

"The Leper King put that in his will, when he felt himself dying. He knew his only male heir probably would not live long. He decreed that the Kings of England and France and the Emperor of the Germans should meet to choose the rightful King of Jerusalem." Guy said this as if he had said it often before. Clearly it was large in his mind. In this game his only counter was Richard. His gaze went to Richard again. "Will he live?"

Her gorge rose. Her brother's life, reduced to a pawn in this man's little scheme to win a meaningless crown. Richard favored him, and she knew why: because he was Poitevin, and Conrad was from Montferrat. That seemed tenuous to her. But she knew her place in this, and she acted it. She put her hand on his arm.

"We shall support you," she said, quietly. "You need not fear for that."

The taut, handsome face before her altered slightly, easier. The damned man thought of nothing but himself. "When will he—get well?"

"Soon, I hope."

"Does it still hold—the oath to take Acre by the next full moon?"

"While Richard lives, his word lives," she said. "And Richard surely lives."

Another page had appeared at the tent flap; Johanna's hand still lay on Guy's arm, and she nudged him that way. "Keep faith, my lord." She drew her hand back and crossed herself.

The coming of King Conrad was only another problem in the sea of problems. She saw King Guy out and let Humphrey de Toron in.

He came with his usual flock of attendants, whom with a look she drove away to the far corner of the tent, among some boxes. Their lord went at once to Richard's bedside and stood there and said some Latin under his breath and crossed himself. Johanna waited for him under the peak of the tent. He came back to her, his hands out.

"My dear lady Johanna, God keep him. God keep us all, these days. I am so sorry."

"He will be well soon," Johanna said. She took his long, ringed hands. "God willing."

"God heed our cause and his." He glanced back toward Richard, then faced her again, his smile fading. "The King's sickness is unfortunately the news everywhere, including the Saracen camp. The truce is thrown down; there will be no council with Saladin, at least until he is well." He squeezed her hands. "He's strong. God is with him."

"He has a good doctor," she said. "We are all praying for him. I was told Conrad is coming."

"Yes, likely tomorrow." His eyes were half-closed, no longer guileless. He let her hands go. "Guy told you? Yes, of course. He needs Richard."

She nodded. "Do many of those here favor Conrad over Guy?"

"Well, they wouldn't be here, if . . ." He tilted his face slightly, watching her sideways. "Guy has his enemies. He has a . . . way of making enemies. In the end, you know, it all depends on Richard. And the shape of the moon."

Once again, her brother's oath to take Acre in a single month made everything harder. She said, her hands cold, "He will be better soon."

He smiled at her, abruptly looking young and guileless. "I am Your Highness's servant." He bowed. His gaze turned toward Richard and she saw the smooth mask slip a little and some fear wrinkle his face, some other longing, and then he was leaving.

So Philip Augustus was sick also. Johanna flexed her fingers together, feeling better. It could not then be her fault, if both of the Kings were sick. She did not bother to plumb the depths of this reasoning, and she did not think much about what else Humphrey had said. She went to sit by her brother and let Lilia go for a while.

◆ ◆ ◆

Richard's fever raged all day, and then fell; in the late afternoon they managed to feed him a little bread. He was never fully conscious. Sometimes he spoke gibberish or reached for things no one saw but him. Johanna prayed and got Lilia to pray, and Edythe kept him covered and gave him wine when she could. *Please*, she thought. *Please*. She was afraid to think he was getting better. People came and went with news. King Philip was very sick, plucked bald and spitting teeth, but unlikely to die. There was some general evil in the camp, which had carried off many people in the first day, among them Baldwin of Alsace, the Count of Flanders. Even some of the Germans, who avoided all of the others, were burning with fever.

Still, after its first killing assault, it was losing its power. Everybody had some notion about this: the influence of Saturn, corrupt air, a Saracen curse. Fevers had swept regularly through the camp for two years and nobody had ever had any answer, except that they all passed by.

During the long, grim day Johanna heard everyone and did what she could, which was not much. Edythe admired her calm. Everywhere things looked bad. There was no bread left. The wine was almost gone. The meat was spoiled. At noon on the third day they heard that Rouquin was fighting by the wall, trying to raise the belfry against it; at midafternoon, that he and his men had swarmed over, but no one could get to their support before the defenders closed. Rouquin barely escaped, last of the Crusaders to reach safe ground.

They ate the meager supper of beans and onions, and Johanna and Lilia went to sleep again on the far side of the tent. Edythe sat by the King's pallet; she dozed as she had before, her head on the foot of it.

The trembling of the pallet woke her. He was shaking all over, his knees drawn up, his teeth clattering together. His eyes were open. She put her hand on his head and his eyes turned toward her, lucid and full of pain. She wrapped him with the blankets, tucking them in tight around him, looped a corner over his head, and rubbed him through the blankets to warm him. Her arms began to ache, but after a while his shuddering lessened under her hands. She rubbed his muscles flat and smooth, all up and down his back, until he was quiet and the spasm passed.

Suddenly he said, "I have to piss."

She went for a pot and brought it to the side of the bed; he was trying to push himself up, but his arms buckled. She put one arm around his waist and heaved his upper half against her. He swung his legs off the bed, one on either side of the pot, and leaning on her, he reached down and sent his stream into the pot. He sighed at the release.

He said, "It's a bad thing . . . when a man can't even stand up to piss." It took all his breath to say it.

She laughed; she thought it was true, and also that the act of will to say it was a good sign. When he was done, she dabbed at the end of his penis with a cloth she then tossed aside. He was falling out of her grip, lying down again, his arms under his head. She swung his legs up onto the bed and wrapped him in the blankets.

She took the pot to the front flap of the tent, where there was light from a torch outside. She sniffed at the urine and looked at it in the light; it was very dark but there was a lot of it, and it smelled clean and sharp. She tossed it out the door, startling the two guards drowsing on either side.

She closed the flap and went back to the pallet. The King was awake. He lay on his stomach, his head turned to one side, and his eyes gleamed at her. When she sat down on the edge of the pallet, he said, in a whispery voice, "Where's Rouquin?"

"I hope he's sleeping. King Conrad is coming."

"Ooh, is he. Well, things were too simple." His body was cool, almost without fever. She began to rub his arms and shoulders, to get his humors moving. His skin was scaly.

"Could you keep down some broth?"

He dragged in a deep breath. "I could keep down half a cow. Who's been here?" His voice was stronger.

"Johanna has never left." She gestured toward the far side of the tent, where the other women slept on. "She told me that King Guy came, while I was asleep." She hoped Berengaria was at least praying for him.

"Good for Guy. He's not a coward, at least."

She got up and went across the tent to the brazier, where a pot of bones had been cooking all night; she drew off some of the juice into a cup. The cup was hot, and she wrapped a corner of her skirt around her hand to hold it. When she came back, he tried to sit up. She helped him and, gasping at the heat, he gulped down the broth, which seemed to make him stronger.

"Johanna said also Humphrey de Toron was here," she said.

"Humphrey," he said. He lay back down on the bed, his head turned to watch her. By the way he spoke the name she knew how it was with him. He must have seen it in her face, because he said, "You think I am a monster."

"My lord," she said, surprised. He was hers, now, whatever his sins; she loved him. "Do you want more?"

"Yes."

She went for the rest of the broth. What men did together, making women of each other, that was sinful, cursed, and apparently very common, to judge from jokes and stories. Those who said it was evil agreed also that she was evil. That set their righteousness at nothing. What Richard did was Richard's humor. She sat down beside him and helped him drink again. His color was better. His head still wobbled.

He pushed away the cup, then lay down again, and his gaze poked at her. "Who are you?"

She sat back away from him in a little jerk of warning. She had loved him too soon. She folded her hands in her lap, her back straight. "Edythe. I'm one of—"

He rolled onto his side toward her, one arm bent under his head;

the light from the front of the tent shone on his face. He said, "I mean, who are you really?"

"My lord, I don't understand. I will fetch some wine." She started up.

He grabbed her skirt. "No, stay. My mother sent you?"

She sat down. Her hands knotted together in her lap. She had let him start this, and now she had to go where he hunted. "Yes, my lord."

"And Mother got you somehow from an English nunnery."

"I—yes." She looked off toward the door, in case someone was listening.

"You're lying. You don't sound English, you don't even sound Poitevin. You're from France, somewhere."

"I—"

"Tell me." He was trying to prop himself up on one elbow, his head unsteady, the blanket down around his waist.

"I was born in Troyes. But I swear—"

"Troyes. That's not a Troyenne accent. No." Abruptly, as if he had caught a fresher scent, he went off on a new track. "Your father was a physician, wasn't he? That's how you know all this, from Papa's knee."

She jumped, cornered. She said nothing; against her will she saw in her mind the gaunt bearded face above the dark clothes, a book in his hand, pointing to places on her doll and explaining humors. A brief pang struck her like a tooth in the heart.

"My mother is broad-minded," he said. "She loves clever, accomplished people, no matter who they are. She knew a famous physician in Troyes. He sent her herbs and recipes, gossip and stories, and gave her much wise counsel. She might have saved him from the French King's purge, what was it, ten, twelve years ago, if she had been free, and still in Poitiers."

She watched him like a rabbit seeing a snake coil steadily closer through the bending grass. He said, "But she did save you, didn't she?"

"My lord," she said, her voice thin. "I don't know what you're talking about."

"Not a Troyenne accent," he said, "because in Troyes you didn't speak French. You spoke that other thing—Zephais—Zephardic. You're a Jew."

"No," she said. She licked her lips. Unwillingly she thought of the evils his coronation had brought upon the Jews of London— when the crowds rioted through the Jewry and killed many. He had stopped it but for money. "No," she said again. "Not anymore—I'm a Christian." She remembered to cross herself.

"Were you ever baptized? You shouldn't be on the Crusade."

"Oh, please—" She flung out her hands to him. Eleanor had decided against the baptism, in itself a dangerous admission. "I want to go to Jerusalem. I have come all this way, and we're so close, I can't go back now."

He said, "You must serve God. Be a true Christian. When we take Jerusalem, we will bring the Kingdom of Jesus, and when He comes again, He will know you, and you will be saved."

"I serve God," she said. She settled back, her hands on her knees. She understood what this meant: To serve God was to serve Richard. "I promise."

He smiled at her. "I believe you." He hitched himself up on his elbows; he was tired. "I think you're one of us, anyway, damned thing and outcast. If I take Jerusalem, we're all saved, you with me."

"Yes," she said. She wondered what he meant.

"Good. Bring me something to drink."

She brought him the jar. At the first swallow he made a face. "This tastes awful." But he drank it all and had her bring him more.

When that was gone, he lay back on the pallet, drowsy. "How long have I been sick?"

"Just three days. You fell late two days before yesterday."

"Good. Now send for my brother," he said.

"Who?" she said, surprised.

"My cousin. Rouquin."

He was falling asleep. She went to pull the blanket up. He said, his eyes closed, "Get him."

"Yes, my lord."

He settled himself into the bed. He whispered, "It's all well if I do this well." At once he was asleep. She thought awhile about forgetting the order and letting him rest, but in the end she sent a page for Rouquin.

Six

ACRE

At dawn the servants brought a basket of bread and cheese. Edythe made sure Richard got the best of the bread and forbade him the cheese. After, with a page and a basket, she went around the camp and begged and bought all the meat bones she could. There were few, and they cost her much; most men were eating only thin bean porridge, and everybody had money.

As she went from fire ring to fire ring, the men around her sent up a constant shrill lewd pipe and whistle, and some reached out to grab at her skirt. She moved quickly, to keep them off. She should have brought a knight, she thought; the page was only a child. She could have asked Rouquin. The idea warmed her, and she wished she had.

When they would not sell her their scraps, she said, "This is for the King. Do you deny Richard?" Then they sold her what they had. Hearing Richard's name, they kept their hands away.

She was tired and the sun seemed too bright and her throat felt scratchy. With the page behind her hauling the basket along, she went back to the royal tent to find at the doorway a large wooden frame, a bed in the middle, and a gang of half-naked men crouched around it.

She bade the page put the bones on to cook and went by into the tent. Inside, men in mail and surcoats made a wall of backs between her and Richard. She crept along past them and got close enough to see that he was eating, sitting up with Rouquin's help. Johanna pulled her away by the arm.

"You have to sleep."

"I need—"

"Sleep," Johanna said, and towed her to the Queen's own bed and made her lie down. She slept at once. When she woke, thirsty, she saw that Richard was gone, the tent empty except for Lilia, dozing, and a few idle pages playing dice. A pot full of bones bubbled on the brazier. She slept again and woke around noon.

The tent was quiet. Johanna and Lilia had left. She put on a fresh gown and a kirtle and brushed her hair a few strokes, skipping over the knots. She summoned in the page and said, "I need to talk to other doctors. You must find me other doctors." He went out. She ate the last of the bread; the cheese was gone.

The page took her across the camp to the west, toward the sea. As she went, her skirts gathered up in her hands, she looked over the siege before her.

Every day the place seemed less a city and more a vast heap of stones. From here she could see the broad dent of the moat, dry and stuffed with rocks and dirt and what looked horribly like dead bodies. Out on the knob of the promontory the tall, thin tower stood, too far for any catapult to reach, and from the big ruined fortress in the harbor the black flag of the Saracens flew out on the stiff breeze.

But the ships that crowded the harbor were all Christian, Richard's ships. They could not get near the Black Tower, wreathed in half-submerged rocks, but everywhere else the Crusaders held the bay. No supplies could get into Acre, and the Tower itself looked abandoned, in spite of its brave flag. They were winning, she thought, and her heart leaped. There was an end to this.

She shaded her eyes with her hand. A red galley she had not seen before was rowing toward the shore, and from the beach a flock of little boats hastened toward it.

The page led her across the camp, weaving a way between the camps, and the men followed her with their eyes but made no sound. Their stares unnerved her. She walked as fast as she could, and the page got her quickly under cover—a strange rambling shelter, half tent and half wooden shed.

She went forward a few steps, looking around. The only light came through the doors and the tent fabric, and she could not see well for a moment. Lining either side of the long, narrow space were heaps of straw spread with coarse blankets, and on these makeshift beds lay bodies. A stout man in a monk's cassock came toward her; the page had just announced her, which, since she had no power of her own, had taken all his breath.

The monk said, in bad French, "Well met, then. The Queen Sicily is known to me. I self Sir Markus Staufen."

"Do you speak Latin, my lord?" He was a monk. Of course he spoke Latin. "Have you a doctor?"

"Alas," said the German knight, who spoke less Latin than he believed, "our doctor has dead. Many having dead here, Lady."

She said, "I have a patient with a recurrent fever."

He gestured toward the beds on either side. "All these fevers, Lady." He was being courteous; she was a guest, somehow connected to Lionheart; still, she was only a woman.

"How do you care for them?"

He talked about the Zodiac, retrogrades and necessary causes, fire and earth; his hands milled in the air. It was important when the disease began. Where the planets were. If the patient fell sick at the full moon, he would be driven mad. The old doctor had told him this. As he spoke, she got, in hints and pieces, that he was not a monk at all, but a knight who had come to fight the Saracens. When they saw the bloodshed and the sickness, he and some of his fellows broke up their ship to build this place for the sick and the dying to come. Mostly he carried blankets and chamber pots and fed people. But he believed he had found a vocation and would enter holy orders as soon as he got home.

"And, my lady," he said, "where to study you?"

Having no ready answer for this, she made none, and he said, with infinite condescension, "Ah, so. An empiricus." Edythe left knowing nothing more than when she went in, except the German knight's bad Latin.

On the way back, she came on a market above the beach, a row of vendor stalls under a canopy, that had not been there before. Johanna, in a cloud of pages and squires, was buying everything she could pick up. The vendors crouched in wait for her and launched volleys of words to draw her to them, but she walked through them as if they were not there. Lilia trailed her, and two knights stood at the head of the market, keeping back everybody else who wanted to buy. Once when a vendor got too insistent, Johanna only lifted her gaze toward the knights and the local man backed hastily away.

Behind them, Edythe went along the makeshift stalls, looking over the nuts and flowers and onions. The vendors jostled for her attention. "Zingiber?" she said. They mumbled together but no one had zingiber. She bought dates and two combs of honey wrapped in a big leaf. A thin man who knew a lot of French sold her a thumb-sized pot of a potion to make people sleep.

"Jews?" she said, quietly. "Are there Jews here?" She should send a letter to Eleanor.

If she found more Jews, would they know her too?

The Syrian shrugged. His cheeks sucked hollow. His head shook just a little. He did not ask about among his fellows, as the vendors usually did when they did not have what she wanted. "Jaffa," he said. "Jaffa, maybe."

In front of his stand, two boys, naked under their long, thin shirts, held out their palms and jabbered at her; she did not understand the tongue but she knew the cupped hands. She gave them each some dates.

The crowd was steadily thicker. The page had gone with the Queen, and Edythe ran a little to catch up. Ahead of her in the swarm she saw Lilia bump into a young man who never looked at her. They moved apart as if it were all an accident, but now Lilia had something in her hand, which she slid quickly into her sleeve. Edythe caught up with them and they returned to the circle of tents, inside the shell of their guards and attendants.

At the height, where they could see out over Acre again, Johanna cried, "Look!" and pointed toward the city.

Edythe turned. Quiet all day, now men burst up from the yellow rock pile and charged toward the wall. From the other side the Saracens were scrambling to defend it. Johanna pointed not at this, but at the hill before them, where Richard sprawled on his litter. The bearers had set it down but still stood at the corners. One of each pair carried a shield, but the litter was as open as a bed. Rains of arrows and stones volleyed down toward it. The King paid no heed and everything fell just short. A crossbow lay beside him; he was reloading another. The bearers stooped to pick up his litter again.

Johanna said, "God shield him. God keep him." She jerked her

gaze away; she would not look. She led the other women back
through the dirt and clutter of the camp to their tent. Edythe hung
back, her head turned over her shoulder. With a bellow, suddenly
the litter jounced down straight toward the wall, into a cascade of
arrows and rocks, Richard firing his crossbows as he went. Rocks
crashed around him. He waved one arm, fending off a blow. From
beyond the wall, on the Saracen side, came a furious banging of
drums. Edythe slipped into the tent, and as she did, Lilia passed her,
leaving.

◆   ◆   ◆

The dark was coming. Another day consumed. Johanna knelt down
at the back of the tent and prayed for her brother, for herself, and
even for King Philip, who she had heard was scorching with fever,
his hair and teeth falling out. The French were saying Richard had
poisoned him. And then himself, by mistake. As proof of this they
said he had also poisoned Baldwin of Alsace, the lord who had challenged Richard in the council, and who had died.

Richard might die, even saved from the sickness, die before her
eyes, felled by an arrow or a sword or a stray rock, trampled like her
brother Geoffrey. She crossed herself, her eyes closing. He could
not die.

She wondered why she let herself care so much again, after everything that had happened. She would do whatever God asked of
her henceforth—Masses and prayers, alms for the poor and barefoot pilgrimages—if her brother lived. But she had offered it all
before, for her baby, her husband, and they had died anyway.

If Richard lived, perhaps he had never been so sick. And she
owed God nothing.

Meanwhile, she would send in secret to King Philip Augustus, wishing him well. Reminding him what she had said, that he should leave the east, which was doing him such evil.

·   ·   ·

Edythe sank each honeycomb in a jar of wine, put covers over the round mouths, and weighted the covers. Johanna was at her prayers still. A page came in the door, stood to one side, and said, "The King of Jerusalem."

Johanna rose, shaking her skirts out. "All right. Send him in." Her voice was low; Edythe knew she was tired of this.

Edythe expected Guy de Lusignan, but the man who walked in was taller than Guy, younger, with thick dark hair and a dark drooping mustache. A soft wide bonnet sat tilted over one ear. His Byzantine cloak had a deep hemline of shredded gold and a gold clasp at his shoulder. Other, lesser men swirled around him, but he had a fighting-cock strut that drew all eyes, a look proud and cold. This, then, was the second King. Edythe backed away, watching Johanna in the center of the room.

"My lord Conrad," the Queen said, coolly.

Edythe put her hands together. There was likely some danger in this. He performed a flourish of a bow, wrists turned back, fingers spread. Edythe remembered that he had been at the Byzantine court; he had very Greek manners. He said, "I am delighted to set eyes on the beautiful Queen of Sicily, whose fame has preceded her."

"Well," Johanna said, and crooked a finger at a page, who ran up with a stool. "You could have done that much sooner had you let us into Tyre when we first came there." Edythe could hear the tension in her voice: She had to measure every word, for what she said here could be exactly wrong for Richard's cause.

The black King bowed again. "A misunderstanding, certainly, my dear lady." He lifted a hand and one of his men came forward with a pouch. "I come to you, my beautiful Queen, as a mere messenger." From the pouch he fingered up two long folded letters, sealed, which he handed to her.

"Mother," Johanna said, looking down at the first letter in her hands. She dropped the second without a glance to the floor. "By your leave, my lord."

Conrad was already going. Edythe realized he had gotten what he wanted: acceptance by a Plantagenet. Johanna had opened the letter from her mother and was deep in reading it, her face bright, laughing now and then. The tent door swung shut. Edythe craned her neck to see the other letter, lying on the floor by the Queen's feet.

"Mother says to tell you, 'Well done, O good and faithful servant.'" She glanced at Edythe as she said it, then saw her trying to read the other letter and gave her another, narrower look. "Go ahead, pick it up, see who it's from, since you're so curious."

Edythe flushed. Johanna laughed. "Oh, do." She went back to her letter.

"Is all well in Poitiers?" Edythe said, guardedly. She picked up the letter and turned it over, not recognizing the hand or the seal.

"She says so. She caught John at a plot to take the treasury and made him apologize until he cried; it's a very merry tale she makes." She folded the thick paper into thirds again. "You know everybody between here and Poitiers has read it. Who is that?"

Edythe broke off the seal. "I don't know. Oh. Isabella of Jerusalem. Here."

Johanna took the letter; her gaze leaped down the page. After a moment, she was frowning.

"I'd hoped for something more friendly, after we talked so well together, back in Tyre."

"Likely she thought it would be read, also," Edythe said.

"Well," Johanna said, turning the page over, to look at the seal. "It was." There were old traces of wax on the paper; whoever had opened it hadn't even bothered to reseal it carefully. "I do nothing that is not spied upon." She flung the letter down.

Edythe took it, curious, wondering why then Isabella had sent it at all. She balanced it on her fingers, noting the thick paper, the ink nearly purple, the letters formed in an even slanted hand.

"My lady, mark this, it's two sheets."

Johanna swiveled toward her. Edythe was trying to pick apart a corner of the letter; her nails were short and stubby and no use at this, and Johanna tore the letter from her grip and ran her thumbnail along the edge.

Like splitting a walnut shell, the letter came apart into separate leaves. Johanna said, "Aha," pleased. She gave Edythe a quick look. "Well done, O good and faithful." She bent over the hidden letter, delighted.

Edythe thought, *Yes, Plantagenet.*

. . .

Around sundown, Edythe went across the circle of the tents, to Richard's tent.

She sent a page in ahead of her, and when she went in, they were all looking at her. She stood and made a nice bow to cover a glance around the tent.

Like all of Richard's housings, it was a jumble of war gear, chests, and armor. The air stank. The bare ground was packed hard and uneven. A mail shirt hung on its cross by the lamp, its circlets glimmering like an animal shell. The iron skull of his helmet hung crooked on the upright. He himself sat on the pallet in his shirt, and Rouquin stood behind him. Half a dozen other men took up the room around her: his cousin Henry of Champagne, and Guy and Hugh de Lusignan, and some Hospitallers.

She said, "I crave your pardon, my lord; I came to see how you did. I will come back."

She could see that he was shivering, and his shirt stuck to his body, soaked with sweat. He had a cup of wine in his hand. He said, "Oh, excellently well. Well. Well." He took a deep drink of the wine. He turned his gaze at the other men. "Everybody get out, now. My physician is here."

They all filed out. Rouquin started to go, and Richard turned his head. "Stay." He smiled at her. His teeth chattered. "Be our duenno." Rouquin, behind him, rolled his eyes.

She said, "My lord, you should lie down. Change your clothes." Going up beside him she put her finger to his throat, where a deep narrow artery let her feel the pulse of his brain. He shut his eyes. The pulse beat evenly: a good sign. Half his ill now was exhaustion, his humors balanced again, but very low, easily disturbed. He shivered under her touch.

He said, "What did the letter from my mother say?"

She backed up. She had to serve God again. She glanced at Rouquin, behind him. But this was fairly harmless; Johanna would show him the letter.

"I didn't read it. Only chatter, I think. Your brother John was plotting and got caught and Eleanor made him cry over it." She could imagine this; John gushed tears when he was in a rage, and Eleanor knew how to work it out of him. "Please, my lord, you need to sleep."

"What did she say to Conrad?" he said.

She was still a moment. This was not exactly spying, but close. She licked her lips. She said, "She never called him King. But he was announced as the King. She said that he should have let you into

Tyre, when we were up there. He said that it was a misunderstanding. You need to lie down."

"Yes, yes." He glanced at Rouquin. "You're ready, then—
tomorrow, in the forenoon, we can try this?"

"I will—"

Then there was a scuffle at the door, and Guy de Lusignan
burst in. Edythe went out of the way. The King of Jerusalem hurried
toward Richard, his hands out, beseeching. "It's all over the camp
that you have received Conrad—You swore to me you would support me."

Richard hunched on the pallet. Edythe went quickly up and put
a blanket around him; Rouquin had gotten Guy by the arm and was
shoving him out the door. Richard lay down on the pallet and she
tucked the blanket close around him, and rubbed his arms to warm
him as he shivered.

He said, under his breath, "Good little monster."

Rouquin came up. "What's going to happen with that? Does
that mean Conrad is the King?"

Edythe stood; she remembered what Johanna had said, that everybody spied on her, and knew it was true. She told herself she
could not have done otherwise. That seemed shaky. She looked
around the room. They had brought in wine in casks, and she took
Richard another cup. She would find him some broth. She set the
cup beside him; he was talking to Rouquin, his voice a labored
whisper.

"It doesn't make any difference. The announcement doesn't matter, and she's only my sister in any case. Guy's safe, he has no choice
but me. Go away, I'm tired." She went out across the circle of the
tents again, wondering whom she served.

. . .

The priests and bishops with the Crusade told Mass every day in their tent-church, and every few days in the open, before the whole army around them. The women sat on the slope, separate from the men, Edythe behind Johanna, and Lilia beside her. Berengaria sat a little apart from them. The little Queen looked pale and sad, but she prayed with a fierce passion that rocked her on her knees, back and forth. Edythe did the outer motions, but she felt as separate from them as if she were standing on a star. She could not stop thinking of herself as a Jew, and yet she hardly knew what that meant, except she was not like the others.

*   *   *

The Crusaders attacked Acre across the belfry in the morning, all together, as fast as the narrow space would let them. Rouquin's men went first, with Richard's on their heels, and swept the wall clear; the Templars and Hospitallers followed, and they surged toward the gate. Then, climbing the belfry, King Guy's men began fighting with King Conrad's and the drive lost its force. The Saracens fired flaming arrows from the crevices of the ruin and catapulted stones down on them, and they had to fall back.

The sun was near the peak of the sky. Rouquin looked over his tired, dispirited men and sent them to their own fires, to eat whatever they had. With Mercadier at his heels he trudged up the slope toward Richard, who had been watching all of this from his litter. Beside him, under a canopy made of a cloak draped on lances, was King Philip.

Guy de Lusignan got there before Rouquin, chattering like a squirrel.

"You see how it is, my lord—I cannot turn my back—"

Richard snarled at him, and he quieted. Rouquin came up nearby; Richard was scowling down at Acre, the lines deeply graven

into his face. His pale hair was damp with sweat. The rest of the
army had dispersed and the Templars had gone to their prayers, but
Henry of Champagne was coming this way, everybody's fair young
cousin, always smiling. Rouquin wiped his face on a rag. He felt a
gouge over his eye and looked at the rag and saw new blood.

Philip said, "I say try the gate instead." He sat twisted on his
cushioned stool, his hands in his sleeves. A white hood covered his
head and his eyes looked rheumy. Rouquin turned his gaze down
on the city.

In the noon light Acre looked like a lumpy mass of gold, with
the citadel poking up out of it and the sweep of the seawall cradling
it against the blue water. It was hard to see what else they could
knock down. The rubble from the bombardments got in their way
now as much as the wall might have.

"Hold," he said. "What's this?"

Beside him, Richard turned, and Rouquin pointed: The gate was
pushing outward, and a man with a white flag came through.

"Hunh," Richard said. "They want to talk." He sat up and swung
his legs off the litter and made himself stand. "Get this thing out of
here." The bearers hurried the litter off.

Philip squirmed on his stool, but he did not rise. He blinked
rapidly, his gaze directed at the little group of men plodding up the
road toward the Crusader Kings.

"My lord, look there," said Mercadier.

Rouquin lifted his head. Off to the east, just beyond the edge
of the Crusader camp, a troop of horsemen rode up over the spine of
the ridge.

"God's blood," Richard said, "they know everything that goes on.
He's miles away and I'm in between, but everything that happens is
by Saladin's direction." He sent a page for Humphrey de Toron.

Rouquin blurted, "They are great soldiers."

Richard said, "Who else is worth fighting?" He was standing strong enough, and he moved away from Philip, hunched on his stool like a schoolboy. "But we'll beat them."

Several others of the Crusader camp were fast approaching, seeing what was up: Conrad of Montferrat strode in between Richard and the stool. On his heels was the German duke. Conrad thrust his chest out. "You won't want to conduct any talks without me, since I speak most excellent Arabic." Seeing Guy, he sneered, and Guy sprang hotly forward, his face flushed, his mouth open to yap.

"Stop," Richard said, and they fell silent. Guy looked down at his feet. The Saracen horsemen were almost there, and the group from the city was creeping up the road. All around, the Crusaders on the slope were standing, drawing closer, quiet and heedful. Even some of the women had come out of their tents. Humphrey de Toron slipped in among them, bowing.

Conrad said, "What is he doing here? He doesn't even fight." His lip curled. "Along with what else he doesn't do."

Richard said, "He will translate for us." He glanced at Philip, who was tugging on his lower lip, frowning.

Conrad veered toward him. "You need no—"

"If he makes a mistake, tell me," Richard said. "I see no fault in this."

Humphrey gave Conrad the briefest of glances. The Saracens drew rein a few yards from them, and several of them dismounted and came forward. Humphrey spoke to the one with the fanciest headgear, who was obviously the leader, and that man gave him a slight bow and replied. It was clear they knew each other.

Humphrey said, "My lords, I present to you al-Malik al-Adil Saif ad-Din, the brother of the servant of God Yusuf ibn Ayyub, Salah ad-Din, Sultan of Egypt and Syria."

"Yes, yes," Rouquin said, under his breath. He had heard of this man already, several times; the Crusaders called him Safadin. "Get on with it."

In fact Humphrey said a deal more, and Richard bowed, and Philip, finally, got to his feet and bowed, and the Saracen bowed back. Humphrey turned and spoke Arabic to the Saracen, taking just as long to present each of the Kings to him. Finally they all bowed again. Conrad stood the whole time with his arms folded over his chest and his mouth crimped shut. Rouquin glanced at the people from Acre, leaning on their flagstaff in the hot sun. One of them abruptly sat down in the road.

Richard said, "What is their purpose here?" He spoke to Humphrey, but he was looking with an intent curiosity at all of the Saracens, especially the men from the city. Philip lowered himself back onto his stool.

The man with the flagstaff spoke to Safadin, who said something short in reply, and then faced Humphrey and spoke. Humphrey said, "They want terms."

Philip sighed. The men around them began to murmur and quickly hushed, solemn. Richard said, "They'll surrender the city."

"Yes. They want to know the price, if they yield, to spare them all."

Through the crowd a crinkling, half-hushed excitement leaped. All across the whole slope, no one spoke. The Saracen Safadin stood straight as a pike, his head back and his eyes sharp.

"How many men are we talking about?" Richard said.

Humphrey and the man by the flagstaff spoke back and forth, and Humphrey said, "He doesn't really know. Maybe three thousand."

Richard said, "We will take the city. The garrison is free to go, under this ransom."

He held up one finger at each demand. "Two hundred thousand dinars. Saladin will free all of his Crusader prisoners. And he will return the True Cross to us. Then every man in Acre walks free."

Safadin burst out at once, barely letting Humphrey get through the change of words. Clearly the Saracen himself understood French; his dark, furious look showed his mind even before Humphrey was done. "Such an enormous sum! It is not possible."

Richard spoke straight to the Saracen; one hand swept toward the defenders by their white flag. "These are valiant men. They have fought like devils, or angels; they have given you their heart's blood, and you with the coffers of half the world say a little money is too much to redeem them."

The two Kings of Jerusalem stirred and nodded. On the stool, Philip muttered, "For once I think we agree." He glanced at the man beside him, who went off and came back with a cup. The crowd packed around them all craned forward, breathless.

The black-haired German Duke Leopold began, "Maybe if we—"

Richard spoke to Safadin. "Do you argue for the honor of Acre? Or for the convenience of the Sultan?"

The Saracen again barely let Humphrey get the words out. His voice was edged, emphatic. "There is not so much money in the whole of Syria. I would give my hope of heaven to free these men, but I cannot do that either."

Leopold said, "Maybe—"

The King of France tilted forward. "Then they decline the terms."

The man by the flagstaff was talking to the others with him. The man sitting on the road struggled to his feet. They all spoke at once, leaning together, as if they propped each other up, their hands lifted toward Safadin as if they prayed. Behind Richard, Humphrey whispered, "He says they have had no supplies and can get no more, they've had nothing fit to eat for months, even the rats are gone, they cannot keep on."

Richard grunted. Rouquin had been through a few sieges and knew what rat tasted like; he said, again, under his breath, "They are great soldiers." Richard glanced at him and moved off a step, away from everybody.

Philip said, "You have our terms." He shot a pointed look at Richard. "I say we have them by the balls. Make them pay."

Richard was looking toward Acre, the broken golden city below him. He said, "What's the moon?"

Rouquin said, "Fat, but not full yet."

"Then I have a few days more." He turned to the Saracen and spoke directly to him. "Those are the terms. Accept them or no peace."

The Saracen lifted his reins. "You are a hard man, Malik Rik. Let the contest continue." He gave a long look at the man by the flagstaff, mounted his horse, and galloped off. His men followed him. The defenders dragged their truce flag back down to the gate.

"Well, now," Richard said.

Philip gave a dry chuckle. His red-rimmed eyes darted toward Richard, and he turned and let his servants half-carry him back to his tent. The rest of the crowd was turning away, too, disappointed. Rouquin let out his breath, and went to see to his armor.

Seven

ACRE

The sun went down in a bloody haze of smoke and dust. Edythe stood at the door to the Queen's tent, where the air was cooler, if not sweeter. Back in the tent, Johanna said, "When we have Acre, at least, it will be done. They can call it done, and go."

Edythe thought nothing so halfway as merely taking Acre would satisfy Richard. She let the tent door drop and went in to set more candles. Johanna looked tired. Edythe brought the Queen a cup of oxymel for comfort. Lilia had disappeared again. They went to bed early.

In the night the blare of horns woke her with a start; sitting up, she could hear horses galloping, somewhere in the distance, and shouting. The horses were coming nearer. She threw the thin cover back. Lilia was still gone, and she was alone on the pallet. She called, "My lady," and then someone screamed, right outside, and she heard feet running, dozens, hundreds of feet pounding past the tent, and the brass shrieks of horns near and far.

"Edythe," Johanna cried, and she went from her pallet to the

Queen's. Johanna was standing, pulling her gown over her head—Edythe helped her get the skirts down straight and tied her laces.

"What's going on?" Edythe said; she wore only her shift, and she looked hastily around for more clothes.

Johanna said, "I don't know—" A man in mail strode in the tent door, carrying a sword.

The two women shrank back; Johanna flung out her arm to cover Edythe's nakedness and Edythe looked for a weapon. The knight's face was wild, but not from the sight of them. He saluted them and cried, in a trumpet voice, "We have guards around you, lady—fear not—stay as you are—" He dashed out again.

Johanna said, "We're being attacked." Her hands rose, to pray, or to thrust something off.

They were alone in the tent, even the pages gone. Edythe flung a kirtle over her head and down, yanking at the laces on the back. She got the dress settled on her shoulders and tied the belt awkwardly backward and could not get it tight enough. Johanna trimmed up the wick of the only lamp burning and the light bloomed, yellow.

Edythe thought suddenly of Berengaria.

"My lady, the little Queen—"

"Go bring her," Johanna said. "Better we're all together." She lit another lamp from the first. "Where is Lilia?"

Edythe went out the tent flap into the dark. A guard stood on either side. One was trying to get a torch to burn. The air was windy, warm, full of grit and the stink of smoke and garbage. She could hear drums down behind the ridge where the tents stood—east toward Saladin's camp. Down there also a wild shouting rose, and the neighing of horses. The Saracens were attacking—they must be striking through the midden there, a battle in the garbage.

The torch caught flame and cast its heavy light around them. A crowd of men and boys ran by her from the south, headed toward the fighting, some in mail, some waving swords, many barefooted. The ten yards along the ridgeline to the church tent, where Berengaria certainly was, looked impossibly far. She burst into a run just as another swarm, these on horseback, thundered across her path.

She stopped; she stood, frozen, not breathing, while they crashed by on either side; a horse brushed against her and she staggered, but they were away and she went only to one knee. They hurtled on past the tents and on to the fighting down the slope. An arrow slapped into the farthest tent, and then another, but stuck halfway through, only making the cloth shake. She fled across to the narrow opening into the church tent.

Much bigger than Johanna's, this tent was deep and dark, except for a space near the back where a lamp glowed. That was the altar. Around it the young Queen and her maids were huddled, praying. As Edythe came in, Berengaria's thin white face tipped up toward her.

"What is? What does?"

"We're being attacked," Edythe said. "Queen Johanna says we should all be together. She wants you to come there."

Berengaria licked her lips; she cast a look at the two Navarrese women and then faced Edythe again. "No. We stay. God help us. No other."

Edythe said, "No, please, you must—"

"I stay." Berengaria bent over her hands again, praying. Edythe gave up and went back to the tent's front opening.

Outside, in the dark, the crash and uproar of the battle sounded as if it were rolling toward them up the slope. The wide open space before her was trampled but empty. There were no sentries before the church, and the men who were supposed to guard Johanna's tent were gone, too, the torch dead on the ground. That meant Johanna was alone. She started forward, but before she had taken a step, three men dashed up from the rear of the camp into the open.

They whirled for an instant to look back, their faces hagridden, and then raced away. After them, between the tents, half a dozen others struggled toward her, marching backward, spread out in a line, still trying to defend themselves. On foot, they lashed out with swords and daggers and even a broken lance. They could not hold back the enemy; a shrieking wave of horsemen in fluttering white robes hounded them up the slope, and one by one the men on foot were going down.

Edythe could not move. These oncoming horsemen were Saracens, killing her people, and they would be on her in a moment. She felt nailed to the ground, struggling even to breathe. *Johanna*, she thought. *Johanna*. Then two black horses hurtled in between this tent and the next. Their riders' white surcoats shone like sails in the dark. They swung their lances down and charged straight past the retreating Christians into the Saracens.

Edythe yelled, breathless. Before the two black knights the white-robed Saracens looked suddenly small and frail, and the knights plowed into them like a row of dolls and rolled them back all down onto the slope, past the tents. In a moment the space between the tents was clear, except for two bodies lying twisted in the open. Edythe darted swiftly to the nearer, to see if she could help him, but she knew at a glance he was dead. The other was dead, too. She straightened. Around her was quiet and nothing moved, but in the distance rose a thousand-throated screech. Drums thundered. Johanna. She glanced quickly over her shoulder toward the Queen's tent, saw nothing, and turned back toward the battle.

The sun had not risen but the air was brightening. On her left, past the King of France's tent, she could see all along the snaking line of the ridge toward the sea. The fighting raged along it, in the murk of dawn one great mass of tangled thrashing shadows; she saw an arm rise, and a horse rear up, and sometimes a helmet, but everything else was a single broad seething struggle, as if it all dissolved into that black rift. Steadily more knights galloped up through the camp behind her and disappeared into the fighting. A riderless horse plunged along the ridge a few strides, reins flying, and on its own turned and charged into the battle.

Then Berengaria was coming toward her, the two Navarrese women stumbling and lamenting after her. The Queen's face was white. She held her skirts up in both hands and picked her way across the ground, going wide around the two tangled bodies. Edythe straightened, her hands out, and from between the tents Johanna hurried across the open ground toward them.

They all came together at once. Johanna's face shone; she cried out, "What's going on? Where have you been?" She flung her arms around them. "They've abandoned us—the guards have disappeared."

"Hurry," Edythe said. Berengaria had her tight by the hand, and she curled her free arm through Johanna's and drew them all toward the nearest shelter, the side wall of the French King's tent where it came down so close to King Guy's. From this space all they could see was stained canvas and a slice of the sky turning pale above them. Nearby a man screamed, and a horn began to bray, over and over.

Berengaria crossed herself. Johanna pushed on toward the far gap between the tents, and Edythe followed her. From the opening they could see down the long slope. Off to the east a thin line of red showed between the night and the day. The sun's new light spilled over the edge of the world, casting enormous shadows over the trampled ground. Still in darkness, the fighting boiled through the ravine at the far foot of the slope.

Johanna whispered, "Armageddon." She reached back and clutched Edythe's hand. Berengaria had come up behind them, close, her shawl around her.

But it was over now. The battle was over, just men running now, in the distance. Edythe had seen the end of the world, the black rift opening, but now it had closed, and the world was still here. The women stood, looking toward the distant fighting. Johanna said, "God be thanked, they're giving up."

"Go back," Berengaria said. "Come. Inside."

Johanna rushed after her back through the gap between the tents. Edythe followed. Her hands were shaking and she felt a sudden need to cry. Berengaria, she saw, was not going back to the church tent, but following Johanna. Even she needed company.

A great shout went up from down the slope, a roar of triumph, that echoed a long moment off the ridge. It seemed not to have come from the throats of mere men, but from one great beast. The Crusade. Not the way to peace but an endless war. She went quickly after the other women, feeling cold.

When they went in the door of Johanna's tent, Johanna stumbled; Berengaria recoiled away, her hands rising; and coming after them, Edythe saw the body lying on the threshold there and gasped.

"It's Lilia," Johanna said.

"Oh, my God." Edythe dropped on her knees beside the girl and laid her hands on her body. Lilia was stiff as wood. She had been dead for hours. Berengaria turned away and made for the prie-dieu. Johanna hovered over Edythe and the dead maid.

"What happened?"

"I don't know." Edythe could find no wound, and a wound anyway would make no sense; she must have been dead long before the fighting started.

Johanna said, "Damn them. Damn the Saracens, my poor Lilia. Almost now I want the Crusade."

Edythe said nothing. She pulled back Lilia's hair and the neck of her gown; under the maid's chin her throat was all bruised. In the purplish mottling there were long marks, like the imprint of fingers. Her belly tightened. *Poor Lilia*, she thought. The lover was not so sweet after all. Her eyes burned. *Poor Lilia.*

The tramp of feet wheeled her around. Rouquin came in the tent door and walked past her to Johanna's side. His hair stood on end; he wore no mail, only his swordbelt over his shirt.

"We drove them clear back over the plain. This was their last chance; we've beaten them now. Tomorrow maybe we'll take Acre." His head turned; he looked down at the dead woman almost at his feet. "What the hell? How did this happen?" He sank down on his heels and put his hand on Lilia.

"We went out," Johanna said, "and when we came back, she was here. We had no guards. If we had all been here, they would have murdered us too."

Rouquin straightened up again, staring at her. "What do you mean, you went out? You left the tent? What is wrong with you women?" His voice rose, whining. "Stay where we can take care of you."

"Oh, you took such care of us," Johanna said. "Not a guard the whole time."

"We won," Rouquin said, hard. "If you'd stay put, at least we'd know where you are." He looked down again. "I'm sorry about this. I'll take care of it." He yelled for men to carry off the body.

Edythe got to her feet. She needed to be by herself, and she went to the side of the tent, where the pallets were, and got busy shaking out the rumpled linen. Johanna sank down in a chair and wept. Berengaria prayed. Edythe's hands were trembling, and for a moment she could not get the sheet to lie flat on the Queen's pallet.

A few minutes later she went outside to find a page to bring them food, and Rouquin came up beside her.

"Wait," he said, with his usual grace.

She stopped and faced him. "My lord."

He said, "You asked me a question once; now I have one for you. What's going on here?"

She looked up at him, startled. As if anybody really knew what was going on. "What do you mean?"

"That girl wasn't killed in the fighting. What happened to her?"

"She had a lover," Edythe said. "She was seeing someone— someone high, or so she thought, but I don't know who."

"She wasn't killed there. She was dumped there. That's like a warning. Or a notice. Something."

Edythe felt a little quiver of alarm down her back. She lowered her eyes. She tried to remember everything Lilia had told her; she thought of the young man brushing against the maid in the marketplace, delivering a summons. "I don't know," she said.

He said, "Keep watch. If you find anything out, send for me."

"Yes, my lord."

"Be careful," he said, and went off. She stood a moment, struggling to make one piece of all of this, and gave up and went to find the page and their breakfast.

.   .   .

Johanna went to Mass, and said prayers for Lilia; when she was coming away, the Templar Grand Master came by her, as if by accident. For a moment he walked step by step with her, his eyes straight ahead, as if he did not see her.

He said, "I shall have speech with you, my lady. Wait for my call."

"What—"

But he was moving away, his back to her. He had commanded her, as if he had some power over her. She tried to understand this in any way other than that he knew she had gone behind Richard's

back to Philip Augustus. And she thought of Lilia, and her whole
body went cold.

•   •   •

In the morning the white flag flew again at the gate of Acre. Edythe
went out with the other women to watch as Richard and the other
high lords of the Crusade met the leaders of the garrison. With
their underlings all around, the Crusaders made a great pack, waiting at the top of the road. The rest of the army, scattered over the
slope around them, was slowly moving closer.

Edythe went in among these people, going toward the Kings. The
crowd was drawing steadily together, surrounding the road where
the Crusader lords stood, and the weary men from Acre dragged
their truce flag up toward them. Against her will she looked for the
French King and saw him, wrapped in a fancy gown, a white scarf
around his head.

Now she could hear Richard talking.

"They know my terms. Nothing has changed. They are the same
as the last time."

She began to pay attention to this; Humphrey de Toron was
there, and translated what Richard had said to the man standing
under the white flag.

This was the commander of the defense at Acre. He was in rags.
The bones of his shoulders showed even through his shirt, and he
was bracing himself against the flagpole. His lips were crusty with
sores. He spoke, and Humphrey turned to Richard and said, "He
agrees. They surrender."

She gasped. Her spirits, which had been so downcast, flew up
like a swallow. Around her a roar rose among the Crusaders close
enough to hear, and then it swelled and spread, rippling out across
the whole camp.

"God wills it—God wills it!"

The ragged man slumped against the flagpole. Richard turned to the other lords.

"My lords? Do you agree?" His voice was bland, although he had to shout to be heard over the din.

Guy and Conrad were bowing and nodding already in a happy babble. The French King faced Richard like a dog in a fight. The cloth on his head had slipped back, showing his bare bony scalp. His lips writhed above the stumps of his yellowed teeth. Edythe, a few feet away, heard nothing, could only see that he spoke, because of the thunderous cheering and whooping erupting from the camp. All across the slope the Crusaders were moving, were plunging toward Acre in an unruly tide.

Her elation faded. She lowered her eyes, and doubt filled her. She wondered what all this meant; was it over? Then she saw someone else riding into the camp, another white flag, but this one from the east. These were Saracens again, the envoy from the Sultan Saladin. Their real enemy. She had been right: Nothing was over.

She stopped. Humphrey stood with his hands folded over his belt. Richard stared unblinking at the French King until Philip Augustus at last lowered his eyes. Richard turned to Humphrey, and Edythe saw his lips move but she could not hear him. Then the newcomers rode up and someone gave a yell and the wall of retainers parted to let them through. The crowd had flooded downhill so far they were no hindrance between the oncoming Saracens and the Kings.

Three of the Saracens dismounted from their horses and strode forward. Brusquely, with no greeting to the Kings and lords around him, the leader went up to the ragged man leaning on the staff and spoke to him in their own tongue, a long question. The ragged man said only one syllable, and the Saracen flung his hands up and looked up at the sky and said something very plainly not a humble prayer of thanks.

Richard said, "Well, hail, my lord Safadin, welcome to Acre."

The Saracen stood still a moment. He was tall, not young, dressed in plain white robes; he was, Edythe thought, the most handsome man she had ever seen, making even the elegant Conrad seem coarse as clay. The Saracen's carved dark features were bold and strong above the pointed black beard, his thick brows bent into a frown over his large dark eyes. He wore a magnificent embroidered robe, a sash of cloth of gold, a turban intricately braided.

He said, suddenly, in clear French, "What are the terms?"

"The terms are the same as I spoke them before. I will give over the remains of this garrison for two hundred thousand dinars, all your French prisoners to go free, and the return of the True Cross."

The Saracen, Safadin, threw his hands up. "The Sultan will not agree to this." He wheeled toward the man under the flag and said another splatter of their own tongue and turned back to Richard. "We cannot agree. You cannot accept this surrender."

"My lord," Richard said, and flung his hand out to the city. "None of us has any choice."

Safadin wheeled toward where he pointed, and all the other heads turned in unison toward the city. A cry of dismay rose from all the Saracens, but the Crusaders yelled, triumphant.

Edythe followed their gaze. Down there the surge of the Crusaders toward Acre had taken them across the beaten ground and in over the broken wall. They were flooding into the city, and now, suddenly, above the remnant of the Tower by the gate, a banner flapped and caught the wind.

The King of France crowed; it was his green pennant. But then beside it Richard's great blue flag unfurled flat, and higher.

The roar that went up from the Crusaders made Edythe's ears

ring. Safadin threw his great-turbaned head back, turned on his heel, and stalked to his horse. In a moment he and his escort were galloping off across the almost-deserted Crusader camp. Edythe had her hands over her ears; she lowered them, looking down toward Acre, wondering if now they would go in there and actually live in a house. Beside the banners of the two Kings a third flag appeared, black, with some yellow emblem.

She sighed. She turned toward the camp again, where she could see Johanna now, come out of her tent, watching what was going on. The pack of the Crusader lords was breaking up. The French King hobbled away, a page coming after with his stool, and the two Kings of Jerusalem glared at each other for a while until they allowed their underlings to talk them apart. Richard stood there with Rouquin. He glanced at the city, his face shining, his eyes brighter than the sky.

"We did it," the King said. "And the moon not even full yet." His eyes narrowed, vexed. "Get that Austrian's banner down off the tower." He walked off, shouting for his horse. Rouquin went down toward Acre; after a few steps he was running. Edythe walked on up through the trash and char and dust of the camp toward Johanna.

Eight

ACRE

Johanna stood in the middle of the tent and directed the packing. After the battle, Berengaria had not left them; nor had she said much. She had changed, somehow, a quizzical look on her face, a kind of deference, although not to any of them. She sat by herself most of the time, her forehead creased. Now she perched on a stool beside Johanna while her women and her pages packed her goods.

Edythe had been folding bedding and shaking out gowns and shifts; she bent and pulled out one of the chests from beneath the pallet to store them in. Behind the chest, she saw another little box, hidden away there. Lilia had slept in this bed; it was surely hers.

"What shall I do with Lilia's things?"

Johanna glanced over. "What things?"

"Her clothes." Edythe laid the dead girl's second gown on the pallet, remembering Lilia wearing it, how she had loved the fine silky cloth. Johanna came up beside her. At once she saw the little box.

"What's that?"

Edythe busied herself with stowing the bedding in the chest, putting Lilia's gown on top. The Queen stooped for the little box. She called over the pages to break up the pallet and take it away, turned slightly into the light, and tipped back the lid.

The box was two hands long and one wide, and not deep. Johanna picked with her finger at the few baubles and ribbons and combs. "Not much. Poor girl. What's this?" She took out a little bundle wrapped in silk.

Invited, Edythe went over and looked. "What are they?"

Johanna had peeled back the silk. She twitched, and her voice went thin. "Just some reeds. There are a lot of them." She thrust the bundle back into the box and dropped it all into the brazier. "I told her not to be so free with men." She walked off, brisk, her back stiff.

Edythe watched her go, puzzled. The Queen had been much on edge of late. She wondered what the reeds had to do with it. Her mind went back to the day on the beach, when she had seen Lilia take a secret summons; that might have been such a reed. So they did have to do with a man. Still she wondered at Johanna's anger. She looked down at the brazier, where the box was flaming, the reeds already burned.

. . .

The Crusaders had been pouring into Acre from the moment they knew they had won it; the surrendered garrison had withdrawn behind a line of pikes into a little walled quarter with a gate, to wait until their ransom was paid. King Philip, by demand, took charge of guarding them, but Richard had arranged to feed them. The rest of the Crusaders streamed into the city and took over what they willed.

The Queens and their little households came in near the end of the day, when the camp was all but deserted and the city streets not so full. They entered through the main gate, where now only the

French King's banner and Richard's flew. Rumor had it the Duke of Austria, whose banner there Rouquin had torn down, had immediately left for the West.

The army was very short of horses. Richard had sent mounts only for his sister and his wife, so Johanna rode first, with Berengaria beside her. The rest of the women walked after them in a little parade.

The gate was smashed, still, although already Christians were working on the wall on either side, hauling the great stones back into place. The pavement of the narrow street was broken and dusty. The way took them by the first blasted houses of the city, where the war had reached in, crushed walls and roofs to rubble, and turned the gardens to dust.

Nonetheless, Acre was theirs; they had brought the city back to Christ. Edythe, walking behind Berengaria, felt her spirits lift, and she looked around her eagerly. They went through the momentary cold darkness beneath an archway. Beyond a gate, the street widened suddenly into a square.

They were deep inside Acre now. The houses here still had roofs and walls, although all the gates were broken in, the doors beyond were gone, and the gardens in between only dirt and stones. What had been a scaly feather-topped palm tree on a corner was only a rotting six-foot stump.

Yet it had been beautiful. Here and there on the tops of the walls some decoration still stood, six continuous feet of a filigree of stone, a single carved trefoil. The shapes of the houses invited her. Blank walls sealed them off, but through the open gates and doors she could see the buildings within, painted bright colors, with tiled floors, designs and pictures painted on the outside walls. On some were dark brown handprints that seemed stamped in old blood.

The place seemed still abandoned. The Crusader army had moved into the city, but it was so big it had swallowed them; she heard a shout, somewhere far off, and a couple of pages ran through a cross street, but the houses they rode by all seemed empty. They rode along a crooked street, past the high blank yellow stone of a wall; balconies jutted above like jaws under the edge of the roof, covered with lattices like strange teeth.

Her nose picked up the tang of the shore, but none of the teeming odors of life. This place was dead. No birds flew, no pigeons, not even vultures in the pale sky overhead, not a cat sunned itself on a high wall, no dog prowled.

They came into another paved square, where at the gates of the walled houses guards stood. In the center of the square was a ruined fountain, a stone angel in the middle, his head and one wing broken off. He spilled invisible water from a shell into an empty basin, crusty with dried weed.

At the foot of the fountain lay a bundle of rags, which the horses shied from. Johanna had ridden past it before a hand reached out from the ragged heap and a feeble voice croaked, "For the love of God. For the love of God."

Ahead of Edythe, Berengaria's horse shied, and one of their escort dropped back to catch its bridle. Edythe's steps lagged. As they passed, her gaze stayed on the ragged beggar, wondering if this was a man or a woman, Saracen or Christian. It had spoken French. In the shreds of its hood a few gray strands of hair showed.

No one else was paying any heed to it. Johanna was riding on, Berengaria on her heels. Edythe followed, her head turned to look back at the fountain. The street bent around a corner and they came to a gate, with a square tower beyond, three levels high.

Guards stood by the gate, and when they went into the courtyard they found it jammed with knights and pages. Johanna said, humorously, "I sense my brother is here somewhere." Grooms came for the horses, and they all went through the massive front door.

Into a house. Edythe followed the two Queens in through the door and stopped, overwhelmed. The square stone walls around her were bare and scarred and there was no furniture, but this was a house. For the first time in months she stood under a roof, the walls around her solid and straight and permanent. The pleasure washed over her, as real as food, spiced with simple gratitude. Johanna exclaimed, and Berengaria clapped her hands, her face lifted; they felt the same.

Edythe drew back, thinking of the beggar. Johanna could manage all this without her, and she went back to the courtyard. If Richard was here, then there was food, and she skirted the main hall, where she heard the glad cries of Eleanor's children meeting, and down a stairwell to the back.

Behind this tower the wall closed in on both sides, to a point above the sea. A ruined garden filled the space, but when she went around the corner of the citadel tower, she found wagons, and men lined up to get bread. She could not wait, and she moved around the people, peering over the sides of the crowded wagons. In one, she found a basket of dates, and took a handful.

She went out again, through the courtyard, to the street, and along it to the square where she had seen the beggar.

The ragged bundle had shifted, sat up, pressed against the bowl of the fountain, bracing itself on one fleshless arm. Edythe sank down beside it.

"Alms." The other hand jerked out toward her. Edythe knew the word, but it was in Greek, not French. She put two of the dates into the withered palm.

"Unh." The creature lifted its hand to its nose and sniffed. "Aaaaaah."

It was a woman, either really old or really sick. Mad, certainly. Most of her hair was gone. Her face was sunken to the bone, her eyes gummy, the hand with the dates a bone cage. She blinked at Edythe.

She spoke again, this time, Edythe thought, in Arabic, and put the dates to her mouth. Her lips moved on the food; a fierce shiver went through her. Staring into nothing, she mouthed the dates with toothless gums. The long narrow seeds slipped out between her lips as if by their own power.

More Crusaders were coming up the street. Edythe said, "Old woman, come to the citadel, I will care for you."

The bleary pale eyes groped toward her. Maybe she was blind. How had she lived? She swallowed, but her mouth was still working over the dates. "Go in there?" Date juice trickled down the side of her mouth, and she licked at it. "Do you know what happens in there?" She thrust her hand out. "More."

Edythe gave her the rest of the dates. "When did you come here?"

The old woman made no hurry with the food. She felt over the plump sticky fruits with her fingers, murmuring, almost smiling, chose one, and put it in her mouth. She said, "I have never left here." Brown date juice collected in the corners of her mouth.

"You were here during the siege?"

"I hid."

"How did you eat?"

The old woman put another date into her mouth. The boat-shaped stone of the previous one slid down her chin.

"You were here then when the Christians were here. We're here again. You're safe, now."

The clouded eyes turned toward her. "Safe. From what? They will lose, too. Everybody loses here."

"No," Edythe said. "This changes everything. Richard will throw down Saladin and take Jerusalem, and the new kingdom will rise up."

The old woman gave a sound like a laugh. Her hand reached out again. "More—More—"

Edythe had no more; she got up and backed away, wary, now, shaken. "Come to the citadel," she said. "Tell them the Lady Edythe summoned you." Richard would win. Then the old woman would understand. Another pack of Crusaders was coming up the street and she ran toward the archway, to get back before Johanna decided to look for her.

She was almost to the citadel gate when the bells began to ring. All around her, everyone stopped and turned; the porters put down their bales, the guards tipped their lances against the walls, the grooms hitched the horses to the walls. Heavy in the air the great brazen voices boomed, slow, demanding, and all started toward the sound. In the street before the citadel the mass of people all walking together was so thick Edythe could not but join them. They went on a few blocks as more and more people pressed in among them and went in under an arched doorway, and were inside a church.

The space around them packed them still closer together. Edythe moved steadily forward, pushed on by folk behind her. As she went, she raised her eyes to the old church. It had been looted, the walls stripped and scarred with burns and scrawled Arabic signs. Ahead, before the altar, the wall that had borne the icons was torn apart, the pulpit broken, the sanctuary laid open. One of thousands, packed together, she stood almost against the altar, in the middle of the great hall, and now, suddenly, from hundreds of throats, a great shout rose.

GLORIA

Her hair prickled up. The song swelled, a thundering joy, a massive wall of sound, so loud her ears rang.

GLORIA IN EXCELSIS DEO

A Templar walked up into the narrow strip of cracked pavement, carrying a bundle; he climbed up a step and fixed his burden there. The crowd fell to a rapt, emphatic hush. Edythe stood on her toes to see. The Templar stood down, gripped the wrapping on the bundle, and pulled it off.

At the sight such a cry went up from the packed crowd that Edythe sobbed, utterly taken out of herself. There hung a crucifix, the Sacrificed Christ, their Savior.

They were kneeling around her, and she knelt, her hands together, her heart pounding, lost in their midst. Their voices rose again, in praise, in a savage, exalting joy.

LAUDAMUS

Tears spilled down her cheeks. Around her they were crying out to God in gladness, certain they were heard, children running to a happy Father.

LAUDAMUS TE—

She clutched her fists to her breast, shaken. She knew no such certainty as this. Christ had died to save them, not her. This victory proved, again, that their God loved them, that they were worthy. But not her. Alone among them she could not stir this faith to life.

Please, she thought. *Something for me, please, let there be something for me, too.* She lowered her head on her hands, sobbing. *Please.*

·   ·   ·

The sun had gone down; in the western sky the evening star shone bright as a lamp. Johanna went quietly along the top of the sea wall, looking out to the murmuring dark water. She had told no one she was coming. She knew that was part of this, to tell no one.

Where the sea wall met the beach, a stair went down into a narrow square behind the blank backs of houses. She waited there a moment, her hands at her sides; the way was steep and went down into darkness. Then from the foot of the stair a man appeared, walking backward, to show her he was there, and she went slowly down the stair to the street.

He at once came to her and steered her to one side, where the angle of the wall and the stair hid them from all eyes. As he did so the church bells began to ring again, this time for Vespers.

"You came as bidden," he said. "Indeed, well behaved, for a Plantagenet." It was Robert de Sablé, Grand Master of the Templars.

Johanna said tautly, "I got your message." She threw the reed down on the ground at his feet. It landed with the bell and star showing. "What do you want?"

"My lady," he said, "surely you know what I know of you, or you would not have come at all."

Her heart churned like a mill of ice. "I did nothing."

He said, "You betrayed your brother to Philip Augustus, his enemy. Do you deny it? What secrets you gave him, the enemy?"

She said nothing. She remembered the bundle of reeds in Lilia's box; she knew how he had learned of this, and likely he knew more.

He said, "How would the King receive this news, do you suppose?"

"Don't tell him," she said. She turned away. Like a gray web her guilt covered her; she could not bear to imagine the look on Richard's face, even if he forgave her. He might never forgive her. It had seemed right, at first.

"Then for my silence I shall require some favors," he said.

She gritted her teeth. She saw how what she had done had led her to this; it was truth that a woman found a twisting path to everything. She lowered her head.

"You must stop trying to turn Philip from the Crusade. Already he talks of going home."

"Then he is unlikely to change," she said, looking at the stone wall.

The man behind her was only a voice. "And you must bend your brother the King toward supporting Conrad for the crown of Jerusalem. Guy has no gift for it. Lionheart must stay, and take back a few more cities, rebuild the kingdom, and then Conrad will fill all our coffers."

That was it, she saw; he needed the war, because through it the Templars throve. The price of his silence was that she betray herself. There was a ruthless order in the world, she knew, and she saw it here again, and despised him all the more.

She said, "Richard prefers Guy."

"Change his mind." The voice was farther away. She turned. He had gone. Her hands were clammy. She put them to her cheeks, terrified.

· · ·

The court settled quickly into the citadel. The tower stood three floors high; the great hall filled the ground floor, the women took over the center level, and the King the highest. The Christians driven out when the Muslims came were returning to Acre in streams. They looked more like the Saracens than the Crusaders, the men in long gowns and turbans, the veiled women in black. They chattered in some other language, but most of them spoke good enough French, although with many odd words. Palestino, some of the Crusaders called it.

Richard had given Guy de Lusignan lordship of the city because he had led the first assault. Guy rushed around judging various claims, allotting this house to that one, and stopping the fights. Richard and the other lords held endless councils on the top floor.

Everybody, even the knights, worked to rebuild the city wall and the ruined houses. One morning soon after they came in, Johanna heard a rooster crow. A few days later pigeons fluttered through the market square.

The weather was baking hot, the sea so blue it hurt the eyes. There was no sign of the Saracen ransom. The captive garrison stayed behind its wall, and every day Richard sent in a ration of bread.

Johanna had been living in a tent for six weeks, but now swiftly she gathered around her cooks and kitchen knaves, pages, porters, grooms, washerwomen, and seamstresses making them all new gowns of the local cloth. Every day merchants came to her door with the meats and fruits of the whole area, with traded goods and local. She hired several cooks and a Turk to haggle for her. After the camp food anything would be better, and now they ate for hours: shaved meats and cheese, sauces, breads and nuts and fruit, beans, mashes, compotes.

As hard as Johanna worked, yet the Grand Master's threat hung heavy over her. She woke up thinking of it and could not sleep at night because of it. But a new secret message from Isabella lightened her heart. This at least was a work with only good in it, and she could make right many wrongs. As soon as she could, she found her cousin Rouquin where they could talk without being overheard.

"The Queen Isabella has asked me to help her get an annulment of her marriage," she said. "And she has excellent grounds. She believes Conrad is still married to a woman he met at the Imperial court. He's her sister's first husband's brother, making him well within the forbidden bonds of kinship, and she was wed against her will, no matter what her mother says."

She had met Rouquin in the courtyard, which was still crowded with donkeys and wagons; he had been out of the city for two days, on some work for Richard. His men were leading their horses off, and she had guided him back into the shade of the wall, overhung with a flowering vine.

He said, "So what? All this was true a year ago, and he married her then." He looked tired. There was blood on his surcoat and he had his helmet in one hand.

Johanna leaned toward him, breathless with this scheme that did so many things so well. She had the secret letter, and she held it out to him. "We will get her marriage annulled, and then you, you marry her—you will be King of Jerusalem."

His jaw fell. Unaccountably he was angry. She had not seen him this angry at her since they were children. She had forgotten the red rage that took him. His eyes glinted. He bristled. He said, "Apparently, anybody can be King of Jerusalem. Is this your way of buying me? Am I a slut you can pay off?" He slapped at the paper in her hand. "Forget this, Johanna. This is trouble." He walked off, shouting for Mercadier, his officer.

•   •   •

She told Edythe what had happened, because she had to tell someone. "I don't know what he meant. It was wicked of him to be angry. I only meant to advance him."

"Do you think he would want to stay out here?" Edythe said.

"No," Johanna said, reluctantly. She was beginning to see it differently and that meant thinking about things she preferred to forget, and she gave up the idea.

But the one good thing she could do was gone, now. She felt heavy with ill feeling. At any moment de Sablé could expose her to Richard, a worthless, two-faced sister who had betrayed his Crusade.

She was putting her whole will into the work of making the household, and yet it did not please her. The food was too little, not good enough, not hot when it reached the table. The new gowns were ill-fitting. She was sharp and scowling, and nothing anybody did served her. More than ever, she longed to go home.

· · ·

Almost at once a market appeared in the main square, where also the fountain began to flow again, although the broken angel disappeared. Edythe went there, to get away from Johanna's viperous tongue and constant whining, and in among the jostling of the other market wives she found some very fine mushrooms, and more zingiber, and short hollow sticks full of a sweet juice. Honey cost more, and she bought several of the sweet canes to make Johanna's oxymel. Sending the page back to the citadel with the full basket, she went on alone, ignoring the screams and pleas of the vendors, looking at the lace, the pots, the plucked chickens, and the strings of dried peppers. Few of the voices around her spoke French. The vendors rushed out at her from their stalls, shouting as if they were old friends. Among the crowds of women swathed in their shawls she felt out of place. Then suddenly, someone was plucking at her skirt.

"Lady! Lady!"

It was the old beggar. She turned, startled. The crone's hand went out. "Alms. Alms."

"I have nothing." She backed up.

The beggar lunged at her. "Alms." Her hands like talons plucked at Edythe's skirt, at her belt, felt along her hands for rings. Edythe wheeled and ducked away into the crowd.

She went quickly down a lane, turning corners every few yards, and then across another square; when she looked back, the beggar was gone. She stood, panting, at the corner. She had no idea where she was. The beggar still made her scalp tingle. The old woman was horrible, a walking corpse, who should be dead but wasn't. She crossed the square and walked down the opposite street. Nothing seemed familiar. On either side blank stone walls rose from the edge of the street, higher than her head, topped with tiles or cutwork; behind them, she knew, were houses, yards, orchards. But she was lost. She passed a gate. The little niche set into the wall had been stripped to one last row of glazed brown tiles. Someone would put an icon there again. She turned right, and then at the end of the next lane, through a broken archway, she came into another market.

On either side baskets and hemp sacks offered nuts, spices, heaps of bright green powder; cages packed with live chickens hung from the roof poles. A vendor rushed at her fluttering a length of cloth. "Lady! Lady!" In a stall a man was hacking up a hanging headless carcass, its body a hunk of red muscle and white muscle sheath and bone.

"No," she said, "No," and shook her head, dodging people waving bowls and boxes at her, screaming, "Lady!" She passed a huge tawny beast squatting on the ground; on its long, narrow moth-eaten neck, its head was eye level with hers. As she went by, it let out a horrible aggrieved moan. She stepped around a heap of dung. "Lady!" Someone dangled a silver chain in her face. A hammer clanged. A small boy was beating a donkey with a stick. Then, at the end of the square, she saw a fountain, where several horses were drinking, and she recognized the big gray horse in the middle.

"No." She pushed her hands at the chains, the lengths of cloth, a woman with a double handful of eggs, and went gladly to the gray horse, looking for Rouquin.

He stood by the horse's head. He wore his mail, but not his helmet, his long surcoat filthy. When he saw her, he said, "Alone again," as if he had caught her stealing sweets, and came up between the horses to her.

"I was lost," she said. She had not seen him much since they came into Acre. She remembered the times he had helped her with Richard, when the King was sick, his tenderness then, but now, disappointed, she saw only the angry sullen brute he had been at first. He snorted at her.

"What you deserve," he said. "I guess I ought to take you back." With no more courtesy than that, he set his hands on her waist and hoisted her up sideways on his great saddle, led the horse away from the others, and vaulted up behind her.

She held to the saddle, her feet high above the stirrup. His arm with the reins came lightly along her waist, and his other hand rested on the pommel of the saddle, encircling her. She was trapped; perhaps he didn't mean this. Perhaps he did. She had to keep him talking.

She said, "Thank you."

"You shouldn't be out here by yourself. You should realize that by now."

She was silent a moment, in no position to argue. She searched for a safer line of talk. "Where will the Crusade go next?"

"First Richard has to get this money. The ransom for the prisoners. Philip is threatening to leave. A lot of people want to go straight to Jerusalem."

He was riding down a narrow way, past a donkey and two shoemakers, a wall seamed with the dry crusty roots of vines, not the usual way to the citadel.

"How close are we to Jerusalem?" she said.

They came up to a gate, and now, beyond the wall, she saw the tower of the citadel: This was a back way in. "Not really close enough," he said. "For my liking." He slid from the horse and lifted her down, and, stepping back, opened the gate.

She went through the wall into the ruins of a garden. The little trees were brown, and many had broken branches like dead dangling arms. The plants in the herb beds looked like thorny black claws. "I didn't know this way was here," she said.

He had left the horse and come after her down the measured little path. There was nobody else around; they were far behind the citadel's kitchen, the closest building, with a line of spindling trees between. She could hear the sea dashing up against the far wall. The garden was laid out in quarters, each framed in a waist-high course of stone. Even the stones were chipped and broken and fallen out of place. She said, a little breathless, "What a hell war is."

Rouquin said, "Yes. But then life is hell, isn't it?" They had come to the end of the path, where she had to turn, and he sat on the wall there so when she turned she faced him.

"But why make it worse?" she said.

"I'm not sure it is worse," he said. "I know what I'm doing when I'm fighting." He took hold of her hand.

"Fighting for God?" She drew her hand away, and he let her go easily enough, his fingers rough with calluses.

"This isn't about God, whatever Richard says. This is about power." He took her hand again.

"Please," she said.

He lifted her hand to his mouth, kissed the inside of her wrist, his tongue against her pulse, his eyes on her to see how she took this. She trembled. Some wild urge woke in her. She remembered again that night when he helped her with Richard, his gentleness, the hidden sweetness under his harsh temper. He said, "What, are you afraid of me? You're not afraid of anything." He drew her closer. She put her hands on his chest, meaning to push him away, and felt the hard body under the mail, and suddenly she leaned forward and kissed him.

He murmured. Their mouths pressed together, tentative, tremulous, soft. She felt suddenly that they were surrounded; where be-

fore they had been too much alone, now anybody might come on
them at any moment. She shut her eyes, all her body quickening.
His lips parted. He slid his tongue into her mouth, his hands on her
hips. He pulled her against him, one hand stroking her hip, the
other smoothing down over her backside.

She broke the kiss; she stepped away, her mouth dry, and her
heart thundering. "This is not honorable," she said, and ran toward
the back of the citadel.

.   .   .

Rouquin went to the end of the garden, where it overlooked the sea;
a slop of white foam showed momentarily above the top of the wall.
He thought: *honorable.*

She had kissed him first. She had given him her mouth, she
should give him the rest. He had heard the story about her. Some
man had abducted her from a nunnery, or she had gone willingly,
and Eleanor had rescued her. Either way, she had surely lost her
honor then.

He thought, uneasily, she must have been very young then.

It had nothing to do with honor, anyway. It had to do with her.
Her touch had saved Richard. Johanna depended on her. And her
kiss . . . She had kissed him first. He wanted more than just to have
her. He needed something of her.

He did not know exactly what. He stood looking out at the sea,
his mind clogged, stuck on some thought he could not pick apart
into words.

At least his bone had wilted. He wondered, briefly, if the Templars' lambskin drawers ever let them stand tall. He raised his hands
to his face and smelled her body on them; his chest felt the pressure
of her leaning against him. His mouth remembered the shape of her
mouth. The touch of her tongue against his tongue. The bone was

coming back. He walked swiftly to the gate, where he had left his horse.

·   ·   ·

Edythe watched him go from behind the pistachio trees. She had almost yielded to him. Even now part of her longed to go after him. She thought of his lips on her wrist, and her knees weakened.

She could not love him. She had no rank, and he was high-born, far above her. She remembered what Johanna had said: He could be King of Jerusalem. If he married Isabella. He would marry an heiress.

He would never marry Edythe. Even if she were a Christian. He wanted only one thing. All she could do was refuse him.

She shut her eyes; she imagined the house in Troyes, the people in the house, burning. She carried them along, somehow, a burning only she could feel, at the center of everything. She went into the citadel, toward somewhere dark and alone.

Nine

ACRE

"He won't let me go to his council." Johanna was pacing up and down the room. "He won't even let me sit there."

Berengaria was there, her hands idle. She turned to Edythe. "What is this? She is mad today." Her French had much improved, being around them more.

Edythe watched Johanna swoop around the room, sending the maids scurrying out of her way. The Queen could not be still, and her fingers picked at each other, as if she would tear herself to tatters. Edythe turned to Berengaria, whose eyes followed fascinated after Johanna, and said, "Please, my lady, would you take everyone out to the garden?"

Berengaria murmured. "It is not pretty out there," she said.

"Well, then," Edythe said, remembering the broken sticks of the garden, remembering also what had happened there between her and Rouquin, "you can make it pretty, my lady. You can enjoy yourself in doing it. Get the servants out. They'll know how to do the work. Go."

Berengaria's head sank down between her shoulders, but her gaze went toward Johanna, still shouting at the far end of the room. Her eyebrows twitched. Turning, the little Queen clapped her hands, calling her other women after her. She spoke in her own tongue and led a little procession out the side door.

When they were alone, Johanna wheeled at the far end of the room, and Edythe faced her. "What is it, my lady?"

Johanna strode toward her, her face stormy and her hands clutching at each other. "I cannot tell you." She sat down on the divan there and put her head in her hands and wept.

Edythe sat beside her and curled one arm around the Queen's shoulder, to steady her, to give her a place to rest. "What has happened?"

The Queen straightened, turning out of her embrace, her shoulders hunched. This new habit of worry had worn creases into her face. She took Edythe's hands tight in her own. Her eyes shone too bright. "You must swear to tell no one."

"My lady, you know this."

Johanna's gaze searched her face. As if what she saw there convinced her, she said, "The Templar. De Sablé. He knows. About me and Philip Augustus. He holds it over me like a ransom." She wrenched her hands from Edythe's and turned away. "And they will not let me go to this council, where I could at least seem to obey him—"

"Obey him." Edythe leaned toward her. "You mean he has given you commands?"

"He will that I support Conrad for King, and keep Philip here," Johanna said. "Or he might— He will tell Richard. He will make it seem much worse than it was. If he tells Richard—" Her hands were jerking and tugging at each other again.

Edythe said, "Draw the thorn. Tell Richard first."

"What?" Johanna swiveled toward her.

"Tell him," Edythe said. "He should know all, anyway—about de Sablé."

The Queen's wide eyes regarded her a moment. Her face smoothed out, her lips softer. "If I tell him, then he will find out—everything. And he will hate me." A tear shone on her lashes.

"He will not hate you," Edythe said. "He loves you, more than anyone, I think. Tell him."

"I cannot. I cannot. He would look at me so—" She turned, and clutched Edythe's hands. "You must not tell him. Swear you will not."

"My lady, I swear it," Edythe said. "But at least do not stoop to heed the Templar. He won't do anything. If he tells Richard, then his hold on you is gone. He must have other hens to pluck here; he is just boiling the water."

Johanna's mouth dropped open. "You think he is only feigning."

"All know Philip wants to leave—how could you make a difference? De Sablé wants to get you in the way of obeying him—like teaching a dog."

"Ah, God," Johanna said, "what a way to say it." But she looked much easier, and her voice had lost its whine.

"And," Edythe said, "You know very well there is a way we can go to the council, and hear all, if not speak."

Now Johanna actually smiled at her. "Oh, you are sideways wise, as my mother said."

"Then, come," Edythe said. "And see what happens."

* * *

Philip said, "We have won a great victory here. We have repaid Saladin for the disaster of Hattin, I think." He spoke a little mushily. He had lost many teeth in the fever. A dark velvet cap covered his head, which was allegedly bald as an onion. He coughed.

Edythe and Johanna crept into the front of the empty musicians'

balcony on the wall above the high table. Through the latticework of
the balcony's front wall they could see down on the heads of the chief
men of the council, stretched along the back of the table, their pages
and vassals moving constantly around them. Philip was directly
below Edythe, Richard to his right; she could see some of Richard's
face but only the top of Philip's head. Swiftly Edythe looked around
the crowded hall and near the far corner of the side table found a
pack of black and white knights, Robert de Sablé among them, the
red cross vivid on his chest.

She thought suddenly of Lilia, who had known about Johanna
and the King of France, dumped as a warning on Johanna's doorstep. Now she wondered less that Johanna was afraid. She glanced
at the Queen beside her; Johanna was looking intently down through
the lattice, her brows fretted.

Edythe pressed her lips together. She regretted promising to tell
no one, but she would regret more breaking the promise. Below
them Richard lifted his cup. "God be praised, and all our brave and
valiant men, that Acre is ours again!"

The hundred-odd men in the hall all shouted, exuberant, pleased
with themselves. All around they lifted cups and saluted one another, and the boys with the ewers ran back and forth filling the cups
again. The men below the gallery were talking again, and Edythe
cocked her head to hear them.

The King of France was saying, "In fact, this victory is so great I
believe I have fulfilled my vow."

Johanna made a small noise in her throat. Her right hand pressed
flat on the latticework. Below them, Richard's yellow head, circled
by his crown, wheeled around toward Philip. "What are you saying?
All week now the whole city has buzzed that you are planning to go
back to France, with the work undone."

Guy de Lusignan sat on his left hand, and Conrad of Montferrat on Philip's left; both of these would-be kings tilted forward to attend this, and the rest of the crowd hushed.

"Well, yes," Philip said. He twisted on the cushioned bench. Edythe wondered why he wore no crown. Perhaps his scalp was still tender; excess of yellow bile made the skin sensitive. He looked very yellow. Likely his humors were still unbalanced after the sickness, his body as crooked inside as it was outside, and he had a bilious temper, bitter and cold. He said, in a smooth voice, "I have taken Acre. I have come to God's help in His own land. I have served my King the length of my fee, and I will go back to France. Ah, dear France—"

"The Crusade—the service of God is greater than dear France! You swore to take back Jerusalem."

Edythe flicked a glance at Robert de Sablé, who was watching, as ever, smiling, as ever.

Beyond Philip, Conrad yawned, like a cat, tipping his head back, his teeth showing; his earlobes glittered in the torchlight. "In truth, you know, the Crusade is finished, my lords. The Saracens are alerted. They will not let us do too much more. We have got Acre back, at great cost. Why put that at risk? They have ruined Jaffa and they are destroying Ascalon now, which is as far south as we've ever gotten. Without those seaports we have no chance of holding the hinterland. What remains is to choose the rightful King for what we do have, so we can get the most out of it."

Richard's head swiveled; he leveled a brief, savage look at Conrad. Edythe remembered what he had told her that night in the tent. He needed the Crusade.

In a bright, clear voice, Guy said, "I will not leave off the Crusade until we hold Jerusalem and the True Cross is in our hands again."

There was a little cheer from those who heard. Richard straightened. His hands appeared on the table before him. "That's why you are the King," he said, loudly. He picked up the knife on the table and began jabbing it at the cup before him.

Conrad banged his fist down. "By what right? By what right? I am married to the heiress of Baldwin the Leper—"

"The Leper at least held the kingdom," Richard snarled. He slammed the knife down so hard it rebounded with a twang into a long arched flight down the room. "We shall take Jerusalem! Go, if you will, then, King Philip—I swear, I shall not leave here until Jerusalem is Christian again!"

Johanna sat back, her hands on her knees. "The devil." Another cheer rose, not much stronger than the one before. They were growing used to his pledges, Edythe thought, to these vaulting catapult flights of words. She put her eye to the latticework, holding her breath to listen.

Philip said, "Conrad is right, the Crusade is dead."

"How can you say that when we just took Acre—"

"A pimple on the backside of Asia," Conrad said, with a sneer. "Like Tyre. Like Antioch. They cling to the edge. But the land belongs to the Saracens, and Jerusalem is far inland."

Guy said, in that same mirror-bright voice, "Yet we can take it, with Lionheart to lead us."

Edythe muttered, "The foot-kisser."

Johanna nudged her. "Then he's kissing the wrong part." Edythe clapped her hand over her mouth to smother a laugh.

Below them, Richard shot up to his feet, shouting. "What right have you then to choose a King of Jerusalem, if you count it already lost? Let Guy be the King, who keeps faith!"

In the ranks of knights and lords watching, half of the men said, "Guy. King Guy," with much less enthusiasm than they had cheered themselves.

Conrad stood, his ears twinkling, his face dark with choler. "I am the King! The blood of the Kings lies in my arms at night—my son will be grandson and great-grandson of a King of Jerusalem— So shall his father be—King!"

The other half of the gathered nobles said, "Conrad. King Conrad." They seemed no happier with that. They knew what they did mattered nothing anyway. Their eyes were on Philip and Richard.

Philip said, "He has the stronger claim."

Richard swung toward him. "You damned serpent-tongued coward. You swore sacred vows for this Crusade."

Philip was watching him only through the sides of his eyes. He said, "Master of talk. But what you say means nothing."

"I said I would take Acre—"

"You said we would divide everything. Where's my half of Cyprus?"

"Cyprus!" Richard's voice rose. "You weren't anywhere near Cyprus. Where's my half of Flanders, then?"

Philip sneered at him. "Talk, talk. This two hundred thousand dinars, which the Sultan will give to ransom the garrison here, do I get half of that?"

His head was tipped a little; Edythe could see only the side of his face but she read the cunning in his eye. She thought, Johanna had no influence on him anyway. Beside her, the Queen was stiff as a plank.

Richard said, "Why do you think I asked so much?" His hand slapped the table. They had been more than a week in Acre and no word had come from the Sultan about the ransom.

"Well," Philip said. "I can wait awhile longer, for one hundred thousand dinars, and half of the True Cross."

Johanna whispered, "Oh, good, maybe . . ." She bit her lip. Edythe put an arm around her.

Conrad said, harshly, "But I shall be the King."

Richard flung himself down on the bench again. "Well," he said, his head turning slowly in Conrad's direction, "if he leaves, and there be only me to lead the Crusade, then I think you shall not be King."

Conrad's face stiffened. Just beyond him, Guy shone, bright as the flashy jewels in Conrad's earlobes, but he had the rare sense to stay silent. Conrad was rigid, his fists at his sides. Sweat popped out on his forehead. He turned and looked out at the nobles of Christendom and Outremer, gathered in the council, and no one moved or called his name.

In the glaring silence, Richard said, "When Guy dies, then you can be King. Because of Queen Isabella, who bears the Leper's blood. Which was blood, you know, ultimately, of an Angevin." He almost spat this at Philip.

"Devil's get," Philip said, quietly. "Doubly so, because of the whore your mother."

Edythe twitched; she loved Eleanor. Richard only sneered. "So? And who was your real father, anyway?"

Philip's body screwed itself tighter; his cap slipped, and she saw the blue-white of his scalp above his ear. But he knew, surely, the dangers of word-fighting with Richard. He said, "Thus even more is the Crusade clearly doomed. I am going home." One hand reached up and smoothed the cap back where it belonged. "I have given much to this place."

"Aye," Richard said. "So I hear. All sorts of relics, and you aren't even dead yet. What a saint."

Johanna said, "Here he is, coming."

Edythe looked up. De Sablé was walking toward the Kings. Her hair stood on end. He would betray the Queen now; he would accuse Philip of scheming with her—but he was bowing.

"My lords, my brothers and I must go to Vespers soon. I have come to ask your leave, and also to assent to your decision here."

Johanna's breath came out in a rush. The Kings spoke, and the Grand Master bowed, and then the Hospitallers came, and a steady parade of the other men. The council was over. They were taking Richard's solution. Richard was staying; Philip was not. Therefore they would follow Richard, no matter who was King.

The women stole out of the balcony and back down the stair. On the landing Johanna took Edythe by the sleeve. "Philip is going. He may halt a little, but he wants to go and he will. This must all be over soon."

"My lady, I hope so."

"The Templar said nothing."

"My lady, he gets no good of it, he loses all his hold on you, and Richard would hate him for it. He would not dare . . ." She left off what he would not dare.

"But—still—" Johanna lifted her head. "How can I be sure? Pray God he leaves me alone now." She lowered her gaze to Edythe. "Again, swear to me in your truest voice, you will not tell my brother."

"I will not, my lady."

"Come, then, before someone catches us."

.   .   .

Days passed. The Saracens did not send the ransom. Saladin's brother Safadin came, to ask for more time. The summer heat wore on. In the garden of the citadel, Berengaria had a force of servants prune and pluck and dig and carry water. Nothing much changed, except the place seemed cleaner. It was cool there, in the evenings, when even the citadel was too hot for comfort.

The city thronged with Crusaders filling the taverns and the whorehouses, which only days before had been empty ruined buildings. In the alleys women sold themselves to men while other men waited in line. The markets sprouted around the open squares, and every day the cost went up of everything sold there: bread and oil and wine as well as the beautiful cloth, the sweet dried fruits, the henna green as pistachios, the ironwork and goldwork and leather. Strings of the huge groaning beasts Edythe now knew to call camels lay folded on their scabby legs in the harbor while naked brown men unloaded their cargoes onto ships. Donkeys stacked with hay trotted switch-tailed down the streets. The reek of sweat and piss and rot lay over everything. Drunken men and beggars littered every corner, every square. In the late summer heat, even in the citadel the noise went on all night.

·   ·   ·

Berengaria said, "Is it not better?"

Johanna sat beside her, looking around at the garden. "Oh, much better, my lady." She turned to Edythe. "Bring me a cushion."

"Yes, my lady." The woman scurried off, her eyes lowered and her head bent; Johanna wondered at this odd cringing attitude in her. Johanna herself had been feeling lighter of heart since the council passed with no trouble. Maybe Edythe was right, and she could forget de Sablé. She looked around at Berengaria's garden.

It was hard to see much change. Some patches of yarrow grew in the back, and in the center a straggling rosebush, more stem than leaves. Some of the low bushes in front did look greener, and the rock walls were mended, and Berengaria had caused little lamps to be hung in the trees and set into niches in the walls, so the long blue evening was spangled with light. On the raked soil between some of the half-dead bushes were spiders of stems and leaves. "You should have them pull up the weeds, though."

"No—" Berengaria looked at her, her brow wrinkled. "I bade them not. They grew—they belong here. I want to see what they become."

Johanna laughed. "They will become weeds. No, do as you like, sister, I like it already."

She had brought her court out to enjoy the breeze from the sea, and the garden was pleasant, cool, out of the wind. It reminded her a little of Palermo, except of course the gardens in Palermo were splendid. Edythe came back with a cushion and sat behind her, her eyes downcast, and Johanna wondered again briefly what was wrong with her.

Sitting on the pavement with his lute in his lap, a Norman trouvère played, a handsome little song about the glories of King Richard on Crusade, with pennants and splendid horses and beautiful ladies waving their silken sleeves. This trouvère had already said he would write a song about the whole Crusade, and many people were making sure he knew their names and deeds.

The pages brought them wine, bits of fruit soaked in sugar, tiny pastries folded around dates, dates stuffed with pistachio and honey. Johanna licked her fingers. Surely now it was over with the Templar. The trouvère stood and bowed, his lute in his hand, and she patted her hands together in applause. He was better at the words than the lute, but she sent him a purse anyway, since the words were probably more important.

Henry of Champagne, her cousin, took the lute and played. Like all his family, he was excellent at music; he knew songs from the matter of Britain, Parsifal, and gentle Galahad. In the gusty balmy dusk people picked up the refrains. He played well enough for a knight, and his voice was deep and true. He sang the questions in Parsifal in a rolling booming tone that got them all crying out.

"Whom does the Grail serve? Why does the Lance bleed?"

A woman across the way wailed, overcome, and people clapped. Johanna crossed herself. They did this all for God; she would not lose sight of that. She thought, *When we are done, perhaps, the song of the Norman will sound so.* When the bad had faded away, as it must, while the good was pure, uncorruptible gold.

She turned to Edythe. "If my brother were here, he would play. Richard plays as well as any troubadour." She lifted her voice. "Rouquin! Rouquin, take the lute, and show them."

Across the garden, in the dark behind the glow of the lamps, Rouquin shook his head.

Johanna cried, "Oh, do, please."

He shook his head again, and then he was leaving, going away out the back. Beside her, Edythe straightened, her head rising, and sighed. Johanna gave her a long glance, and called to someone else to play.

Ten

ACRE

Edythe knew the city better every day. She went through a maze of narrow streets where shoemakers sat crosslegged in the shade with their awls and knives and scraps of leather, where women sold eggs and figs and children played in the dust, and found a sign she recognized: a little jar with a stick in it. The shop had no door, only three walls around a space two people long and one person wide.

Inside were drawers and shelves built into the walls, holding tiny stoppered pots, silk envelopes, and bowls with lids. A scale stood on the table at the end. Even as she stepped under the roof a man was bowing to her, smiling, rubbing his hands together.

"Welcome, lady, welcome."

She said, "I am a physician."

He bowed, smiling, as if anything could happen.

"I have a patient with a recurring fever."

He went to his shelves and began taking down jars and pots, opening them, giving them to her to sniff the oils they contained. "This for stomach. Good for stomach." It smelled like mint, like orange. "This for fever, this for throat." She sniffed deep of the complex scents.

"Ah."

"For restlessness. For sloth." He put another pot to her nose. "To bring man."

She drew in a disquieting animal aroma.

"To make man hard and strong." His eyebrows jacked up and down.

She laughed. None of this seemed what she needed, but she coveted it all, just to smell. She bought several jars; having Richard's purse, she needed not haggle. She said, as if an afterthought, "Are there Jews here?"

"Jews. No Jews in Acre." He shook his head, regretfully. "Jews have magic over herbs." She paid him, and left.

She wanted the Jews now not only to send messages to Eleanor, but to answer her own questions. She crisscrossed the old city but found no houses with the holy scroll beside the door. At last, collecting her courage, she went to the big central fountain and found the old beggar sitting in the shadow of the broken palm tree.

"Alms—"

Wordlessly she sat down beside the heap of rags, took the claw-like hand, and put a piece of bread into it. The old woman smelled bad. Her eyes were like raw mussels. A steady passage went by in the street: horse hooves stirring the dust, the padding bare feet of ordinary people, running children, a stray chicken, the curled toes of donkeys. She fed the old woman dates and bread, until the beggar said, "You came before."

"Yes."

"You know me."

"No," Edythe said. "Only what you told me, that you had been here awhile." She had drawn back behind the palm trunk, to keep from being seen from the street, and she folded her knees up and wrapped her arms around them.

"Then you want something." The old mouth chewed on the air. "What is it?"

"Were—" It was hard to get the words out. "Were there ever Jews here?"

The old woman growled. "Jews. The dogs. They brought the Hagarites on us. Everybody said so."

Edythe said nothing, wondering what Hagarites were. She felt cold, afraid she had given away too much. The beggar rocked back and forth, her old scrawny head tipped back.

"They went down by Jaffa. The old man had some sons, I think. Mordecai. They were rich, once."

"Mordecai," Edythe said, startled. But it was a common name.

"I know everybody." The old woman yawned. "I know." Her head moved to one side. Edythe waited for the old woman to say more, but then a gentle rumble of a snore came out of the pile of rags, and Edythe went away.

• • •

On her bed Johanna found a little flat bit of reed, only a few inches long. Her skin went cold. She glanced around, to make sure she was unwatched, and picked it up. There was a daub of ink on the underside. With a gesture like shying from a snake, she cast it into the chamber pot.

Nonetheless, she was there, the next evening, alone, at the foot of the stair by the sea wall. She faced him, brave, her head up, ready to be chided, and to defy him. She reminded herself what Edythe had said. He bowed to her.

"What happened happened, I know. Not much to be done." He sighed, as if they were both disappointed.

She began to say, "I will no longer—"

He said, "But I would have the letters of the Queen, which surely is within your grasp."

For a moment, shaken, she wondered which Queen he meant, and almost asked him; instead, she blurted, "I burned them."

He moved into the shadow of the wall. "I happen to know that is not so." His voice was smooth as wax. "Should I speak to your brother?"

She swallowed. "No. Wait." How could he know about the letters? He had some other spy. She was ruined; he would know everything, the plot with Isabella, everything. She thought of Edythe in a sudden gust of suspicion. But Edythe had promised her.

He said, "Bring them to me, here, tomorrow." He was drawing away. "And your brother is the power in the Crusade; you must no longer try to turn him aside." She lowered her head and let him go.

*   *   *

The Sultan sent his brother again to ask more time to raise the ransom. Philip ranted through the hall, jeering at Richard.

"You still believe this? I've heard talk he's killed his own prisoners. Meanwhile you're feeding his, what is it, forty bezants a day now for bread for these infidels—he's stalling! He will never pay. I am leaving."

In the middle of the room, Richard wheeled on him. "You cannot leave off the Crusade—you swore—"

Philip's shoulders hunched, and his eyes gleamed. "Well, I will not. Leave off the Crusade. I'll give up my half of the ransom, one hundred thousand dinars, to keep French knights here to fight for Jerusalem." His smile licked across his face; he gave a little smug nod of the head. "I'll order the Duke of Burgundy to command them."

Richard straightened; he hated Hugh of Burgundy as much as

any man alive, and he saw by Philip's sleek grin that the Gnome knew this. He wrenched his mind toward the hundred thousand dinars, now magically doubled. He needed money, he always needed money; it was a lowering thing, to be King and yet always grasping for pennies, but true.

"While I am on Crusade, my realms are in God's hands," he said to Philip. "You may walk on no crumb of dirt that's mine, you may receive no enemy of mine. I owe you no duties."

"Agreed, by the rule of the Pope," Philip said, sleekly. He had won. Richard could hear it in his voice, and it rankled him; he looked away, his neck rough. But if he got all the ransom from Saladin, then Philip would have lost. He would put Hugh of Burgundy in the rear guard, where even a stupid dirty-mouthed cunt-plugger couldn't make much trouble.

A few days later Philip did leave, finally, taking a long and wordy parting of Johanna; Richard saw how his sister's smile stiffened at the corners as the sad good-byes went on and was pleased at that, at least. Whatever had gone on between her and Philip in Sicily, she had lost interest now.

Still, he could not help feeling Philip had cozened him.

The next day he sent word to Saladin, that they should all meet before the gate of Acre at noon on the day after the full moon, to deliver the ransom and exchange their prisoners; and he said pointedly that the time had come once and for all to fulfill their oaths before God.

◆   ◆   ◆

Johanna paced up and down, up and down. Edythe saw her knitting her fingers together, and she said, "Is it de Sablé again on your mind?"

The Queen would not look at her. Edythe turned her gaze away, uneasy; out the window, she could hear someone singing in the garden.

Johanna came suddenly and sat down by her. "Edythe. You would not betray me."

"In God's name." Edythe turned and took her hands. "Not you, nor any child of Eleanor's. Oh, my dear, what is this?"

Johanna's fingers tightened around hers, but her gaze turned elsewhere. "He has . . . sent to me again."

"He means only to threaten you."

"Easy for you," Johanna said bitterly. "No harm comes to you." But she was still clinging tight to Edythe's hands.

Edythe said, "Who harms you harms me."

"I believe you. I believe you." The Queen flung her arms around her and they embraced. Edythe held her tight; she had again the idea that she had to give Johanna somewhere to rest.

"Have you seen him? Answered him?"

"I—" Johanna stirred. "I—no."

Edythe said nothing but held her fast; she knew Johanna was lying. Whatever had happened, she was under de Sablé's whip hand even more now.

Johanna said, "What shall I do?"

"You cannot go against your own heart. Don't see him. Give him no answer at all. Don't do what he wants."

In her arms Johanna sighed and was still. Edythe wondered what she was not saying; she felt a rush of tenderness toward the other woman, who got herself into such tangles. She thought, *Well, who doesn't?* Unwillingly she thought of Rouquin. She patted Johanna's shoulder and murmured reassurances, wishing she could put him out of her mind.

•   •   •

Johanna had never really thought Edythe was spying on her for the Templar. But someone was, or how would he know she still had the letters? Maybe he had been guessing. But she could not be sure. She had to keep him quiet. She wrapped up her mother's letters in a bundle and sent them to him. Her mother said nothing wicked anyway, not outright.

She kept on arguing against the Crusade, but she made sure nobody overheard.

She said, "Now that Philip is gone, you can go home, too. We can all go. Philip will not keep his word, you know that. He will start trying to take Normandy from you before he is even back to Paris."

Richard was sitting by the balcony, where there was a breeze, one leg folded with the ankle on the other knee. He said, "Now that Philip is gone, the Crusade is all mine."

Rouquin was staring at her, his eyes hard with temper. "We came to take back Jerusalem."

Johanna said, "Is Aquitaine not good enough, or Poitou, or Anjou, or Normandy, or England, all the sweet lands our father left you? It's not just Philip; even our witless brother schemes—"

Richard laughed. "Oh, yes. Wicked John. Whom Mother, apparently, outdid like the sluggard schoolboy he is." He turned to Rouquin. "Have you scouted the way to Jerusalem?"

Rouquin drifted over toward the table. Johanna had sent off all the servants, and he poured his wine himself. "I will if you order it."

"That's unlike you. You've done nothing?"

Rouquin swung around, bristling. "Jerusalem is far from here, and the country's harsh and dry and full of Saracens. That much I've found out."

"Well, then," Richard said. He turned to Johanna. "May I call a page now?" His voice was silky with exaggerated courtesy.

"Yes," she said. "Of course." She watched as Rouquin drained his cup in a swallow, filled it again, and went over past the divan, toward the balcony, away from Richard.

The King sent the page for Humphrey de Toron. There would be a few moments while they were alone again; Johanna said, "You risk so much, staying here. Everything Mother and Father built—"

"John can't beat a one-legged man to the privy," Richard said.

"But Philip can," Johanna said. "You know this. He is not the fighter you are, but—"

"Damned right he isn't," Richard said. "And he'd better heed the Pope's letter, too. While I'm on Crusade, everything is safe."

"It isn't working that way for John," she said.

"Nothing is working for John," Richard said. He raised his voice. "My lord de Toron, come attend us."

The young man joined them, slender, elegantly dressed, with his perfect manners and his lifetime's knowledge of the country. Johanna drew away, toward Rouquin, who had his back to the King and the handsome courtier called in place of him.

The sun was going down and the courtyard outside was filling up with shadows. Now suddenly Rouquin went closer to the balcony; he was looking down into the courtyard below. Johanna followed him.

Behind them, Richard said, "We were talking about Jerusalem."

Humphrey answered, "I am at your service, my lord."

"Can we march there straight from here? What is that ground like?"

"Aaah—"

"My cousin says it's rough, and a far way to the city."

"Then my lord de Rançun already knows the country."

Johanna stood just behind Rouquin; she thought the lord de

Rançun knew when he was being edged out, too. Past his shoulder she looked into the courtyard below.

"It's a long march," Humphrey was saying, "through some very hilly places, and full of bandits."

Still staring out over the balcony, Rouquin said, through tight lips, "In the Leper's time, the port for Jerusalem was Jaffa."

"My lord de Rançun is as always well informed," said Humphrey de Toron. Somehow he made this sound like a pat on the head.

Johanna leaned on the wall by the balcony door. Down there the servants were gathering in front of the kitchen, waiting for the last meal to come out. The door sprayed a bright yellow flood of light out into the deepening blue twilight. Rouquin was still staring down into the courtyard. She wondered if he was watching something particular or just keeping his back to Humphrey.

"Jaffa," Richard said. "That's south of here? How far?" The divan creaked; he had leaned forward. "What's the coast like?"

Humphrey's musical voice answered him. "It's one straight long beach from here to Egypt. There's some high ground—the hills you can see from here, at the southern end of this bay—and there are some ruined cities."

Out there, a dark form walked into the courtyard from the garden. Rouquin put his hand on the side of the door. The form became a person, who Johanna saw was Edythe. She wore her plain long dress, and the square-necked kirtle; her coif was coming loose, and her hair showed. In her hands she had bunches of herbs.

Johanna remembered the night in the garden, when they had both acted strangely at the same time. Abruptly much became clear to her.

She said, quietly, "Rouquin?"

Humphrey was saying, "Jaffa to Jerusalem is only one-third as far

as the distance between Acre and Jerusalem, and there is a road.
Supply lines, support."

"Then we should take Jaffa first," Richard said. "How far is it
from here?"

Rouquin turned stiffly and went out of the room, without asking leave, without saying anything. Johanna watched him go. She
thought, *Well, it's best if she does refuse him.*

Humphrey said, "Ten days. Two weeks maybe. Depending."

"On what Saladin does," Richard said.

"On how you both do," said Humphrey.

They would be fighting again soon. He would forget her then.
Johanna felt her eyes burn. She wondered how Edythe felt and re-
called some moments from a new view and thought, *She loves him.*

Yet it was no wonder she denied him. She was no child, but a
knowing woman. She would see that between a servant and a prince
there could be only one arrangement, in which he would have everything. This unaccountably made Johanna sad. She went back to the
divan and sat down, not listening to her brother talk about the coast
down to Jaffa.

·   ·   ·

The wind was blowing off the land, hot and gritty; Edythe drew the
tail of her coif across her mouth and nose to keep from breathing
sand. Johanna, beside her, moved closer into the protection of the
wall. Below them the great gate of Acre was full of men, some on
horses and some on foot, milling around talking, many times looking up the road, and into the sky.

Out beyond the city a little, on the slope, the captured garrison
was lined up, thousands of men jammed together, their hands tied
together and to each other, surrounded by mounted knights.

It was almost noon; the Saracens would soon bring the ransom and their prisoners, and these would go free and Saladin would return them the True Cross. Then, again, Johanna would hammer on her brother that the Crusade was fulfilled and he should go home. She had confided this to Edythe at the same time she had warned that someone else was spying on them for the Templar Grand Master.

Edythe plucked at the front of her gown, trying to peel it away from her body. The heat of the sun pounded down on her, and sweat soaked her shift; she thought with all the coming and going in the citadel that de Sablé likely needed no real spy but only to ask a few questions now and then. She wished she could ease Johanna's mind, but Johanna believed the worst, because she did not dare otherwise.

Edythe frowned. The road up and over the hill toward Saladin's camp was still empty. This was taking too long. She looked up at the sky; the sun seemed to be at its peak.

Down there Richard nudged his horse forward, looking at the ground. He wore a fine white silk surcoat over his mail, and on his head was his gold crown, each engrailment studded with a jewel; his shield with its three leopards hung from the cantle of his saddle. He looked impatient. Edythe could tell what he was watching now; the shadow his horse made, however he moved, stayed directly underneath. It was noon.

He rode back toward the gate, scowling. On the wall around Edythe and Johanna and the other women, a crowd of people was pushing closer to the edge to watch, more and more coming up every moment. Someone whispered, "I've heard Saladin has killed all his Christian prisoners. The devil. He cannot meet the terms." A woman sobbed, her hands to her face.

Edythe glanced at Johanna, who was leaning over the wall. "Look there," the Queen said.

She rushed over, hoping to see some sign that this was coming to a good end, but it was only Richard in the midst of a crowd of yelling, shoving men. They were all on foot around his horse, and their arms stretched toward him like waving tentacles. Edythe looked up the road again: nothing.

Below, King Conrad shouted, "Time, sire, he needs more time, surely—"

"They aren't coming," Edythe said, under her breath, and Johanna grunted.

A brawny knight in a red surcoat shoved Conrad out of the way. "Sire, he's making a fool of you. He's broken the bargain. Now we should make these prisoners pay their own ransom in blood."

Richard recoiled at that. Edythe thought, *Oh, God, he won't. He can't.* His horse half-reared, his hand tight on the reins. King Guy shouted, "Yes, yes, he's had time, he thinks you will yield, again, sir, he's testing you." Richard's head turned, taking in the other men around him, all clamoring at him.

The brawny knight flung a fist up. "Our dead cry from their graves for revenge! Let these prisoners pay for what we've all suffered!"

"Who is that?" Edythe asked.

"Hugh of Burgundy," Johanna said. "Richard hates him; they had an argument once and Hugh called him an awful name. There's de Sablé."

"The Saracens—" someone yelled. "Kill the fucking Saracens!"

The Grand Master of the Templars was forcing a way through the babbling mob around the King. "Sire—Sire—"

Edythe felt almost dizzy from the heat; Johanna wiped her face with her sleeve. Below them, de Sablé was saying, in a voice that pierced all the babble, "Sire, after Hattin, when they massacred my brothers, it's said Saladin looked on with joyful face. Now might we repay."

"Revenge," somebody shouted, and other voices picked it up. "Revenge!"

Johanna said, "He needed that money."

"Besides," Edythe said, leaning on the wall, faint, "now Philip is winning."

Down below Richard spurred his horse, driving away from the press of men, as if he fought free of enemies. Alone on the road, he swung the horse neatly on its hocks and faced them.

"Yes, kill them. I can't feed them, anyway—I can't let them go—I can't leave them here—kill them all."

Edythe gasped. Johanna covered her face with her hands a moment. Then she lifted her head, and her eyes turned toward Edythe; she reached out and caught the other woman by the arm. "Let's go home. Let's go home."

Edythe felt as if the sun's heat pinned her fast where she was. Below her the knights were riding toward the captives on the slope. She saw the swords drawn, and the captives saw them, and began to scream. Johanna was pulling her. She stumbled away after the Queen, down to where their horses waited. She thought, *This is why you are a monster, my lord. Not the other thing.* The screams rose, out there, shrill with terror, and inside the gate knights and men-at-arms fought to get out, to join in the slaughtering. Their voices rose, howling. She shut her eyes, following Johanna away, away.

• • •

She went into the garden, where Berengaria had coaxed some green things back to life; Johanna followed her like a lamb after the bell. Neither of them spoke. Berengaria was indoors, the little Queen having more sense than they did, knowing to stay out of the heat and away from the men. Edythe kept having to dash tears from her eyes. She concentrated on picking bunches of yarrow, which she would grind later into a paste. She had found some beautiful jars in the apothecary shop to store such balms in. A healing balm. Her stomach twisted.

A page came in the garden gate. "The King."

She straightened, moving away. He had shed the crown, the surcoat, the mail; he wore a Byzantine tunic with a plain border, scuffed riding boots, a belt of braided gold. He had just murdered three thousand men. Her stomach was cramped. He was hers, still, hers, no matter, but her belly hurt.

He came up before his sister, who had stood to greet him, and they kissed. Johanna took one of his hands. "Will you have some wine?"

"No. I have a lot to do, Jo, I can't stay long. I wish I could." He put her hand away. He looked tired, or distracted. Not especially remorseful. Edythe realized he would never speak of what he had done.

"You're leaving Acre," Johanna said. "You won't reconsider."

"No. I'm taking the army down the coast to Jaffa. You can stay here."

Edythe drew closer; she said, under her breath, "Jaffa."

Johanna said, "Richard, you must take care. This is a strange place, and they have such strange ways—I am afraid." She put her arms around him, and they held each other; he laid his cheek against her hair. Edythe thought, again, *Of anyone, this is whom he loves*. Johanna stood back.

"Will—the Templars go?"

"Yes," he said. "Of course." He glanced at Edythe.

Johanna's face smoothed out, calmer. One problem solved. She sat down on the stone bench behind her. "Very well, then. But we should go with you. Berengaria and I."

Edythe thought she said this to be dutiful; surely she knew

he had already made up his mind to leave them in Acre. Berengaria had come in the gate and stood there listening.

Richard said, "This will be a rough march. We'll have some fighting, maybe a lot of fighting. And I don't know what we'll have when we get there. You should stay here until I send for you."

Johanna bowed her head, as if submitting to this. Then Richard was turning to Edythe. "Can you treat wounds?"

Edythe said, "I—I have—" Thinking of the bumps and scrapes of pages, a lapdog's broken leg, and digging a needle out of Alys's finger.

Johanna surged up off the bench. "You can't take her—by herself—she's a woman!"

Richard said, "She is the only doctor I have, and she's done well at it. I'm taking the fleet down, too. She can go on shipboard. She'll be in no danger."

Edythe said, "I want to go."

Johanna said, "Why?" and Richard said, at the same time, "Good." He moved a little closer to Johanna, and his voice fell. "She's good luck to me. And if I get sick."

Johanna was staring at Edythe. "But I need her."

"It will only be a little while," Richard said. He patted his sister's cheek and turned and went, passing Berengaria as if he never saw her at all. Edythe turned back to picking yarrow. She was going to Jaffa. She was going to Jaffa to find out what it meant to be a Jew.

Eleven

ACRE

Johanna said, "I shall miss you very much. I don't know why you're going."

Edythe said, "I can do some good." She kissed Johanna's hand. "My lady. Pray for me."

"I will," Johanna said. "And pray for me also, I will think of you every hour."

Edythe went down the plank to the galley; the captain met her, short and lively, with bright blue eyes in a dark face. His name was Ayberk and he spoke strange but fluent French. He said, "Welcome, lady, welcome. Richard the Basileus has placed you in my care." He crossed himself, Greek-wise. "I will watch you close, and you will have fear of nothing." He took her to the foredeck, where a little tent was rigged.

Almost at once the galley set its huge triangular sails. One of half a hundred ships, they went south across the long shallow bay, turned the hilly cape at the far end, and anchored in the shallows just off a white beach.

Night fell. They fed her excellently, stewed meat and yogurt and bread. She slept in the tent; Ayberk himself slept on the deck just outside. In the morning, the army still had not appeared on the shore. Ayberk seemed unconcerned. And in fact by midday groups of horsemen were straggling down over the hill toward them. There was no sign of any Saracens. They made a camp, and Edythe spent another night there on the ship.

The next day they sailed south again, going close along the coast, the army marching just beyond the sand of the beach. The heat and the idleness had her half-asleep; she pushed the little tent open, to get some breeze. She missed Johanna, and she was wishing she had something to do, when Ayberk came up.

"Saraceno."

She jerked upright. Shaded her eyes with her hand. Ahead of them, under their great sails, the galleys stretched in a line into the south, hardly a length apart and only a hundred yards off the beach. Just above the white sand the Crusader army rode, studded with upright lances and little pennons. Beyond, on the hills, a white dust cloud was rising.

Her scalp prickled up. She could hear them, even over the relentless sawing of the oars: a faint warbling scream, and then the low rumble of their drums.

Ayberk was calling, motioning with his hand, and the ship slid in closer toward the beach. "Rocks," he said. "Rocks all everywhere here. Look." One hand on the mast stay, he leaped onto the gunwale of the galley and stared to the east. She went to the rail and looked down; through the clear blue-green water she could see the sand, far below, pale between shoals of flat mossy rocks like the ones at Acre. The ship glided above as if through the stumps of teeth.

Out on the land the dust cloud swirled closer. On all the galleys in their wavering line ahead of her, men with bows were climbing up onto the wooden frames around the mainmasts. Ayberk turned to her.

"You see, the Basileus Richard good on this." He tapped the side of his head. "The flank we cover. See?"

She leaned on the rail, breathless. They were near the tail end of the line of galleys, and most of the army was ahead of them. She wondered if she imagined the main body moving faster than the rear guard, this disorderly crowd of horsemen and men on foot on the shore directly opposite her.

They were close enough that she could see the men turning toward the cloud of dust approaching from the east. Then, out of that oncoming dust, a flight of arrows rose and pelted down.

Ayberk yelled to his helmsman again, and their ship slowed. On the wooden castle at the mast, ten men stood with crossbows. Edythe clutched the railing. Ayberk maneuvered his ship closer to the beach and kept them at the flank of the Crusader army there; if the white wave of horsemen tried to sweep down the beach and surround the Christians, they would come within range of the crossbows. She saw that this was well done and looked on him with more admiration. The Saracens, their arrows loosed, veered and rode off.

Moments later they came back from another angle, loosing another storm of arrows, their shrieks thin in the distance. They were striking with all their force at this rear guard, she saw, but she saw also that they could not overwhelm the Crusaders. Armored in their mail, their shields up, the Christians rode along unscathed through the waves of arrows. The bolts hit and stuck, in shields, in mail, but they did not kill. Arrows poking out of them, men went on as if nothing had touched them. On the edge of the pack of knights, the men-at-arms with crossbows and javelins kept the Saracens from coming too close, and the crossbows of the fleet held the other flank.

She saw a horse go down, and the rider leap from it and begin to walk, still carrying his lance. Someone quickly brought him a fresh horse, and other men ran to the dead one and stripped off its harness. The Crusader army paced on steadily, and the Saracens, wailing, fled away again.

This time they came from the rear, and the last few ranks of the Crusaders wheeled and lunged to meet them.

Ayberk said, "Bad. See. They stop. Bad."

She looked down to the south, to the front of the army, which had pulled away. And now the whole rear guard had stopped marching, was bunching together and turning to face the Saracens.

The gap widened between them and the main army. The high-pitched screaming of the Saracens took a keener edge, and the waves of arrows came closer and faster. Then, from the south, a horn blew.

She turned, looking that way. A line of horsemen was galloping up the beach. As they rode, more and more men peeled away from the army, until hundreds of knights pounded up along the sand toward the embattled rear guard. They came in a thundering pack, their surcoats fluttering, their lances upright. They reached the end of the main army, where there was more room, and without a signal that she could see, the pack stretched out, the men behind galloping up to the front, so that they formed into a single rank. The horses at full stride, the men riding long-stirruped and tall, they flowed over the land like a great sword. She caught her breath, her heart pounding, caught by the power and beauty of this charge.

"The Basileus Richard," Ayberk cried, and pointed.

The first of them all, she saw, wore a crown over his helmet. Then Rouquin was there somewhere. She beat her fists on the rail. They streaked down past the bedeviled rear guard, and in a ragged pattern the lances swung to level, and stirrup to stirrup and head to head the charge hurtled into the lighter Saracen horsemen.

The white-robed archers went down as if a wave of iron had broken over them. Ayberk whooped, delighted. The rest of the Saracens were whirling, fleeing, but on the sand behind the charge lay trampled bodies, a crippled horse trying to stand. The Crusader charge took them straight in among the rear guard, and every Saracen was running.

"No," Ayberk cried. "Stop."

She glanced at him, turned back to see what he meant. The inland few men of the charging Crusader line had veered off to chase the Saracens back toward the hills. This seemed a daring move to her, and she wondered they did not all follow it. Then halfway to the hills the fleeing Saracens turned, circled, and engulfed the men chasing them.

"Oh, no," she said. Cut off from their own, and scattered apart as they rode, the handful of Crusaders were caught in the midst of hundreds of horse archers. Now the lighter, faster Saracens had the edge. She gasped; her hands beat the railing. The trapped Crusaders were struggling to get back to the others, but steadily they were surrounded; their horses stumbled; a knight staggered on the ground, trying to fight, and then fell. The Saracens raised their tremulous cry of triumph. The rising dust hid them. Nearer, by the beach, the rear guard had begun moving again, faster, she thought, as if flogged, the men-at-arms running.

Ayberk said, "Ahead is camp."

She licked her lips. She could see the first ships of the fleet turning in to the beach. Up above the sand were ruins, archways, piles of bricks. She craned her neck, looking back the way they had come; the rear guard was catching up with the rest of the army again, and she could scarcely see the fine film of dust, toward the hills. No Christian knight came back from there. She thought, *If I stay here, I will never find out.*

Then, she thought, *I won't stay here.*

But it was twilight before she managed to wade ashore, carrying her sack of potions and balms and jars. The army had begun laying out its camp in the meadow by the ruins, putting stones in rings for fires and marking out spaces with saddles and lances. She had no trouble finding Richard. He alone had a tent, a great sway-backed sprawl of cloth draped over poles and rope, the edges held down under bales and casks. A sledge heaped with wood was drawn up before it, and as she drew near, a man was building a fire out in front. A groom led around a weary horse, stripped to a halter. In the midst of a swarm of squires and pages, Richard stood giving orders and drinking a cup of wine. He already had his mail off.

When the last man had gone, he turned to her. "What are you doing here?" he said. "I was just about to send for you. Come on, then, here he comes."

Her heart turned to an icy rock. Someone had been hurt. Three horsemen were trudging up toward the King's campfire, and she recognized Rouquin's gray horse.

But Rouquin was hale and in the saddle. He swung down into the firelight; three arrows stuck out of the shoulder of his mail. She caught her breath. Then he was helping the man behind him dismount, and that man leaned hard on him and sobbed in pain.

Richard said, "You stupid ass, Mercadier, you should have died out there. Get over here." He turned to her. "Fix him." He drank from his cup.

She stood, heart pounding, while Rouquin and the two others brought the injured man up into the firelight and sat him down.

She squatted in front of him and looked him over. Mercadier had no arrows in him; his helmet was off, his short black hair plastered to his head, his eyes open. His round brown cheeks were drawn hollow, but in spite of the pain creasing his face he did not seem to be wounded. She said, "Mercadier. Where does it hurt?" Then she saw his right arm, hanging by his side, the forearm twisted out.

"His horse went down," Rouquin said, behind her.

She stood up. "Can you get out of the mail?"

Mercadier struggled left-handed with his mail, and then another man bent and helped him. Still he was gasping and soaked with sweat when they got it off. The other man unlaced the Brabanter's padded jack and pulled that off, too. She glanced at Rouquin; Richard had given him the cup of wine and stood behind him worrying the arrows one at a time out of his mail.

She turned back to Mercadier. Even without touching him, she could see by the way the arm hung that the bones had come apart at the shoulder. She had seen this relocation done once, a long time ago. Then it had seemed wonderful to her, the way the body wanted to be whole. Now she hoped she remembered it that well. "Somebody sit back to back with him."

The other man sat down, and Mercadier leaned against him. Edythe squatted before him again.

"This will hurt," she said.

"Hurts now." Sweat lay in droplets on his forehead and his black beard.

She took his injured arm by the wrist and elbow and laid the forearm over his belly so that his upper arm hung straight against his side. With her left hand she held that elbow fast, and with her right on his wrist she began turning his forearm out away from his body.

He gasped and gulped, his eyes popping, and the man behind him gripped his other arm to hold him. She felt the bones turn, the joint snagged briefly, and then the top of his arm rolled over the rim of the socket and dropped into place. She sat back, her hands empty.

He shut his eyes, breathing hard, but his face was suddenly smooth. The man behind him let him go. Mercadier lifted his other hand to his shoulder and opened his eyes toward her. "Thanks."

"Be careful with it." She said. "I'll bind it up for you."

Richard said, "If my own men won't heed me, what good is this? We have to keep the march. Don't break after them. When they attack, they can do nothing if we stay together. The mail stops the arrows, see?" He flung down the two arrows in his hand, which he had just tugged out of Rouquin's mail. "Just stay in the march, damn you; I thought you were a good soldier." He was yanking on the last arrow. "This one is deep."

Rouquin grunted at him. Edythe got up, her gaze on him; he looked well enough, although he was breathing hard as Richard wiggled the last arrow loose. She had not let herself look at him since the kiss. Now she had an excuse, and she took it.

She said, "Let me see that."

He said, shortly, "It's nothing." He kept his eyes down. He gave Richard the wine cup, and Richard tossed it to a waiting page.

"Let her look. I need you, and a few of those felt as if they bit." He swung toward Mercadier. "You damned near got your lord killed, see."

"Sire—"

"Shut up."

Rouquin stripped off his mail and the padded jack under it. His chest was soaked with sweat, the red hair plastered to the skin. She glanced at the arrows; the long heads were bent and nicked from the mail. Two of the three had penetrated far enough to make small nasty wounds.

"Sit," she said. She took the flask of vinegar and a pair of pincers from her pouch. He sat on a barrel. The arrows had carried shreds of cloth and fiber from the jack into the star-shaped holes, and she picked those carefully out with the pincers. She washed each cut with the vinegar and smeared it with yarrow balm. He looked bigger with his clothes off. His chest was massive and hard-muscled under the great arches of his shoulders. Touching him, she remembered kissing him and wanted to kiss him again, everywhere.

Remember, she thought. *Remember why you are going to Jaffa. Don't be distracted by a man beyond your reach anyway.* He didn't care; he wasn't looking at her.

Richard was saying, "Hugh of Burgundy is a complete fool." He nodded at a page offering him a cup of wine. "Give it to him."

"You put him in the rear guard," Rouquin said. The page brought him the cup. She was standing by his knee working on the deep wound in the front of his shoulder, and for an instant as he reached for the wine their eyes caught.

His look was so intense she gave a shiver. She tore her gaze away, hot down to her heels. Her fingers pressed on the heavy muscle of his arm. She rubbed the yarrow over the slit in his shoulder, her knees trembling.

"I'll send the Hospitallers to the rear guard," Richard was saying. "At least they obey orders." He gave a deep, humorless laugh. "That was a nice charge. We'll teach the Saracens not to try to stand up to us."

The other men growled agreement. They were turning chunks of meat over the fire, and slowly they all fell to eating. She backed away; a serving man brought her a piece of bread with a bit of meat on it. Richard said, "Make her a place in the tent. I'll be her dragon." He laughed. Rouquin was by the fire with the rest of the men, eating. She went back into the tent and sat down; by the door a torch already burned.

The meat was almost raw. The juice dripped down her chin. She remembered how Mercadier's arm bone had moved under her hand, how it had slipped back where it belonged, and a deep satisfaction flooded through her.

She thought of Rouquin, and shut her eyes. Remembered why she was going to Jaffa. But she wanted him, and now she saw that he still wanted her. She ate the bread soaked in blood and wiped her hands on her kirtle.

◆　◆　◆

The sea was pleated blue and silver; where the breakers rushed over the rocks the foam was lacy white. Humphrey de Toron leaned his arm on the seawall. The pile of the monastery loomed behind him and he could hear the monks chanting Vespers. He had been waiting all day, and she had not come. Soon the sun would go down and he would have to admit they had failed.

When the Crusade left Acre to go south, he had come north, up to this little monastery on top of the white rocks called the Ladder of Tyre. In the sea-washed caves below there once had been hermits, but now the monastery favored a more comfortable way of life. He watched the sun sinking, wondering what to do next.

"Freo."

He wheeled around. Isabella came out the door, alone.

"Oh, my God," he said, and she came to him and they embraced. Married as children, they had had only each other all through the bad times of stepfathers and stepmothers and wars and hostage, and he would always love her best of all. And she was adorable. He stepped back, looking into her eyes.

"You are the most beautiful Queen in the Holy Land." He laughed. "Believe me. I've seen a few." He leaned on the wall again. "Including she of Sicily, who is keeping Conrad in Acre, so that we could meet. But she won't be able to hold him there for very long, now that Richard's gone."

"The dog," Isabella said, with force. The end of her coif fluttered in the wind. She was supposed to be in common dress, which for her meant a long dark gown with thin gold trim, gold slippers, gold on her fingers and in her ears. She went on, "How could he disdain the Crusade? Call himself King and yet not go to the rescue of Jerusalem?"

Humphrey said, "There, actually, I agree with him. We cannot hold Jerusalem."

"Oh, Freo." She came up into the wind. "Then it is all gone, isn't it, what so many have died for, gone." She turned on him, her cheeks ruddy in the wind. The sun was going down and spilled its light all over her, so that even her tears were golden.

"Why did you not fight for me? Why did you let me go like that?"

"He would only have killed me, Bella. He wanted to kill me. And then he'd still have taken you. God, if I could have saved you that way, I would have, I swear it, but it would have been for nothing."

She put out her hands to him, and he took them. "Freo, he does every night what you said. Every night. It's like having a grunting dog lying on me. Worse."

"I'll help you. Johanna is in Acre now, and she will help you. If you can get out of Tyre, we can help you fly beyond his reach—Antioch, even Constantinople."

"If we could find a priest to give me an annulment—"

She chattered on awhile about the annulment, which was highest in her mind, as if she could erase Conrad utterly from her life with a priest's few spoken words. Humphrey knew there would never be an annulment. If Conrad had been grunting on her, he knew very well that Humphrey never had. Conrad had already sneered at him about that. He hated Conrad for a lengthening string of insults, the forced marriage, the challenge Conrad knew he would not accept, the gossip behind his back, the sneers and sideways smiles to his face. As if by making out Humphrey less, Conrad himself would be more.

"Bella," he said. "If we get an annulment, you would have to marry again."

"Anyone but him. If I can't have you again, anyone."

"We'll find someone good." They embraced again. With their arms around each other, he remembered how it had felt, before, when the world was whole, changeless as adamantine, and made for them. Before Guy lost the kingdom and it all came down like a tower of glass. Before Sybilla died and Isabella suddenly was the blood knot.

"I have to go," she said. "I must be there by Compline."

"Trust Johanna; she'll help you get out of Tyre." He would deal with Conrad. The trick was to find some way that would not lead back to him, since Conrad had many allies who would be quick to avenge him, and Humphrey anyway wanted nothing against his name.

He had no wish to be King. He had seen what became of Kings, sacrificed on the altar of a sword. He thought that Richard would get enough of the kingdom back to give the title some flesh, but it would not be his flesh. He wished Richard himself could be cajoled into staying here and being King. Maybe then even Jerusalem would be within reach.

But the Lionheart had brought back Acre already, and soon he would have Jaffa, and then maybe even Ascalon, and the whole coast between, a fit kingdom of merchant cities, thriving with the trade of both sides. Richard was rebuilding the glass tower, if not the same, yet good enough. Humphrey thought he had never met a man before like him. He watched her go away, slim and beautiful, Isabella, whom every man wanted, but he only wanted Richard.

. . .

King Conrad spent more time than Johanna liked in Acre, where, with the other lords gone, her court was hardly more than a household and could not interest him. He spent much of the day looking over the city, its walls and defenses, rapidly being rebuilt at the direction of Templar masons. In the evening he yawned through the lute-playing and singing and got too drunk, and she was very glad to hear him say he was going on to Cyprus.

He said, "I can make some arrangements with the merchants there to bring their ships to Tyre, and to Acre also. Thus we will all get rich." He smiled at her. He was always trying to take her hand; his palms were sweaty, his fingers creased and ugly in their coiled rings.

She said, "My lord, I should be glad of a few traders in." When he kissed her hand, she wiped it on her sleeve. He left with many bows, and she sent at once for paper and ink and a quill pen to write to Isabella, in Tyre, that her husband would be gone to Cyprus and she should escape at once. This she managed to send that same morning to Tyre.

In fact, more ships were coming to Acre's harbor, and the markets were growing. A few days after Conrad sailed away to Cyprus, she got another packet of letters, and went out into the garden to read them. Berengaria had gone to Mass and would likely be there all day, bobbing and praying. Johanna sat on the bench with the letters in her lap.

Both were from her mother, the first fretting about Prince John and his endless inept scheming, and the second announcing her alarm that Philip Augustus was reportedly on his way back to France. Apparently he had stopped in Rome and tried to get the

Pope to release him from the Crusaders' peace with Richard. The Pope had not relented.

Johanna said, under her breath, "The damned Gnome." But Philip was looking for another wife, and Eleanor took several mean and funny turns on this theme, so Johanna was laughing by the end.

She crumpled the letters quickly in her hand, lest anyone even see them, and looked around for a brazier. If she burned them, she could not then give them to anyone else. She had realized too late what a mistake that was; now de Sablé had proof that she was loose with the family secrets. She wished she had thought more about that. She wished she had asked Edythe. A page came up the garden walk, and said, "My lord Humphrey de Toron."

She folded her hands around the wad of paper in her lap. The slender young lord came up the walk and bowed to her; she was always taken by his elegance at this. All the local lords had this kind of sleek address, as if they lived in a more delicate world than the common Western oaf. In most it was artifice, but Humphrey made it look very fine.

She said, "God be with you, my lord. Come sit by me." And when he did, she said, "I have good news. I believe Isabella will be free of Tyre within the week. I have sent to her that Conrad has gone to Cyprus, and she can flee away."

The lean young face before her did not smile, as she expected. He said, "My lady, Conrad is going to Tyre."

Her heart clenched. She said, "He told me he was going to Cyprus. To make arrangements with merchants."

"He lied. He sailed to Tyre."

She gripped her fists together. "The dirty swine. Does he know, then? About me and Isabella."

"Maybe not. More likely he found out I saw her at the Ladder of

Tyre." Humphrey gave a shake of his head. "Conrad has no use for truth; he lies just to keep his edge. But it's possible—he could know. He could be managing everything between you and Isabella for his own ends."

She closed her hands over her mother's letters. She thought of what Edythe had said about de Sablé, that he trained her like a dog. Suddenly she hated de Sablé the more for what King Conrad had done. "What a snake he is."

Humphrey shrugged.

"Maybe she can still escape."

He sat perched on the bench, rocking slightly back and forth, ready to take flight. "Maybe. Ladymas is soon; there is much celebration in the city then, crowds, processions and Masses, people in the street late into the night. If she cannot, she has the wit to know, and not to try."

"Well," she said. "Then we will have to try again."

"Anything is possible." He bowed his head toward her, and his voice fell, soft, intimate. "My lady, you have my constant gratitude for this. I am in your debt forever."

Berengaria's maids were coming down the walk, and the little Queen after them, with a veil over her face in the Byzantine fashion. Humphrey greeted her with a bent knee and a flourish, and for a moment the three talked of the weather, the quiet of the city with the army gone, the lovely music to be had. Johanna was not staying in the garden while Berengaria was there, and she started up the walk to the citadel, still carrying the letters.

To her surprise Humphrey followed her. She took this for a compliment, that he attended her rather than the Queen of England. A few of his pages followed. They went across the courtyard and into the bottom of the citadel.

There in the empty corridor a brazier burned, and she paused long enough to throw the letters into it. Humphrey saw her; he gave her a sharp look but said nothing.

She said, "Oh, I was just tired of carrying around all that paper." The letters blazed up. He made no comment, and they went up to her hall and sat there and drank wine and gossiped.

Twelve

THE WAY TO JAFFA

The army marched only in the morning, because of the heat, stopping wherever they found water. Edythe rode on shipboard. The ship glided along just off the beach; she could see individual men, the foot soldiers dragging their javelins, the knights making their horses dance, up there past the fringe of sea grass. The galley kept pace awhile across the narrow water with a cart, drawn by mules, a tall staff in the middle holding a red banner. All morning, the dust clouds hung in the air, and the Saracens' wavering cries came and went.

Ayberk pointed to the cart with the banner. "There they take the wounded."

In the afternoon when she came ashore she wanted to find the red cart, but Richard had taken a slice across the ribs from a lance. When she reached him, he was standing by a campfire drinking, his shirt already off, and the gash bleeding down his side. His body was more slender than Rouquin's, his skin white.

The wound was shallow but long, and she had to sew it. She

used silk thread, because he was a King. The hard part was making sure the edges matched. All the while, he stood talking to his officers, sending them here and there, never wincing at the needle. She tied off the last knot, gave him a tonic to drink, smeared yarrow on the cut, and laid a strip of linen over it; since she had seen the texture of the armor padding she had worried that the scab on a healing wound might stick to it, and the linen seemed a good remedy. The squire came with Richard's shirt.

Then suddenly something walked over her foot, and she looked down and saw a huge black spider on her toes.

She screamed and kicked violently; the enormous black mass flew away in a wild high loop through the air. It landed on its back on the ground, many legs squirming above a hairy body the size of her hand. The men around her dodged it, laughing, and Mercadier scooped it up into a helmet.

He thrust the helmet into her face, and she recoiled, with another scream.

Now they were all laughing at her. It was a joke; they had planned it. She scowled at them, outraged, humiliated, and that made them laugh more, even Richard. She could hear the spider's claws tapping on the sides of the helmet. She stood up straight and walked back into the tent to be alone.

·   ·   ·

On the galley she sailed by flat sandy beaches, past deserted villages, rock outcrops, old walls, and broken towers. The heat was relentless, soaking her through to the skin even under the screen of her tent. She kept the sides up, but there was no wind. In the distance rose plumes of smoke. Ayberk told her the Saracens were burning the villages ahead of the Crusaders, to deny them supplies, but of course the fleet carried supplies enough.

On the ship she ate bread and drank sour wine. At night, when she walked into the camp, she ate what the men ate. Every few days they heard Mass, the whole army chanting at once. *Holy Sepulcher, help us.* One evening she reached the tent before the King was there, and a man-at-arms in a green and red striped jacket came up to her.

"Please. Lady, please. My brother. Can you help? Please help me."

He was younger than she was, a scrawny straw-haired boy with buck teeth. His French sounded like hers. She went after him, down through the camp.

Usually all she saw of the camp was going through it on her way to Richard's tent, when the army was just moving in. Now they were all sitting around their fires, cutting wood, bellowing and drinking, half-naked in the heat. She walked through them as fast as she could, following the yellow-headed boy.

Somebody hooted after her. Somebody else hissed. "Take care. That's Richard's witch."

After that she walked easier. She thought now, also, she should have just stepped on the spider.

The bucktoothed boy took her to the cart with the banner, where the wounded were taken. There were several wounded lying on the ground around the cart, and three gowned men standing around, but the bucktoothed boy led her around behind the cart, to where another man lay on a blanket.

She could see at once that he was dying. He was pale and he breathed in little gasps, and his wide eyes were unseeing. Matter dribbled from his nose. She knelt down beside him. One of the gowned men came toward her.

"God's greeting. I am Doctor Roger Besac—can you bleed this man?"

She started, angry. They thought she was a common bloodletter.

She said, "No—he's dying; it won't do any good anyway. Get a priest."

Roger Besac looked at the bucktoothed boy. "I told you," he said, and went around the cart again.

She sat down by the dying man. "How was he hurt?" She touched his throat, to feel the pulse from his brain, and it was thin and fluttery and she knew there was no hope.

"His head," the bucktoothed boy said. "Not even fighting. He fell asleep and fell under a wagon and it rolled over his head."

"Ah," she said. "Ah," and laid her hand gently on the man's matted, filthy hair. The wide dark eyes looked at nothing. The matter issuing from his nose smelled bad. She felt the print of the wagon wheel crossing the bone beneath her fingers.

The priest came with his oil and his mumbles, and she got up to give him room. The bucktoothed boy was sitting on the ground crying. She crouched beside him a moment, but he turned away from her and put his arms across his face.

"I'm sorry," she said, and he shuddered away from her.

Useless, she walked up toward Richard's tent again; her body felt like stone. She began to cry silently, tears dripping down her cheeks. She remembered the beggar saying, "Everybody loses."

"Edythe." Rouquin came up to her.

She gathered herself, shaken, telling herself she had seen men die before, that sometimes it was better to die. The big knight scowled at her. He had taken off his mail but still wore the jack, and he stank. "Where were you? He is looking for you."

"Is he hurt?" she said.

"He's fine. He's the greatest fighter in the army. Any army. Nobody can get near enough to him to hurt him."

She knew this to be untrue. She hoped no one could get so near to Rouquin. Talking steadied her. Drove the dark away. She had to keep herself from reaching out to him. Instead she said, "How do those wounds feel?"

"They still itch a little. It's all right. It's my shield arm. I just let the bastards get too close, pulling Mercadier out of there."

She wiped her eyes. He was watching her intently, and he said, "What happened?"

She started up toward the tent again. "Somebody died. They asked me to help him, but I couldn't."

He walked beside her, unlacing the top of his jacket, sodden with sweat. "Damn, woman, you can't save everybody. You're supposed to be Richard's doctor, not the whole world's."

"I can't save anybody." She thought, *Tomorrow he could be dead. I could be dead. And never have what we both want.* The whole world shrank down to this moment. She stopped and put her hand on his arm.

"Rouquin—"

He faced her with that same hard look. "What?"

She felt, suddenly, everybody watching them. She said, "Nothing." She went on toward the King's tent.

At the fire, a cook gave her meat and bread, and she took it into the tent to eat, where she could sit with her back to a crate. The tent door darkened a moment and Rouquin came through, a cup in his hand, and sat down beside her.

He did not speak, only put the cup between them. The jack was gone and he was wearing a dry shirt, the sleeves torn off, his arms bulky with muscle, scratched and scarred. He smelled slightly better.

She said, "It seems so hard. Fighting like this." She took the cup and drank some of the unwatered wine; it was half-turned. With a glob of honey it would be oxymel. She ate more bread.

"It isn't what I'm used to," he said. "At home, it's all ambushes and raids, home by morning. This marching, marching, the heat, the

Saracens like gnats all around us, and we don't even strike back—I don't know how this will end. We can't beat them; they can't beat us."

"Won't it end in Jerusalem?"

He shrugged. "I don't know. I just follow Richard." His hand scrubbed through his hair. He said, quietly, "It's different, is all. Everything here is different."

Maybe talking eased him, as it had her. She remembered when they had sat together beside the sick King; he was that Rouquin now, not angry, nor harsh, but inward and unsure, even his voice lower. He picked up the wine and drank some and spat it out. "God, this is privy dribble."

She laughed; he turned smiling to her. Then Richard's voice sounded outside.

"Rouq, come here."

He grunted. "I knew this was going to happen." He got up and stalked off; in the light of the doorway, she saw him pull his belt up, square his shoulders, make himself again into the outward Rouquin. She ate the rest of her dinner, hoping he would come back, but he did not.

·   ·   ·

Rouquin roused his men in the dark before dawn; the fleet had already left, with Edythe safe aboard. He harried his men along, getting them moving off before the sun broke up over the horizon. Ahead, in the first gray light, spindling trees covered the rolling coastal plain. Their leaves were turning and the whole wood looked like a smear of yellow across his path. He rode on the left flank, with the Templars, the vanguard spread out in several ranks ahead of him. Their banner had already disappeared into the wood. Rouquin turned to Mercadier and pointed a finger and pushed his palm for-

ward, and the Brabanter officer went up to move the men in closer
to the vanguard's flank.

The sun rose red as blood on his left. Richard, trailing squires,
Hugh of Burgundy, and Guy de Lusignan, rode up beside Rouquin
and reined his horse in. He leaned his forearm on his saddle pommel; his mail glove glinted back the first red daylight.

"You said this wood is an hour's ride across?"

"The rear guard should clear it by midmorning. They aren't big
trees, just clumps." Rouquin had scouted the wood the night before.
Guy was looking from one to the other of them, frowning. Hugh
was just staring at the trees.

"And you think Jaffa is close by."

"The road to it is."

"What day is it?"

"Unh—" He knew the phases of the moon better than the days
of the week.

Guy said, "Sire, I believe it's Friday." He gave Rouquin an apolo-
getic smile.

Richard sat up straight in the saddle and looked south. "Saladin
has been moving along south of us all along. He's south of us now.
I think when we come out of this wood he will attack us. He'll
count on the trees breaking up our line of march. And he cannot let
us get to Jaffa."

Guy said, "Well, there's not much left of Jaffa, really."

Rouquin ignored that; on things like this Richard was usually
right. "So—"

"So we form up as close as we can now, through the wood. No
straggling. Nobody out of line. The Templars in the vanguard. Your
men and mine here on the left, the Angevins on the right side. Guy
and Hugh in the middle, and the Hospitallers in the rear guard.

We'll set a screen of foot soldiers in front. You command the vanguard, all across. Make sure they keep going. Stay tight. If we're attacked, don't let them charge. No matter what, until I say so." Richard's voice was taut. Maybe he wasn't so sure as he seemed. "I'm depending on you."

"I will do it."

Richard smacked his arm, by way of parting, and turned to Guy, who was putting on a gaudy plumed helmet. "Come with me." He galloped off, the other men clattering after him. Rouquin rode forward into the wood.

The trees were small, crooked, many of their leaves still on the branches, so as the sun rose the wood grew shady. He wove a way through, trying to get around the corner of the vanguard. As Richard had foreseen, moving through the stands of trees was breaking up the march into separate groups of riders and men-at-arms, scattered for almost a mile from the edge of the sea to the far side of the forest.

He found his own men first, where he had sent them; Mercadier raised a hand to him, and Rouquin lifted his fists over his head and banged them together and Mercadier waved. He would hold the left side of the front line, just behind the men-at-arms. Then Rouquin turned west, toward the sea, where the vanguard was already deep into the forest.

De Sablé had let his black and white knights spread out, getting through the trees; in the shadowy light, they looked like many more than they were, but they were farther apart with every step, straying out of any kind of order. Rouquin reined his horse up to four of them.

"Where is de Sablé? You've got to keep closer together."

"How far is it?" The Templar he had spoken to wiped his sweating face on the skirt of his surcoat.

"Soon. Where's—"

"What if they set the forest on fire?"

Rouquin waved one mailed hand at that, dismissing it. "Push up. Get into a rank." He nudged his horse on, fighting a way between two stands of the trees, the branches rubbing on his knees. His horse's hooves scuffed up the mat of dry leaves on the ground, crackled on fallen branches. A fire here would cook them like pigeons. If the army came out of the woods scattered like this, Saladin's men could pick them off one at a time.

Through the yellow trees he saw the Templars' black and white banner, finally, up ahead, and steered toward it. The trees kept him from going straight, and he had to struggle to catch up with the Grand Master. Before he reached de Sablé he came upon a pack of men-at-arms, with their crossbows and javelins, roaming along behind the knights singing and drinking, and yelled at them to get where they belonged. They put their flasks away and ran. De Sablé saw him finally and reined in and waited.

"Get your men closer together." Rouquin rode up beside him.

"This wood—" The Grand Master thrust back his visor, so he could see better, and looked all around. "Will they fire the wood?"

"Ah, God—" Rouquin glared at him. "Get your men into ranks! See—" The first knights of the rest of the army were closing up behind them. Between the trees for a moment he saw Guy de Lusignan's red plume in the middle of the pack. Richard was driving the whole army into a tight column as if they were riding down the middle of a road. De Sablé saw this and turned his horse and shouted, waving his arm. The black and white knights on their black horses began to press in toward the center, breaking through copses of trees, filling the gaps between them.

Ahead of them Rouquin could see a solid line of men-at-arms, at last all marching in front. The army as it packed together made more noise, a continual crash and thud like a gigantic beast. Through the yellow trees, beyond the men-at-arms, he could see open sky. At least there would be no fire. They were coming to the end of the wood. He went back and found his squire, on the left flank with Mercadier and his men and now Richard's Poitevins, and got his lance.

*   *   *

Richard, at the inland front corner of the army, left the trees behind and rode out into the blaze of the morning. Ahead the ground rolled away down a shallow slope; the sea glistened on the right. The slope curved slightly into a valley between a low hill on the inland and a cluster of rocks near the beach. As Richard rode closer he saw that this rock pile was a ruined town.

On the hill opposite, rings of white tents crowned the height, the enemy camp.

A low roar went up from the packed army behind him as they saw this, and their pace quickened, but no one broke ranks. They followed him steadily forward into the trough of the valley, between the hilltop camp and the ruin. In the distance now he could see the pale line of a road going to the coast.

Rouquin had said that road led to Jaffa. Richard regripped the lance he held butted into his stirrup; his horse strained at the bit, tossed its head, its hoofs beating at the ground. He lifted his gaze to the Saracen camp, there. Along that hill, all around it, he could see horsemen moving, the light mares of the Saracens like dancers, the white robes rippling like wings. Then a drum began to pound.

His hair stood on end. His horse broke into a jog, its head bowed to the bit, and he held it to a man's walking pace. He cast a quick glance back at his army, a solid pack of mailed men and horses, the rear guard still coming out of the wood. The men-at-arms were running ahead of the column, trying to keep a line. The Saracen drums beat into a frenzy, and with a shriek of horns and a thousand screeching voices a flock of archers swept over the side of the hill and hurtled down toward them.

The air darkened with a rain of arrows and he swung his shield up. *Hold*, he thought. He turned his horse so he could cover its forehand; he felt the thump of the arrows on his shield. *Hold*. The men-at-arms around the edge of the army were shooting back, and the Saracen attack broke and swerved and galloped away on either side. Richard pushed on, down the long shallow trough of the valley, toward the road in the distance.

This place interested him. He looked around again at the ruined town, the slopes on either side, and then over his shoulder at the wood behind them, where now the Hospitallers were finally coming into sight.

Their lines were ragged, and they had lost contact with the main army; their Grand Master was an idiot, and Richard had never been able to handle him. He swung his gaze forward again, toward the hill, the town. Out on the open ground to the east, where they could run forever, the Saracens were regrouping.

He turned his horse, letting the front of the army get ahead of him, watching the Hospitallers at the tail end struggle to catch up. Between him and the bulk of the knights he saw Rouquin galloping back along the army's flank; he had his lance, but he had lost his helmet somewhere. Then the Saracens attacked again.

They were aiming, Richard saw at once, not at the main army, but at the gap between them and the Hospitallers. They would try to break the rear guard off and destroy it. Richard flung a long look at the rest of the army, marching steadily along, down into the valley toward the road. In their thin serried lines on the flank of the column, all the while marching, the men-at-arms fired their crossbows, reloaded, and fired again into the fluttering white torrent sweeping toward them.

The Saracens wheeled past the rear guard, firing a constant hail of arrows. The Crusader crossbows blasted them, and the white tide of fighters reeled back; behind them the ground was salted with dead and wounded men and screaming horses.

The Hospitallers had finally gotten clear of the wood, but they still straggled. Their front lines were still a hundred yards behind the main army, and they recoiled from the Saracen charge even as the main army turned it away. They had lost horses. Jogging closer, Richard saw men walking. He swept his gaze around again, from the hill to the ruined town, to the wood. He could see some possibility here. If he could pen the Saracens up against the hill, or the wood, or the ruin, they wouldn't be able to get out of the way of a charge. He could bring his whole weight against them. A man on foot ran up to him, screaming.

"My lord, my lord, the lord Grand Master begs you—"

"No charge," Richard shouted. "Keep to the march. Wait until I signal." He turned, making sure the squire with the trumpet was next to him. Then the Saracens attacked again.

Free of the trees, the Hospitallers had bunched up, not in ranks or files but a shifting mass of horsemen and men on foot, and when the Saracens attacked they all swung to face them. The gap widened between them and the main army even as the screaming onrush of the enemy flowed in around them on either side, firing thickets of arrows. Kneeling, the men-at-arms shot back and threw their javelins, but the knights could do nothing but take blows.

Now Richard had reached the back corner of the main army; he could see most of the Saracen army, and it seemed to him many more than before. His heart jumped. He thought Saladin had committed his whole strength here. He had been right: The Sultan could not let him take Jaffa.

The main Crusader army was slowing. Everybody would be watching him. He wanted this to happen here, anyway, where there were these interesting features of the ground. The Saracens rolled back again, hooting and cavorting their horses, back to the east and safety.

Let them cavort, he thought. *Let them get tired.* He held up his hand, holding his own men back.

. . .

Rouquin's horse took an arrow through the rump, and he had to ride it awhile before he found a fresh one; when he changed mounts, he realized his helmet was gone. He vaguely remembered hooking it onto the cantle of the saddle he had just left. He rode at a quick jog along the side of the army, shouting to them.

"Hold. Hold." Among them were men on foot. The Saracens killed few men but many horses. He thought they might all be on foot before this was over. There might be no way to charge. Up the slope toward the wood, the Hospitallers were staggering along, trying to catch up with the rest of them.

Then, once more, the Saracens swept down.

"Hold!" His voice was raw. His eyes were full of grit. The storms of arrows burst over them, and he crooked his shield over his head. The Hospitallers reeled under the assault; their red surcoats disappeared in the dust and the waves of white robes. He looked at Richard, a hundred feet ahead of him up the slope, his arm still in the air; a Hospitaller sergeant had run up to him, was pleading with him, and Richard shook his head.

"Hold," Rouquin yelled. He lifted his fist over his head. "Hold—"

He ached to fight, to give blows, not just take them. The Hospitallers were staggering, nearly surrounded by enemies; a thousand Saracen archers had taken the higher ground near the wood and were pouring arrows down into the knights' ranks. In front of the knights the white horsemen fired their arrows and wavered back, as they usually did, to regroup and charge again.

Among the Hospitallers, a yell went up.

Rouquin shouted, hoarse. The knights were charging, against orders, hurling themselves toward the Saracen archers by the wood. And now suddenly Richard's trumpet sounded, shriek on shriek, calling the whole army to charge.

At last, at last. Rouquin's horse was already galloping. Beside him and behind him the whole main Crusader army was moving, charging back up the slope toward the wood. He pressed in closer to the man on his left. All around him, now, ten thousand hooves thundered. A wild exhilaration lifted him, as if he flew. Someone rode up on his right, head to head. He looked west down a rank a mile long, and as he looked, all the lances dropped level.

He faced forward, the lance hooked under his arm, and shoved his feet down and sat deep in his saddle. Between the army and the Hospitallers, a thousand white horsemen were scrambling to get out of the way. The line of the knights crashed into them and broke them down without missing stride.

Beyond the Hospitallers the Saracen archers, taken by surprise, were on foot—they had dismounted to shoot, thinking the Crusaders would never charge. The Hospitallers rode straight over the first of them. Rouquin, three strides behind them, saw three men in white running away, one looking back over his shoulder, a gaping face, and he drove the tip of his lance into the middle of that face. He felt the lance shudder, striking flesh. The body fell and was gone in the dust. His horse leaned into its gallop.

All along the slope the running white robes were going down under the driving hooves. Coming up against the wood, many of them had wheeled, were shooting arrows, trying to take cover behind trees. Horses galloped among them. Rouquin splintered his lance on a tree, threw it down, and drew his sword. Pinned against the wood, some of the Saracens wheeled to fight. He drove his horse into a lighter, smaller Turkish mare and she buckled under the weight, and he slashed at her rider, at the coils of his turban. The man collapsed away. The trees pressed closer around him. A man ran away from him between the trees, screaming, nimble on foot. Rouquin sat back, lifting his fist with the reins, and the horse skidded to a stop. The rein scraped a white lace of foam from its neck. He realized he was alone, ahead of the rest of the army, and wheeled back toward the open slope.

He wove his way back through the wood full of bodies. He came out on the slope and saw that the Crusader charge had scattered back down the slope. The ground was heaped with white robes and sprawled horses. Over toward the beach, near the ruins, a thousand Saracens were regrouping, and down in the lowland the Crusader army was gathering to attack them.

Rouquin rode back down into the sunlight. He was going to be too late to join them. A shout turned him; a Hospitaller was running toward him on foot, his sword in his hand. Rouquin veered his horse over to him. The monk-knight sheathed his sword and vaulted up behind him. Rouquin's horse staggered a few steps under the extra weight and he looked around for another mount, but all he saw were dead and wounded. Down there he heard Richard's trumpet sound.

The Hospitaller shouted, "They're coming—Look—"

He twisted in the saddle. The Saracens gathered near the ruin wanted no more charges. They were bolting toward him across the top of the slope, making for the gap between Richard's men and the wood, where only Rouquin and the Hospitaller came between them and the open land in the east. He was going to be in this after all. The Hospitaller drew his sword. Rouquin switched his sword into his left hand, so they could strike on both sides, and turned his horse to face the oncoming Saracens.

"God's balls, run, damn it," the Hospitaller cried in his ear.

"Wait," Rouquin said.

The wave of Saracens was not waiting; the horsemen saw the two knights alone before them, and their high trilling war cry rose. Faintly through it he heard a trumpet sound. A wide white tide, the Saracens rolled down toward him. Their horses' legs pumped. Their curved swords rose like scythes, all sharp edge. The Hospitaller shouted, "God and Saint John!" and Rouquin held his panting horse still, watching the Saracens rush on him. He waggled his sword over his head, daring them. An arrow skidded through the torn earth before him.

Behind him he heard a rumble, as if the whole earth shook, steadily louder.

He did not have to see it. He felt the charge coming like a cresting wave. The first Saracen was six strides away from him, and then from behind him the Crusader line reached him, lifted him, carried him along. All together, at full gallop, a thousand men across, the iron rank struck the oncoming Saracens headlong.

Rouquin's horse smashed shoulder first into a Saracen horse. For a moment the mare held, her head across the charger's neck. A curved blade flashed at Rouquin and he saw a wild brown face, a black beard, a turban. Dust rose in clouds around him. He struck and struck. Then the mare went down, her legs flailing, her saddle empty.

Richard lunged up beside him, the battle axe flashing in his hand. Ahead of them, the fleet Saracen mares carried their white riders out of their reach, but the wood loomed beyond, and again the trees slowed them. Some thrashed into the trees, and some turned to fight. Rouquin drove his horse headlong into and over the first and slashed on either side. He felt the blade bite but he saw nothing, only a last chestnut rump bouncing away through the wood.

Richard bellowed, and Rouquin drew rein and wheeled. The slope before them was gashed and men lay on it and screamed, and horses lay dead or thrashing. The Hospitaller spoke, and slapped Rouquin's shoulder, and slid down off the horse and a moment later was mounting one of his own.

Rouquin let his reins go. The big roan he was riding blew a long ruffle of air through its nostrils and shook its head so its mane flopped. Around him the other knights, slumped in their saddles, moved slowly in around Richard. The Christian men-at-arms had drawn away almost into the ruin, to give the knights room to charge. The cart with Richard's banner was among them. The last of the Saracen fighters had fallen back onto the slope below the tents of the enemy camp, only a few hundred men.

Richard said, "Does that horse have any more run in him?"

"Oh, yes," Rouquin said, and gathered his reins. The roan's head came up and its ears switched forward. Richard let out a roar; a trumpet blasted.

All up and down the mailed line of knights, the horses strode forward into a single rank. The slope carried them, took them to their full gallop faster, and stirrup to stirrup the whole Crusader army hurtled across the trampled low ground and into the remnant of the Saracens.

The white-gowned fighters could not stand against them. They wheeled and fled, but they were going uphill and their horses were tired and the knights rode up over their heels. Rouquin cut out at a fleeing body and missed, and then, with no one ahead of him, rode in among a stand of tents.

He sat back, panting, his mouth coated with dust, and the horse immediately stopped. Its head sank. He patted the foamy, filthy shoulder and said words for its courage; the stallion had fought as hard as he had. He could hear the other Crusaders hallooing all around him now. Richard, on a bay horse Rouquin had never seen before, rode up to him.

"You crazy fool! Where's your helmet?"

Rouquin put a hand to his head, covered only with the mail cowl. At Richard's grin he began to grin, too. He reached out his hand in its mail glove, and Richard clasped it.

"I've never fought a battle like that."

Rouquin said, "No, that was another thing entirely."

"We trampled them."

"It was pretty one-sided."

Someone yelled, nearby; they were looting the tents. Richard said, "Better stop that," and reined around. Rouquin dismounted, to ease his horse, and went to look for something to drink.

Of course, even then they could not stop fighting. There was still Jerusalem.

Thirteen

JAFFA

The terrace thrust out over the beach, over the edge of the sea; Richard walked up to the railing, his gaze turned toward the west. The triumph of the battle still lay on him like a magical brightness, like the hand of God. Nothing he did could be wrong if God gave him such a victory. Moments of it rose into his mind: the sight of the army coming out of the wood, the thump of arrows on his shield, the weight of his axe in his hand, the vast rumble of the charge. He felt as if he would live forever.

Footsteps grated on the floor behind him; the wide terrace was full of men. No one would approach him until he made some sign that he was ready. He stood with his back to them, staring west, and cherished this last satisfaction, before he had to sink back into the muddy doubtful everyday, and get back to work.

*   *   *

After Richard took control of Jaffa, he sent Rouquin and his company to find Saladin's army, and the Sultan himself, if he could.

Rouquin patrolled the coast back toward Acre and saw no Saracen warrior; he circled back along the feet of the low hills inland toward the Jaffa road, watching the while on the heights and in the gorges.

At a spring he came suddenly on some Saracens and charged them. There were more of the Saracens than the Crusaders, but for a few moments the weight of the mailed knights told, and they fought a brief hard clash. Rouquin galloped side by side for three strides with a chestnut mare, striking at the rider. His sword bit deep, and he saw blood spray from the Saracen's arm, but the mare pulled steadily away from him.

An arrow clanged off his shield. He drew rein, holding one hand up, and his men stopped. With a last patter of arrows the turbaned warriors ahead of them disappeared over a low rise.

"My lord—my lord—"

He turned, looking them over. Two of the knights had taken arrows and one man was on the ground, his dead horse pinning him. Rouquin sent four men to keep watch, in case the Saracens circled back, and the rest helped him drag the carcass off the downed man.

He was alive, panting, blood running down his face. "I'm— I'm—" He got to his feet and walked in a wobbly circle and fell. "All right," he said, looking up at Rouquin standing over him.

"Let's go home," Rouquin said. "I've seen enough."

·   ·   ·

Roger Besac said, "This man has a fracture of the skull bone."

Rouquin snorted. "Put it in Latin." He had known that already. He looked around the long dim room; when they told him at the gate he should take his wounded to the hospital, he had expected to find something run by the Order of Saint John. This doctor, round and pudgy, was no knight. The space around him was no monastery. Maybe he had made a mistake.

Besac had the injured knight lie on his back on a table, although the knight kept saying, "I'm all right." Two lamps hung above the table, and the knight blinked at them but did not move. A servant brought straps and bound him to the table across the chest and the thighs.

The doctor said, "I have sent for my assistant." He turned to the other man, who had an arrow in his thigh. "That will have to come out."

He was a fountain of the obvious. Rouquin began to think he should have taken the men to Edythe. But then, to his surprise, Edythe came in the door, her pouch under her arm.

She and Besac greeted each other familiarly; she was the assistant. She turned to Rouquin at once and smiled.

"See our hospital?" She sounded proud.

"Yes," he said. He saw nothing much, just a long room with heaps of straw for beds. Mercadier was watching from the door. Rouquin folded his arms over his chest. "Where did you get this idea?"

Besac said, "The Hospitallers have nothing better, my lord." He said to her, "This man has a crack in the skull, do you agree?"

She went to the man on the table, who said to her, "I'm all right." The bleeding had mostly stopped. She felt gently of his head.

"Yes, I agree. What will you do?"

Besac went up beside her. "He is awake, so there is no deep damage. But we must examine the crack."

"I'm ready," she said.

"He must keep his head still."

Edythe opened her pouch and got out one of her collection of jars. When Rouquin moved to watch her, she said, "You must not get between his head and the light, my lord."

He grunted at her, almost apologizing, and went around the table to the other side. She took a little black ball from one of the jars and held it to the injured man's lips.

"Eat this."

"I'm all right."

"Yes, but eat it anyway."

"What is it?" Rouquin asked. The injured man opened his mouth and she put the little black ball inside.

"Gum of the poppy," she said. "With some henbane. It will quiet him and keep him from moving. He won't feel the pain as much." She glanced quickly at Besac, who had brought out his kit and was choosing a knife. "What should I do?"

"Have your pincers ready." He was already standing at the end of the table, bending over the knight's head. His fingers padded gently at the knight's scalp, and then with his knife he cut a six-inch slice across it.

Rouquin said, startled, "Hunh." The knight stiffened, his eyes widening. The doctor ignored all of this and, turning the knife, brought it sideways in another long slash across the middle of the first. A thin sheet of blood ran through the knight's hair.

The knight blinked. "I'm all right," he said, in a thick voice.

Edythe stood there with her pincers in her hand; the little doctor peeled back the four flaps of the knight's scalp, hair and skin and all, exposing a patch of bone as big as Rouquin's palm. Another trickle of blood ran down the knight's face. The doctor said something under his breath and made the sign of the cross over the wound.

Edythe used a cloth to wipe off the blood. She bent quickly over the knight's head; her hand with the pincers darted in and out and dropped something on the floor, in and out again. Rouquin said, "What's that?"

"Bits of bone," she said. She was looking at Besac. "It's depressed, there. See the cracks."

"I have to raise the bone," he said. "Make sure there are no more fragments. If they fall beneath—"

"Yes," she said. She put her face close to the skull of the knight, and with the pincers she took out more splinters. "Let me wash it."

"Do that," the doctor said. He had taken something that looked like a drill out of his kit.

She opened another of her endless jars and dripped liquid onto the knight's head; he frowned slightly, but did not move. She daubed gently at the exposed skull. "It's clean."

She stood back. The doctor moved toward the knight, the tool in his hand.

It was a drill. Shocked, Rouquin saw him set the sharp tip against the skull just behind the crack and turn the handle, and the tip screwed into the bone. There was a little collar behind the tip, he guessed so it would not pierce too deep. He realized he was holding his breath. His gaze went to Edythe, watching calmly, her hand with the pincers raised. When the drill was well into the knight's skull, the doctor backed it slowly out again, and peered into the hole.

"Did you hear anything break?" he said.

"No." Edythe put her fingertip to the exposed bone; to Rouquin the crack seemed thinner. There were tiny concentric cracks around the drill hole. "The fracture meets exactly now."

Besac sighed, relieved. "Good." He stepped away, and she went forward, looked into the hole, and with her pincers drew out a narrow white curlicue of bone.

"I have to smooth the edge," Besac said. He had another tool, this one much like a farrier's rasp, but smaller. Edythe backed off, and the little doctor bent to work on the edges of the hole.

"All right," said the knight, and yawned.

Besac stood back. "That went well." His voice was lighter; obviously it could have been bad. "Sew that," he said to Edythe, and put his tools back in the kit. "I will deal with this arrow."

Rouquin drew a step nearer, his gaze on the bared skull; the white dome of bone with its bumps and tiny seams looked like a map, with the fracture for a river. He put his hand up to the top of his own head. She had a needle and thread, and she flopped the four quarters of the knight's scalp back into place, like a woman wrapping a baby, and stitched them together. With the edge of her hand she pushed the knight's hair down out of the way for the needle. Being one of Rouquin's men, he was close-cropped. The ends of the stitches poked up stiff through his hair.

The other knight howled. Besac had pushed the arrow out through the far side of his thigh. Edythe paid no heed, bent over her patient.

She said, "We must keep him here. Until he heals."

Rouquin made a sound in his chest. "I wasn't about to take him drinking."

She laughed, to his surprise. She called to the servants, who carried the whole table away, man and all, into the back of the hospital. Rouquin followed them and stood watching them lift the hurt man onto a heap of straw covered with canvas. The knight was smiling dimly at the ceiling. He was well enough, for now, anyway. Rouquin went back under the lights.

Besac had the other knight on a chair and was fussing over the arrow wound. That knight moaned and yowled; his eyes followed Edythe, full of hope. Rouquin thought he wanted some of the poppy. She was putting her jars away, ignoring his cries.

"My lord, the King will be glad you're back," she said.

"Isn't Johanna here yet?"

"No." She took the pouch under her arm and followed him out the door into the courtyard. "Has he sent for her? The palace is really very rude yet."

"He sent de Sablé to bring her."

She stopped, her mouth open, and then licked her lips and looked away. Rouquin's horse was still hitched to the brass circle by the street, but his men had gone. He said, "I will ride you back."

She said, "I would walk, if it please you, my lord."

So they walked, his horse led alongside them. He liked measuring his strides to hers. He liked her beside him, their shadows in front of them on the uneven dirt of the street. He said, "What's wrong with de Sablé?"

"He—" Her eyes shone. She was about to lie to him. Instead she said, in a thin, angry voice, "He is not supposed to expose himself to us sinful daughters of Eve. Pure and uplifted soul that he is."

A clever diversion, but not an actual lie. He had taken off his gloves, and he reached down for her hand. "Whose idea was this hospital?"

"Besac's and mine," she said. "The Hospitaller place here had been torn down." Her hand lay warm in his. In the shadow now there was this link between them. "Is it not excellent?"

It was not the hospital that interested him. He remembered the deft fingers taking up arrows of bone he could barely see. Her hand tightened around his.

"My lord Rouquin," she said, in a brave voice. "I have to tell you something—"

Then a page was running up to them. "My lord! My lord! The King is most wrathful you have not come."

"Well, damn the King, anyway," Rouquin said, "two of my men were hurt." But he turned to her. "I have to go."

"Yes," she said. "Of course."

"I'll see you later."

"Yes, my lord," she said, in that brave voice. He got on his horse and went to exchange some wrath with Richard.

.　.　.

She did not see him again, not alone, for a long while; Richard had work for him, and Besac was always calling her, and she was supposed to be making the huge old palace along the water into a place fit for Queens to live in. She doubted she could tell him anyway who she really was. She had read the admiration in his face. She did not want to see it turn to contempt, or worse. The dirty Jewess. When she thought of that, she pressed her face to the stone wall and hated God for being so unfair. But the knight with the skull fracture was up soon, eating and talking perfectly well and walking around, and bedeviling her for more poppy, and a few days later she delivered a backwards baby, live and yelling, and his mother hale and walking almost at once.

.　.　.

"My lord the King gave me the honor of bringing you this news," the Grand Master said. "My lady, let there be special Masses sung in thanks. We have won a great victory, near a place called Arsuf, by Jaffa. Saladin's army has fled. King Richard holds Jaffa."

The Queen sat still as a post. None of this was news anyway; the rumors had been everywhere for days. She said, "God be thanked." Humphrey de Toron, standing behind her, slid his hands behind his back; she looked on de Sablé as if on a viper.

Humphrey had been with her when the Grand Master was announced, and she had begged him to stay there. Now he saw why.

The Grand Master strode up and down before her, his arms swinging. "The King was magnificent. He led charge after charge against the Saracens. All fled before him. Of course, my brother Templars and I rode every step with him. It was a day of true glory. We were invincible."

"*Non nobis*," Humphrey said, unable to resist. "*O Domine, sed tuo.*" De Sablé's glance stabbed at him.

"My brother is a great knight," Johanna said. "I trust my cousins did as well, and the other soldiers of the cross."

"We all fought in God's name," de Sablé said, his lips thin, and his eyes still turned on Humphrey.

"God be thanked," Humphrey said.

De Sablé turned brisk again. "And my lord the King has given me the honor as well of escorting you and the Queen Berengaria south to join him, which I stand ready to do, whenever my lady shall wish."

At that, Johanna slid back on the divan, as if she would get as far from him as she could. De Sablé held her gaze, half-smiling, and Humphrey saw that he knew she loathed him, and relished it.

He held some power over her. Humphrey cleared his throat.

"I see you came overland, my lord Grand Master, and will want to refresh yourself before journeying back. My ship is in the harbor, and I can leave at once. The Queen may travel with me, if she wishes, and so reach her beloved brother sooner."

De Sablé lost his smile; his cheeks quivered. He kept the beard required of his order down to a thin neat line around his jaws. His black and white habit as always was spotless. He said, "The King requested this of me. I can find a ship."

Johanna said, "I will happily travel with my lord de Toron. My lady Berengaria may have a different choice."

"My lady," de Sablé said, in a voice with a warning edge.

Humphrey said, "Thus you will not compromise your vow, my lord, associating too closely with women."

The Templar's face was rigid; he gave Humphrey a savage look.

But whatever he held over her, he was not spending it now, on a trifle like this. Johanna said, "You have my leave, sir. You should bear your news at once to the lady Berengaria, who is likely in the garden." She rose. "I shall go give prayers of thanks. Good day, my lords." The three maids in the far corner had risen when she did and followed her out.

De Sablé swung toward Humphrey. "Ah, you interfere."

"Alas," Humphrey said. "I merely try to serve." He smiled at de Sablé as de Sablé had smiled at her.

. . .

"Oh, God, Jaffa at last!"

Johanna came down the ramp from the galley, first of all the women; Edythe went to meet her on the quay. In spite of the heat the Queen wore a dark gown of many layers, trimmed in fur, and a long cloak with a jeweled clasp. Her arms engulfed Edythe. "I am so glad to see you."

"My lady." Edythe hugged her back, glad for the welcome. "Welcome to Jaffa, and happy we will all be to have you here. But I am afraid you will find it a little rough."

"Oh, nonsense. After Acre camp?"

The Queen swept on down onto the quay. The other women spilled around them, murmuring a welcome to Edythe as they passed. Berengaria in a veil gave her a curtsy, which Edythe hastily remembered to do, and then hugged her. To her surprise the Navarrese women hugged her also, but the several others Johanna had found in Acre only bent the knee and bowed their heads and said her name in a little chorus. On the quay they gathered in an excited chatter, talking about the journey and Richard's great victory and now Jerusalem, surely, Jerusalem was next. A seagull shrieked past. The harbor smelled of rotten seaweed.

Henry of Champagne was waiting on the street with some pages and knights, and the horses for Johanna and Berengaria. Humphrey de Toron had come quietly off the galley behind them and already gone. Johanna hooked her arm through Edythe's.

"I have so much to tell you." She flitted her gaze here and there. "We can walk," she said to Henry. "I have no interest in sitting anymore."

He bowed. Edythe led her toward the street, the Queen's warm bulk friendly against her side. A page and two knights ran to get ahead of them. The air smelled of dust, and from several places came the bang of hammers. They went from the broad harbor street into a lane, the honey-colored walls close on either side, a staggered row of darker bricks running along the top.

"My lady, I must warn you, the palace is hardly—"

"Well, then I'll have much to do." She whispered into Edythe's ear, "Do you know de Sablé got Richard to send him for me? But Humphrey saved me." She looked around again. "I have so much to tell you I don't know where to begin."

They went up some steps and across a broad marketplace, where heavy colored awnings hung out over the street and shrill voices hawked nuts and bread and tincraft and deliciously aromatic roasted lamb wrapped in soft bread. Down a narrow seam in the hard beaten earth ran a foul trickle of waste. A white goat ran by them. They turned a corner and went in through the new gate to the palace courtyard, which was only half-bricked.

"This is not so bad," Johanna said, looking around. The long flat palace loomed up over them, featureless. "Does it have any windows?" she said uncertainly, and went up the steps. Edythe followed, beckoning to the porters to bring the Queen's trunks and chests.

"Oh!"

Johanna had gone out into the hall. Edythe went after her, smiling. She had felt the same, seeing the frowning back of the building, and then coming up the steps to this hall, to the huge expanse of the terrace above the sea. Johanna, like everybody else, was at once drawn to the sunlit edge. Edythe went up beside her, and Johanna turned and ran her arm through Edythe's again.

"This is very fine. Jaffa!"

"Yes, my lady."

She felt Johanna's touch like an embrace all around her. She had been long among the men, with their spiders and wounds and killing each other and dying. She took Johanna down the balcony to the end, where the women's chamber was. "The King's is at the far end," she said. "It makes for quieter nights."

Johanna laughed. The room was bare, except for a well-built pallet with a thick mattress on it and a big clothes chest. Edythe said, "I've been trying to find carpets for the floor, but—"

"I will bring everything from Acre," Johanna said. "This is good, for now. Let me show you this." She sent off the men bringing in her baggage, tossed off her splendid cloak, and opened her wallet.

"This came just before I left Acre."

It was a thin sheet of paper, obviously one of Isabella's double letters. Edythe turned it quickly over, on one side the formal letter, on the other the hidden one: They were both on the same piece of paper, unlike before. The back, which had been glued on along the edge, was gone.

"Sister," the hidden letter read, "I must beg you to pardon me, but I cannot leave Tyre now, not now. You must give up on this, I implore you. Your loving sister Isabella of Jerusalem."

She thought, *Conrad has found out.* Aloud, she said, "Were you planning that she should leave?"

"We had—first she was supposed to flee Tyre on Ladymas, and then that did not play out, so we were talking of another. But then this came."

Edythe said, "Where would she go?"

"She was going to take ship for Acre." Johanna frowned at her. "What?"

"Acre is too close to Tyre. They would only force her to go back," Edythe said. "Most of her family is on Conrad's side."

Johanna faced her, brave. "We could withstand them."

"Not without Richard. And Richard wouldn't be there." Probably didn't care, but that was unkind.

Johanna was frowning, her face fixed: Another of her plots gone wrong. She said, heavily, "So you think it's for the best?"

"Yes," Edythe said. "I expect so." She put her hand on Johanna's.

"At least she saw Humphrey again," Johanna said. "I managed that much."

Edythe said nothing. She remembered the shimmering blue and silver Queen, whose touch could make any man King of Jerusalem, and wondered if Isabella ever knew happiness.

Johanna paced around the room. The pages would have taken Berengaria away to her own chamber, in the back of the palace. Johanna ran her hand over the terrace wall. A hole pierced the wide flat stone top, its rim stained brown; once there had been an iron railing here. "I'll have them send down those hangings from Acre, the ones with the lions and camelopards."

"It's actually quite comfortable, at night, the only cool place."

"Good. We'll make it all very pleasant. I told Humphrey about de Sablé. Maybe a bit too much, but he is discreet. And he loves Richard." She giggled. "He's like a girl sometimes. You should hear him talk about Richard."

"You told him?" Edythe said, alarmed. She had hoped that matter was closed.

"Well, he had already thought most of it out. He's very clever, Humphrey; you would like him better if you talked to him more."

Edythe had not realized she disliked Humphrey. Now suddenly she did. She tried to convince herself that she was foolish and stupid, but like a grain of sand the worry settled itself into a corner of her mind, that he knew too much.

Fourteen

JAFFA

On the next full moon Edythe took blood from Richard's arm; the blood was warm and looked wholesome, thickened properly, separated out properly into the other humors. The rebuilding of Jaffa went on, the walls rose higher, and the King himself went around every day to see it. A messenger came from Saladin, but Richard would not receive him, because of the bleeding. Two galleys brought in the first shipments from Acre of furnishings for Johanna's room and the hall. The hall especially was suddenly more comfortable, with long cushioned divans and hangings on the walls, and the raised chair Johanna set out for a throne.

At last, after three days had passed, the King allowed in the Saracen messenger. It was the Sultan's brother again, Safadin, tall and lean and watchful of everything, with a small guard of swordsmen whom he left in the courtyard. The King sat on his new throne to receive him; a Byzantine silk shawl covered it, magnificent with gold and stones. Humphrey de Toron stood by his side, to translate, so that he and Safadin were each talking in their own language. Rouquin stood behind the throne on the other side.

Safadin walked calmly up before the King; he inclined his head an inch. He spoke in a bold voice.

Humphrey said, "My lord Saif ad-Din, in the name of the Sultan of Egypt and Syria, Yusuf ibn Ayyub, Salah ad-Din. He congratulates the great King Richard the Lionheart. They have not lied who spoke of you with awe before you ever came here. Rather, they said not enough. You are the Alexander of the Franks."

Rouquin lifted his head; he felt the praises of this enemy as he would never feel them from a friend. Richard himself got to his feet, walked down from the throne, and stood face-to-face with Safadin, equal to him. He said, "God has sent us worthy adversaries," which pleased Rouquin also.

Safadin talked, not gesturing, his smooth dark hands clasped at his waist. Humphrey said, "The Sultan finds el Malik Rik as excellent in words as on the battlefields. He wishes to discuss a truce, so the Lords of East and West can see if words may solve this issue. You must know, my lord, that their faith does not allow them to make peace with the Dar al Harb"—he bowed to Safadin as he said this—"that is, the House of War, which is all that of the world which does not submit to Allah. But they can make a truce, to recover from a loss."

Richard said nothing for a moment. Humphrey said a few words in Arabic to Safadin, who shut his eyes and opened them. Rouquin thought, *The House of War*. That fit, everything else than that a figment of words.

At last, Richard said, "My terms for peace have not changed. I want Jerusalem, the restoration of the kingdom of the Franks here, and the return of the True Cross."

Humphrey spoke, and Safadin spoke.

Humphrey said, "He says thus: Jerusalem is as holy to us as it is to you. Holier, in fact, since it is there our people will come on the day of the last trumpet, to hear the judgment of the One True God. He has a letter from his brother." Humphrey held out one hand, and Safadin put a scroll into it.

Richard made no move for the letter. He said, "I shall read it and reply as I see necessary. In the meantime, my lord Safadin, permit my cousin to escort you back to your own house." His smile flashed at that. He said, "My cousin is to me as you are to the Sultan, so this is very apt."

Safadin took three steps backward, bowed again more with his eyes than anything else, and turned. Rouquin went after him and caught up with him at the door. He wondered what the letter said and doubted it was much. He thought Humphrey had put this truce idea in exactly the right way. In the courtyard, with a gesture he summoned Mercadier and three other men, who brought horses, and they met Safadin and his guard at the gate.

They rode out of Jaffa and turned inland. Dark was coming. Rouquin was almost stirrup to stirrup with Safadin, but he said nothing; he felt the war between them like a sword. He liked the Saracen's horse, a dark bay mare with white socks all around, who moved as prettily as a swallow. She was too light for a man in armor, more a fine palfrey. He thought of Edythe riding her. Bred to a brawny stallion like his roan warhorse, she might throw bigger colts that still kept her fine lines. Then, where the road went down through a dry streambed, the Saracen reined in and turned to him and said in perfect French, "From here I can make my own way."

Rouquin wanted to see his camp, which he knew was also Richard's design. He said, "The King bade me ride with you to the door of your tent."

"Ah," said the dark, expressive face, taking some amusement from this. His eyes held Rouquin's. "But I could not promise you that you would then get all the way back to Jaffa."

Rouquin felt his blood heat; he said, "Nothing you have can stop me."

The Saracen said, "I myself faced your charge at Arsuf. I hope never to do so again. But I would for the sake of the True Faith. I think also you have felt the bite of our arrows, and an arrow can kill as well as a lance."

Rouquin said, "I have taken your arrows. I am still here."

The quick white smile parted the Saracen's dark beard. "Yes. You are here. Far from home, and we are home. We can drive you away, and you have somewhere to go. We have only here."

Rouquin said nothing. Against his will, he saw the reason in this. The Saracen lifted his hand, almost a salute, and moved off into the falling darkness with his men. Rouquin went back to Jaffa.

. . .

Edythe had been looking throughout the city for Jews but found none. Then, while she was inhaling the cool fragrance of peppermint in an apothecary, the shopkeeper told her he had gotten it from the village at the mouth of the river. "They're Jews, you know," he said. "They can't even live here. But, you know, every herb gathered by a Jew has a special power, every bark and every berry, and they have a doctor there."

As soon as she could, she went down along the shallow river that cut through the sandy low ground north of the wall of Jaffa. Ahead of her a cluster of small white houses appeared under some palm trees where the water ran into the sea. Closer to the real city, Syrian women washed their clothes in the river, wading in with their skirts tucked up between their legs. Screaming naked children ran along

the shallows. She ambled by as if she were only walking and crossed
the empty space between Jaffa and the little village.

The cluster of buildings seemed no different from any other
houses in Jaffa, stretching their clay roofs wide beyond the walls to
fight off the blaze of the sun. Many of them had a low freestanding
stone screen around the outside, as if to protect them from all eyes.
In front of the biggest house three women in dark shawls were sitting
on a bench; one was picking through lentils, and another nursing a
baby, and the third sewing.

Edythe's heart was hammering. She could not remember the
words. She hoped they knew some French. She went up and bowed
to them, very nicely, to put them on her side.

The woman with the baby got up and went in through the gate
behind her. The woman sorting the lentils spoke in a tongue she did
not recognize, and then said, in French, "You want?"

The two women stared at her, unsmiling. They did not seem on
her side. She said, "Doctor. *Iatros. Medicus.*"

They looked at each other, and then the woman with the lentils
said, "Yeshua. You want. Yeshua ben Yafo." She pointed across the
way, to a smaller house.

"Thank you," she said, and bowed again.

Their faces were blank as the walls, unfriendly as the walls. A
chill went over her. She turned and went to the house opposite.

This was small, the white plaster chipped, part of the roof patched
with palm fronds. No one was outside. Hesitantly she went in the
opening through the screening wall, onto a narrow walk. Little trees
grew along the side of the house, their leaves mostly fallen at their
feet, the bare branches spangled with yellow apples.

A door in the house opened, and someone called, not in French.

"Please," she said. "I am—I have heard there is a doctor here—

Please—" She took another step forward, farther into the narrow orchard. All her hair was stirring; her stomach was clamped to her backbone.

An old woman appeared, also swathed in black, and stone-faced. Edythe said, "Please—" The woman backed up and slammed the door.

She staggered, as if the door had struck her. But then the door opened, and an old man came out. He was tall, even if old, and his face jutted out in a wedge, a sharp nose, a long jaw below sparse white hair and a scalp spotted brown.

"You want a doctor," he said. "Are you sick?" His French was slow but exact.

She took her first deep breath in moments. "Yeshua ben Yafo," she said.

He bowed. "I am he."

"My name is Edythe," she said. "I am a doctor with—with the Crusade."

"Ah," he said, and nodded at her. "You are the woman from the Latin hospital, in the city."

Her jaw dropped. He stood aside and waved his hand at the doorway. "Please come in."

She went past him into a room filled with scrolls and bound books, stacked one on the other, wads of paper thrust between them, heaps of books and paper on the floor, on the table, on a chair to one side of the table. The old man went by her to the only other chair.

He said, "You are young, you can sit on the floor." He sat in the chair.

She sank down cross-legged on the floor and tucked her skirts around her. "You know who I am?" she said.

"Everyone knows of you, yes," he said. "You are not a woman of the people, but you serve everybody. What do you need of me?"

She said, "I have a patient with a recurring fever."

"How have you dealt with it?"

She told him—the oxymel, the bergamot she had gotten in Acre, the bleeding, cooling him through the fevers and warming him through the chills, rubbing him down, the lemon potions and zingiber. He listened, his head to one side. His eyes were wide, the irises large even for this dim room, and she wondered if he was going blind.

He said, "None of this will hurt. Often a kind touch will do more than a potion. You should give him a tincture of artemisia when he first shows signs of falling sick. It is not easy to find. I hope your patient is rich, and has a strong stomach."

She blurted, suddenly, "I want to be a Jew again." Tears rose in her eyes. "Tell me how to be a Jew again."

Silence met this. He sat still, his wide eyes unblinking. He was blind, she thought, despairing; he could not even see her.

He said, "What happened to you?"

She said, "We lived in France. In Troyes. The French King made a decree that we all had to go. All the Jews had to go. My mother was near her time with child, and my father would not leave her." The tears rolled down her cheeks. It didn't matter, since he could not see them. "They set a mob on any who stayed. The mob burned—burned—I wasn't there, my aunt had taken me to Rouen. I was thirteen. They sent me off to England, from house to house. To the Queen, who took me in."

"Blessed for that," he said.

"And told me henceforth to be a Christian."

He coughed, or chuckled. "Not that. Troyes, yes, all know of the martyrs of Troyes, of the terrible purge of Philip Augustus. Who was your father?"

"His name was—was Mordecai ben Micah."

He lifted his head. The huge eyes fixed on her. She had been wrong. He saw everything. He said, "Mordecai ben Micah of Troyes."

"Yes."

He rose and went behind the table, digging through the piles of books. His hands caressed them. He picked them up and set them down as gently as babies. At last he turned, one little book in his hand.

He held it out to her, and sat down again when she had taken it. She laid it on her knees. It was plain, bound on the left in a scuffed leather cover, some of the pages ripped at the edges. He was smiling at her.

He said, "That is your father's book."

She gasped. She raised the book in her hands, amazed. It was written in Hebrew characters, which she could not read. The leather cover had faded gilt lettering on it; she knew the character that began her father's name and traced it with her finger.

"It is a copy, of course, not the true book," he said. "It is—as you see—a commentary on the Canon of Ibn Sina. Your father was known all over the world. He had some interesting notions about disease, what it meant, how it moved from person to person."

She drew his initial over and over with her fingertip. Yeshua was being generous; she could read nothing of the book, not even the title. Her father, here, under her hands. "He said the only wealth was knowledge."

"He was right," said Yeshua ben Yafo.

She cradled the book against her and lifted her face to him.

"Why do they hate us?"

He said, "Have you never known a son who hated his father?"

"Oh," she said. "Yes," she said. "Who are the Hagarites?"

"You call them Saracens. Another son who hates his father. They were Jews first, just as the Christians were Jews first. Now they all want Jerusalem, to prove they are not Jews anymore. They hate us, because we remind them they are, really, still Jews."

She felt herself stiffen against this. She thought the Christians and the Muslims she had seen were much different from her and from this man, although she didn't know why exactly. Maybe only that they claimed it so insistently. She said, "You must tell me what to believe. How to pray."

He said, "What do you believe now?"

"I believe nothing." It felt bitter to say this, acid on the tongue. "Nothing."

"You believe that."

She frowned at him, bewildered. "You play games with me."

"No, woman. You play a game with yourself, you make up this problem, to hide from who you are, and what you really think. God made you. You are this woman, God's child, complete in yourself. Anything you try to change or hide is false and will fail. Be who you are. Take the book. Give your patient a tincture of artemisia, very softly heated, in a dilute dose, perhaps one drop to two hundred, as soon as you know he is sick. Come back and tell me, if you wish, how he does with that." He straightened. "Now, go, so I can get back to my work." She rose and went.

·   ·   ·

She walked back up into Jaffa and wandered through the narrow crooked streets, past men raising new walls and hauling big chunks of rock, and through markets and squares. She saw nothing. Her mind was a seething uncertainty. She held the book under her cloak, tight against her breast. She could not fathom what the old man had said to her. The words tumbled in her memory, huge and small, clear and vague. Sometimes it seemed to her like the wisdom of the world and the next moment a rare stupidity. Of course she was who she was. But who was she? She had come all this way for nothing. And yet when she thought of the way she had followed, she was astonished and glad. Surely the old man had understood. But she could not really say what he had told her, or what the words had really meant. In her hands, her father's book, which she could not read. At last, exhausted, she went back to the palace by the sea.

.   .   .

Johanna said, "Where were you? I sent people all over looking for you. Besac has been asking for you. Richard is leaving. He has announced it; he will march on Jerusalem in three days."

"Three days," Edythe said, excited. Everything seemed to be happening at once. In Jerusalem, maybe, she would find the real answers.

Johanna had work for her, and a lot of gossip; Berengaria and she were on the outs again, the little Queen taking all her meals in her own chamber, and the two never even seeing each other except in church. Johanna said, "She's a fool. She wants to go back to Acre, to her garden, and she cares nothing for Richard."

Edythe agreed with that. She had seen Berengaria that morning, because she had a headache, and Berengaria had spoken longingly of the garden and never mentioned her husband. Now Edythe sat with Johanna in the great hall, sewing a fringe onto a great rug to cast over Richard's throne. Johanna chatted amiably about the throne of Sicily, which had been very majestic, and that led her to the fabled throne of Byzantium, which was supposed to speak, float up into the air, and change colors. They were to dine the next afternoon and she wanted some musicians, and a train of luters and tambour players was waiting to be rehearsed. She expected Edythe's opinion on them and kept her for every one. Edythe listened only enough to agree with her. In her mind, over and over, she thought,

Jerusalem. At last, Jerusalem. She worked her needle through the thick stuff of the fringe and slipped it down into the rug.

. . .

She went the next morning to the hospital; she had to hide the book, anyway, and she could put it there on the shelf with her herbal. The hospital always pleased her; she could always find work there. A woman had come in with dropsy, and Besac was withdrawing the excess humor from her belly with a long silver tube. When he was done with that and they had laid the patient down, Edythe said, "Do you know anything of tincture of artemisia?"

He said, "Artemisia, artemisia," tapping his fingers on his chin. She knew this for a sign he had only the vaguest notion of what he was about to say. He said, "You want a tincture? I believe it has some action on the choleric humor."

This made sense, since it was treatment for a fever. She said, "I need to find some."

"I am sending later for some things from Tyre. I shall write it down."

She started after him, toward the little corner where he made his desk, but then a page came in the hospital's front door, stepped to one side, and said, "The King!"

She wheeled to face him and fell into a proper curtsy. Besac went almost to his knees. Richard came in, trailing attendants like a comet.

"Well," he said, "I see the rumors are not idle, then; you have made good use of this."

Besac hurried forward, bending and stooping. "My lord, my lord—"

He showed Richard around the hospital. Edythe hung back, pleased, thinking Besac a little fevered himself over this. Rouquin was not there, only pages and some yawning squires. She thought of Jerusalem again—she wanted to have the artemisia to take on the trek, in case the King fell sick; waiting for Tyre was too long.

Richard came back up the long narrow building. "Excellently done," he said, at which Besac almost rolled over, puppylike, his butt wiggling. Richard's gaze slipped past Edythe as if she were not there. He said, "Master Besac, I want you shriven. You will go with us to Jerusalem on the morrow."

She startled, cold. For the first time she realized she might not go. Besac was actually now kissing the King's sleeve. Above his bobbing head, Richard's gaze finally met hers. But he said nothing, and turned and went.

.   .   .

Later, on the pretext of having some medicine for him, she managed to get into his chamber and maneuver a moment alone with him. She said, "My lord, I want to go to Jerusalem."

He was sitting on a divan, trying to tune an old lute. Humphrey de Toron had just gone out. The cup with the oxymel was on the floor by his feet. He said, "You can't. And you know why." His voice was reasonable, as if surely she saw this the same way he did. "From Acre to Jaffa was one thing. This time we are going to the Holy City. We must all be confessed and shriven pure. I am taking no woman."

She said, frozen, "And certainly not a Jew."

"We must be pure."

She turned away, stiff with rage, her body seeming made of wood and slightly disjointed. He said, "When I have the city, and the gate is open, then you can come in and no one will notice."

At that moment, she hated him; if she had found a knife to hand she would have plunged it into him. Instead, she crept out of the room, went down onto the balcony, and there wept into the salt sea.

*   *   *

She plotted to leave, to go by herself, but she knew that was impossible. The hills were full of Saracens, and even the Christians now were her enemies. She wept again. Johanna saw her and put an arm around her.

"What is it, now?" The Queen laid a cheek to her hair. "This terrible war."

She muttered, not comforted. She helped Johanna rearrange the Queen's chamber, with new hangings on the walls.

*   *   *

At the dinner Richard was lively, calling back and forth to the men around him, and eating very well. Johanna sat beside him and he kissed her often.

He asked Rouquin about some fighting recently, and Rouquin said, "It's like at home. They set an ambush, I set a counterambush, they try to circle around behind me, I circle around behind them. Little raids, nobody really hurt." He had brought in a flock of sheep from his last ride out, which had made excellent mutton pies.

Johanna nudged her brother. "You have not told me of this big battle you had. The trouvère is making many verses. Are they true?"

Richard made a sound in his throat. "Don't ask me. I was in it. I don't remember much but the noise." He stabbed another kiss at her cheek. "All you need to know is that by Christmas you will be sleeping in the Tower of David. On Christmas Eve you will hear High Mass in the Church of the Holy Sepulcher." He turned to shout across the room, exuberant.

The excitement ranged around the room in waves. Edythe, by the wall, felt cold, alone. After all she had done, he had cast her aside. Serving Jesus, serving a Plantagenet, had gotten her nowhere. She left as soon as she could, going around the side of the room to the porch, toward the stairs.

Behind her, a voice called. "Edythe. Wait."

She stopped, in the dark above the steps, and Rouquin came toward her.

She flushed, sure he knew now; she said, desperate, "I served—I did everything he asked—"

"He is asking again, that's all. He needs you to be here. Johanna is in some kind of trouble. He thinks you can keep her in line."

The breath went out of her. She lowered her head. Richard, after all, had kept her secret. Explained not taking her with this false trail. She had no way with Johanna, who would do as she pleased. The mere fact that Richard was leaving her behind would make Johanna suspicious of her. But he had kept the true reason to himself. Finally, she looked up.

"But you are taking de Sablé. To Jerusalem."

"Of course."

"Then there is no worry—it is de Sablé at the root of this." She was glad to say it. Let Richard deal with it. She hated Richard now anyway.

"Maybe the root, but some of the branches have gone elsewhere." He said, "I am going to Jerusalem. I will take something of yours, if you want."

Her lips parted. This was why he had come out here, to say this. She stood on her toes and kissed him.

"That," she said. "Take that. And come back." She kissed him again, and went up the stairs, lighter.

. . .

Two days later the army marched out of Jaffa, all trumpets blaring, and the horses tossing bright colored plumes in their manes, and the

knights waving to the women in the crowds and the men-at-arms
tossing their quarrels up and catching them in fancy ways.

She watched them a long time, from the wall. Their dust moved
up the long brown road toward the hills, Jerusalem at the end, the
heart of the world.

There was no army between them and the David Gate. They
would ride straight into the Holy City. Then she would go.

She thought about Yeshua ben Yafo; surely he was wrong, surely
there was a right way to be, one right way, that would warrant everything. In Jerusalem she would find at last what to believe, how to
pray, whom to love. Who she really was. She yearned after them, up
that long brown road into the hills, as if toward the gate of heaven.

*   *   *

That afternoon, while they sat on the breezy balcony, a messenger
brought in a letter from Tyre.

Johanna laid it on the table, and her gaze flicked toward Edythe,
across from her. Edythe kept her eyes away. As she had thought,
Johanna suspected her of spying for Richard, but the Queen had no
one else she trusted even that much, and finally, she said, "Well, look
at it."

"My lady, it is for you."

Johanna grunted. Impatiently she ripped off the seal and un-
folded the heavy sheet of paper, and in a singsong voice read the
formal greetings of the Queen of Jerusalem. Edythe looked off to
sea. The day was cloudy; she wondered if it rained, inland. Maybe
God showed a distemper to the Crusaders.

Johanna was prying apart the two halves of the letter, and she
read the inside one. "Hunh." She put it on the table. "What do you
make of this?"

Edythe picked it up. "It's on the wrong side again," she said.

"What?"

"When she wrote calling off the escape, remember, the secret letter was written on the back of the front page. Always before she had written on the front of the back page."

Johanna took the letter from her, turned it over, and turned it again. She said, "Well, that's very clever of you. But does it mean anything?"

Edythe shrugged. Johanna arched her eyebrows at her. "Well?"

"My lady, maybe she is trying to warn us. Maybe she had to write this; maybe someone was forcing her to do it."

Johanna's gaze was steady, but the letter in her hand quivered. "Conrad."

"My lady."

"The lying snake." Johanna crumpled the letter swiftly in her hands and flung it over the rail of the balcony. "Well, I shall send her an answer, but very off the point."

"My lady—"

"What, not to Richard's taste?" Johanna gave a nasty laugh. "But I cannot simply ignore her, can I?" She whisked her hand at Edythe. "Go, make whatever report you care to."

"My lady," she said, "I report to no one."

"Yes, yes," Johanna said, but would not look her in the eyes. She said, "I could not sleep last night—make me another potion, will you? A strong one." Edythe, dismissed, got up and went away.

· · ·

Days went by. In the hospital, with the army gone, there were few patients: a drunken man who had been hit by a wagon; another man, not drunk, who had fallen from a new building and broken his skull and now could not move. She was keeping him clean and moving him around in the bed, but she knew he would die soon. His family came around the hospital and prayed by him. When she came they kissed her hand, but she had done nothing.

She comforted herself that Besac could have done nothing, either. As the beggar had said, everybody lost eventually. She went up on the wall and watched, straining her eyes, to see the messenger coming from the east with news of the triumph of the King.

A pouch came from Tyre, with many new medicines in jars and envelopes. One envelope was full of leaves and flowers and labeled in Greek letters. She struggled through the first few letters and realized it was the artemisia. He had said to make a tincture, but not with what. Softly heated. She ground the leaves and flowers together in a mortar jar and mixed them with a sulfurous oil, good for the stomach and easy to boil, and set the jar on a shelf, covered.

After the army had been gone more than a week, one of the French knights came back.

Richard had not sent him to announce a victory, to call Johanna to Jerusalem. Nobody had sent him; he had deserted. He limped in wearily on foot at nightfall, when Edythe was getting ready to leave, and showed her an evil wound in his arm, a deep knife cut, full of pus and rot.

She worked all night to clean it, feeding him strengthening potions and watching for signs that the infection had traveled elsewhere, and over the course of the night when it hurt too much to sleep, he told her of the march and why he had given up. There was no Saracen army, but there were Saracens by the hundred. They assailed the Crusaders from hiding, unseen, unpredictable, a flurry of arrows in the dark, a sudden rockslide, a waterhole full of horseshit. Everybody was on edge, but there was nobody to fight.

And King Lionheart was moving too fast. It was hard to keep up. Even the local men were grumbling: King Guy, the Templars. The wounded man, lying down now, his arm dressed, said, "Then my horse was killed, and I just came back." He shut his eyes and slept.

It was daybreak, and no use going home, she thought. She slept a few hours in the back. By midmorning she was up again, at Besac's desk writing down the medicines that had come from Tyre. She stowed them away in the big chest and locked it. The man with the cracked skull had died, and the hospital was empty now but for the man from the army. She fed him broth and raw garlic and oxymel and changed the dressing on his wound.

She meant to go back to the palace when this was done, but then two more men came in the door, one with a slash in the leg, the other with a broken forearm.

They too were from Richard's army. They were hungry, and as they bolted down bowls of porridge they too cursed the hard march, the Saracens who shot at them from ambush, hurled rocks down on them, and threw dead horses into the streams.

"Why keep going?" the man with the broken arm told her. "They were just killing us."

When she had their wounds dressed, she went out to the city wall again, and looked east. The road was empty, except for an old woman hobbling along on a stick.

Surely these wounded were cowards, weaklings, who fell out of the war. Surely in the east now the Crusaders had cut their way through to Jerusalem. Only the brave deserved to win it. God would winnow out the unfit. A horrible feeling seethed in her belly. She felt her soul yearn out of her body, stretch out along the road after them, until she caught herself standing on tiptoe, straining to fly over the top of the wall. She hated him for leaving her behind, but she wanted with all her heart for him to succeed.

There was nothing to do but wait. She went back to the hospital and tended the wounded men.

"We'll all go to Jerusalem," she said, "when the King takes it."

The young man with the gashed leg groaned and flung his arm over his eyes. His wound was festering and she cleaned it, flushed it with vinegar, and left it open to the air.

Then in the afternoon more men appeared.

They had bumps and arrow wounds and broken bones, more than she could manage, but fortunately Besac was there among them. Unfortunately he had bad news.

"The Crusade has failed." He stripped off his cloak and muddy boots, looking around the hospital. He flapped his arms up and down, his gaze expansive, glad to be back. He said, "Missed me, have you?"

"What happened?" she said. "Didn't you reach Jerusalem?"

"I told you, the Crusade is over. Richard has broken his vow. We turned back. We all failed."

She felt her legs go soft. "Where is the King?"

"He's gone south, to Ascalon." Besac laughed. "He will not dare face us now. His vow a turd in his mouth."

She needed to sit down, and she did, on one of the empty beds. In a rush of fury she hoped Richard swallowed it whole. His pure, shriven, Christian vow. She felt shrunken, as if his failure had dried her like a leaf.

Still stunned, she went up to the palace; the Queen was nowhere. Edythe went out onto the balcony, hearing this, over and over, in her mind: *We all failed.* Somehow they had turned back. She could not fathom it. Jerusalem was so close and yet they could not reach it. Enspelled, it floated in another world, just beyond their grasp.

Johanna came out behind her. Her face was a blaze of high feeling. "Have you heard? They deserted him. There was trouble, certainly, but they would not keep up. Even Guy wanted to turn back, the little lapdog. It wasn't Richard's fault they failed. But they will all blame him." She put her hands to her face and wept. Edythe went to her, and put an arm around her, and they stood bound together, wretched.

Johanna called in a priest and harangued him for an hour, until he agreed to deliver a sermon the next day on the Crusade, saying that the failure wasn't Richard's fault, that the evil men around him were to blame. At the church, when he started in saying this, half the people listening turned and walked out, and a mob of boys stormed around Jaffa, throwing mud at the palace and cursing Richard's name and beating old people with sticks.

Much of the Pisan fleet left for their home port. They took half the Poitevins with them, who had used up their feudal dues. Richard was behind on his payments to them anyway.

Edythe went to the hospital, now overflowing again with wounded men. They whined and complained, and sneered at Richard, and damned the Saracens, and many of them died in spite of all she and Besac could do. But Richard kept to himself in Ascalon, and Rouquin with him.

Fifteen

JAFFA

Johanna said, "Here, read this."

It was another letter. Edythe took it and saw at once it was from Isabella, and written on the wrong side again.

Johanna said, "That came this morning, by ship."

Edythe read, slowly. "She says she will fly Tyre as soon as you send her a safe conduct into Acre. This must be soon. Conrad is gone but not for long. Pray, send the safe conduct soon." She looked at Johanna. "Can you even issue a safe conduct?"

"I don't know. Probably. Enough wax and ribbons will carry it." Johanna said, "What do you think of it, though? It's on the wrong side again."

Edythe turned the letter over and looked at the seal. "I don't think it was opened, like the others."

Johanna said, in a low voice, "Could she have gotten it out without him knowing?"

Their eyes met. Edythe said nothing. She was thinking, *Why then would she need the pretense of the false letter?* Johanna said, "No."

Edythe said, "No, probably not."

Johanna was already nodding. She said, "We are betrayed. This is Conrad's work, the liar. He's worse than a Greek." Her eyes widened. "He wants the safe conduct to sneak into Acre and seize it."

Edythe said, "Maybe . . ."

Johanna gave her a sly look. "You have some thought in mind?" Her voice was bland.

"No, my lady," she said, humbly.

"Good," said Johanna. "Leave this to me. Now help me with this table."

Edythe wondered why it mattered to her that Johanna had this plot afoot, and that Acre was suspended on her whim. Guy de Lusignan had gone back to Acre after the Crusade fell apart. Now Johanna was giving a safe conduct into his city to his worst enemy. Let him sink or rise, most likely sink, from what Edythe had seen of him. Richard would suffer, but ho heigh. They had no loyalty to her, and so she had none for them. It was all one to her, and one was nothing.

But it was not nothing. She tried to grind away the pebble beneath the blanket, but still it rubbed her. She longed to see Rouquin again, who would never leave Richard. Richard had kept his own kind of faith with her, protecting her secret. She hated him less now that he had failed. With the rage against him in the streets, she could not rage against him in her heart. And they had fought so hard for Acre. And she thought of the old beggar by the fountain there, and Berengaria's garden.

·   ·   ·

Johanna had a safe conduct drawn up, allowing the bearer and an escort into Acre, and covered with seals and stamps and colored ink and a big ribbon. She concealed this in a letter to Isabella. She did not hide it especially well, but she knew it did not really need to escape notice, up there.

She wrote also to Guy of Lusignan, who was back to ruling Acre now, that he should be ready to arrest anyone who used it.

This seemed the perfect trap to her, which Conrad himself had devised, and Conrad himself would set off. She kept it out of Edythe's sight. She knew Edythe was Richard's creature, and Johanna wanted to punish Conrad herself, by her own guile. Then she would let him know, the lying snake, that she had done it. Edythe might even admire this. Richard certainly would. Pleased, she sent her letters off.

. . .

"They have come back from Jerusalem," Berengaria said.

She was sewing on an altar cloth. She had excellent skill at this, and in the light of the candles the angel's wing she was composing in gold thread looked as smooth as honey. Her own sleeve was worn, and soiled at the edge; her ladies took poor care of her.

"They never reached Jerusalem," Edythe told her. She was holding the cloth on her knees, to steady it for the Queen's needle. They were sitting in her chamber, where around them the other women went on chattering in their own tongue. Berengaria alone of all the Navarrese had bothered to learn French. "The Crusade failed."

"Well, then," Berengaria said, watching her fingers with the needle and thread. "Will we then go back to Acre?"

Edythe said, "I don't know, my lady."

Berengaria gave her a quick look. "You want Acre too?" She stopped sewing and faced Edythe.

"I want what you want, of course."

Still watching Edythe, the little Queen smoothed the gold thread with her thumb. She said, "I want to go back to Acre."

Edythe was thinking they might never be able to go back to Acre. Conrad, whatever he was, was far too clever for Guy, and if he seized the great city in the north he would not let the Crusaders in again, as he had not let them into Tyre. She considered what Berengaria had just said.

"You could write the King and ask him."

"I could send a messenger," Berengaria said. "I cannot read or write, my lady, alas. You know this." She made no move to do anything, but stared at Edythe, as if she could put her thoughts into Edythe's mind.

Edythe said, "I could write it for you."

Berengaria smiled at her. She had said the right thing. Berengaria said, "You write him. You tell him better." She nodded. "Help me, I help you."

"My Lady, I—"

Berengaria shuffled her hands in front of her. "Just do. Bring paper and pens." And Edythe wrote exactly what the Queen wished to say to her husband, and beneath it, wrote, *Go to Acre, quickly.*

. . .

A letter came back, a few lines of script: He would let them go back to Acre in the spring. Ricardus R. No news, nothing personal. Nothing to Edythe. Berengaria said, "Will I ever be truly Queen of the English?"

"My lady, only God could tell you that. It has been a strange marriage, that I can say. But, you know, I have seen few marriages that are not strange." She was thinking of Eleanor and Henry. "You could make a garden here."

"Here, there, everywhere," Berengaria said, in a sharp voice. This was so unlike her that Edythe gawked at her. The little Queen threw down the letter. "I could as well have heard from my father. I am tired of waiting." She waved at Edythe to go. "I think I will have a headache later. If you would bring me a drink."

"My lady," Edythe said.

. . .

Some time went by. They heard nothing from Ascalon, nothing from Acre. Edythe made the women potions containing mostly honey and wine and spice. She put the tincture of artemisia in a jar with a firm stopper. One day when she went up to the palace, she came on Johanna in a flying rage, storming up and down the hall.

"Have you heard this? Tell her! Tell her!"

By the throne Rouquin stood, taking a cup from a page. He said, "Not likely." He wore a long loose shirt and hose, no armor, but his sword on his belt, his gloves thrust under the buckle. He gave Edythe a brief, hot look. She remembered the last time she had seen him, and her heart jumped. She tore her gaze away from him.

Johanna's face was magnificent with anger. She spun toward Edythe, her arms flying out. Her coif had come loose, and she pulled at it, and released a tumble of her curly red-gold hair across the yellow silk shoulders of her gown.

"They have offered me up to the Saracens."

"What?" Edythe said.

Johanna stalked across the room. Along the divans the other women murmured and bowed as she walked anywhere near them and giggled when she had passed. A table fell over. A cup rolled. As she neared Edythe, she cried, "They have offered me to marry one of the Saracens!"

"Safadin is not so bad," Rouquin said, smiling. He drank the wine.

"No, when he has a scimitar and you have a sword." She stamped her foot. "I will not marry an unbelieving pagan hound."

Edythe drew back with the other women, trying not to smile. Rouquin was clearly not conveying this as a serious offer; she thought Richard himself would have to come before her to make this even a matter of question. Johanna in full fury was like a small storm, gusting up and down the hall, things flying in her wake. Probably enjoying herself.

Now she blew past Rouquin and flung herself down on the throne, where she was wont to sit when Richard was not there. She glared at her cousin. "My brother is being amusing. He cannot mean this."

Rouquin shrugged. "I don't know if Safadin is any more inclined to it than you are." His eyes moved, and Edythe caught his glance, but then he turned back to Johanna. He said, "The King wants you to swear you will not deal anymore with Isabella."

"Oh," Johanna said. She looked suddenly smaller, the air gone out of her. "Is that why you were in Acre?" She waved a hand at him. "Tell me everything that's going on there. And Berengaria will want to know about her garden."

"Guy still rules," Rouquin said. "I don't know about the garden. Let me go, Jo, I have to leave soon."

"Go," she said. "Tell Richard I will have a Christian husband, or none."

.   .   .

Edythe went out onto the terrace, into the dark; she thought, *He would marry his sister to a Saracen, but I am not fit to be allowed into Jerusalem.*

She knew Richard did not mean the marriage offer seriously. It was his way, she thought, of punishing Johanna for meddling with Isabella. He seemed to have fallen into a playful way of dealing with Saladin when they weren't fighting, these mock negotiations, like boys dueling with sticks. The moon was rising, a little less than full, clouds drifting over its face like islands in the air.

Someone was coming, and she turned. Rouquin walked up beside her and leaned on the rail.

"The King has a message for you, as well."

"Oh," she said. "What, is he marrying me off, too?" And put her hand over her mouth, before she said too much.

He laughed. "No. He said, 'Tell her she's a good little monster.'"

She lowered her hand and looked out to sea. "He thinks I'm his familiar, like a toad."

"They call you the King's witch. You saved Acre," he said. "Guy could not have kept Conrad out. He wasn't even ready when the safe conduct came, much less when he saw how many men Conrad had brought, and ships, too. If I and my company had not been there, Conrad would have Acre now."

She said, "I'm glad he doesn't." *Berengaria would have lost her garden, then*, she thought. She turned to him, wanting to hold him there, to keep his attention. "How can he do that? Attack Christians on Crusade, when he thinks he's King of Jerusalem?"

"I think his Jerusalem is different from ours," Rouquin said.

She had not seen him since the night before they marched on the Holy City. She said, "How close did you get, last month?"

One of his shoulders lifted and fell. "A few days' hard riding. But they would not continue. The other lords. They were threatening to leave on their own—Hugh of Burgundy and the French, the Flemings, all the local men, even Guy—just ride away from Richard, run back here to the coast where it's safe."

She said, "Oh, God."

"It was harder every step. The Saracens burned all the villages in the way, all the fields; there was no forage, hardly any graze for the horses. They shot down horses from ambush. We were running out of food. They had poisoned the wells. We'd have to fight all the way back, too, and we had nothing to eat but dying horses. Saladin's army may be gone, but they hate us out there."

She said nothing. Her lips tasted salt; the wind sang off the edge of the roof behind her.

"I don't blame them," he said. "They're great fighters and Jerusalem is theirs, as much as ours. If I were one of them I'd be fighting us too."

She gave him a startled look. "That must be heresy. Are you going to confess that?"

"Oh, come," he said, scornful. "I was born halfway out the church door. Angevins don't confess, it would take too long."

She laughed. "What does Richard say?"

"Richard wants that city. But I'm beginning to think even he . . . There's this marriage offer."

She said, "He can't mean that. As you said. He is just having a little joke with Saladin." *Still*, she thought, *he is looking for other ways out of this.* Her heart clenched; she thought of what the beggar had said, and Yeshua ben Yafo.

"Anyway," Rouquin said, "I came back."

She remembered what she had told him, before they left, and leaned toward him, and he bent and their mouths met.

"I have to go soon," he said, a while later, his arms around her. "When my men are all loaded on the ships. We have to get back to Ascalon; we're building a fortress, and trying to take another place, down the coast toward Egypt." He kissed her cheek and her nose and her mouth again.

"How will you know when the ship is ready?"

"They'll ring the church bell."

"Why can't we come down to Ascalon? Jaffa is boring."

"It's just a pile of rocks, right now. We have some hovels raised. Johanna won't endure that. You stay here." He kissed her again.

She leaned her head on his shoulder. Better he leave. Better they keep this to a few kisses. But even as she thought that, she was lifting her head and he was turning his. He licked her lips and she parted them and he slid his tongue over hers. She shut her eyes. He was groping through her gown; he had too knowing a way with women's clothing. She laid her hand on his chest. She wanted to touch his body, to feel his skin against hers, to taste him, mouth him, to study him and know him. The church bell began to ring.

He drew his hand out. "Next time," he said, and kissed her mouth again and went away. She shrank back to the wall, thinking this could go nowhere good. But she would not turn back; she wanted where it went, whatever happened afterward.

. . .

Saladin had gone to Damascus. Humphrey said the Sultan was having family trouble, maybe an uprising, that the Muslim priests were preaching against him and the Caliph himself had rebuked him for losing Acre and Jaffa to the Christians. Humphrey had told Richard about the *hashishiyyun*, the sect that practiced political murder, and now came a report that Saladin had wakened one morning to find two of their knives by his bed.

In the countryside around Ascalon were men who had not stopped fighting just because the Sultan was gone, who fought, simply as a matter of course, whoever tried to rule them. Richard was hammering these, attacking their villages and running them down piecemeal, driving them to submit or leave. Every day he rode out with enough men to move fast and punch hard and went looking for enemies.

He said, "We found nobody today, not even any sign."

He sounded gloomy about that. Rouquin thought the local small game was no solace for Jerusalem. They were in the hall in Ascalon, small and grim and cold in spite of the smoky braziers. "My sister is well?" the King said, abruptly, turning toward Rouquin.

"Like an ox. She has Edythe make her all kinds of potions and elixirs and infusions."

"Can she make her an infusion that will keep her out of trouble?" Richard slumped in his chair, his feet thrust forward.

Rouquin laughed. He said, "What we need is to plan another attack on Jerusalem."

Richard's head went back, his eyes shut. "There is no army anymore. Who would go? You and I and Mercadier?"

"That would be a start. A smaller army. Better supplies. If we could stash supplies on the way, then getting back wouldn't be such a problem. We know better how to fight them now, too."

Richard lay sprawled on the throne. "I think this is, as usual, more complicated than you make it. Although if I had eight thousand soldiers like you, I could take heaven. That was good work, in Acre."

Rouquin would not let him turn off the subject of Jerusalem. "The winter is ending. We could try an early campaign. I could do some scouting. Start planning the supplies."

Richard's fingers tapped on the arm of the throne. "It's tempting. I just came back and I'm already itching to get into the saddle again."

Rouquin said, "Then scout with me." This was how it felt to lose; you wanted to go win again as soon as you could, to erase the humiliation. The loss rode you like a bear on a stag until you got it down under you and ate its heart. Richard would come around. Jerusalem was still out there; they could still reach it. He went down to the half-ruined city, where his men were quartered in an old mosque.

· · ·

Rouquin would not stop talking about Jerusalem, and Richard began considering a new attack. But first he sent for Humphrey de Toron, who had come down from Acre with Rouquin. He would not stay long, rude and harsh as the place was; Richard thought it would take years to rebuild Ascalon, and the harbor had a problem with sand. Yet the oldest parts of the city were beautiful, even broken and ruined: a dense pattern of tiled arches and courtyards, fountains, grillwork, balconies, part Arab, part Greek, part something else indefinable. He and Humphrey talked of this for a while, the young man standing before him several moments before Richard remembered to tell him to sit.

He liked talking to Humphrey, who was clever and observant. When this was over, finally over, he wanted to do a lot more to Humphrey. In the meantime, there were these conversations. "You were in Acre," he said. "For this plot of Conrad's."

"Yes. Your cousin is a master of these things; he put a lot of men in the right places, and Conrad abruptly changed his mind."

"Rouq' is good on the ground. What he cannot see, sometimes . . ." Richard sat forward, his arms on his knees. "Jerusalem is much farther than it seems. There is more between us and it than mere country. More trouble."

The young man said, "Yes, my lord. I believe that."

"It's so far from the coast. The supply problem is the backbreaker." Richard rubbed his hands together. "The old Kings held it for a hundred years. Baldwin, my great-grandfather Fulk, Amalric, the Leper. Yet now I cannot see how they did it."

Humphrey said, "They never did hold it all. What they did control were the right places—where you must be master, to keep

Jerusalem. Nablus, Kerak, Ramleh, the fords of the Jordan. They
had a truce with Egypt. And they weren't up against Saladin."

Richard sat staring at the floor. He was remembering that campfire two months ago, halfway to Jerusalem, and Guy telling him, "We
can't go on." Even Guy, who owed him everything, telling him, "I will
start back with the others in the morning."

He said, stubbornly, "These lords now are a pack of greyhounds,
who are happiest watching the game from far off." Humphrey, of
course, the prettiest of them.

Humphrey said, "What they wanted, you have given them—
Acre, the coast, Jaffa. Cyprus."

Richard said, "What I want—"

He stopped. The taste of turning back still sour. Even the great
victory at Arsuf was a rock in his gut now. He had to take Jerusalem
to get this over with, but he could not shake the suspicion that
he had let his reach go past his grasp. He stood up.

"What I want is the Holy City. What I came for."

"My lord, you can take it, perhaps, and even hold it while you
are there." The young man rose with him. "But you will go back to
the west, and then we will lose it all again. Because none of us is like
you." In Humphrey's slim young face, his dark eyes widened, solemn. "As Safadin said, you are the Alexander of the Franks." Then
suddenly Humphrey leaned toward him and kissed him.

Richard caught hold of his wrist. But he took the kiss, held it
deep and hard, all the pent-up desire in him like a scorching brand.
In his hand the slender wrist turned, and Richard let go, and Humphrey wound his arms around his neck, his lips greedy, their bodies
pressed together. Richard thrust himself against him. The creak of
a door warned him that someone was coming. He drew back, and
Humphrey stepped away, his face red.

A page came into the doorway; Richard nodded to him and the

boy approached them, a bow to Humphrey, a deep bow to his King, his face clear, suspecting nothing. "My lord, there is a letter—"

Humphrey said, "I take my leave, then, my lord." His voice trembled. He would not meet Richard's eyes, but went out.

Richard reached for the letter, watching the young man go. The hard lust packed him, a heat past fire. Humphrey wanted him, too. He had guessed but not known. He could not speak; his mind leaped on to what came next between them. He had to collect himself. He looked down at the letter in his hand; he felt as if he had just fought a battle.

The letter in his hand bore his mother's seal, much tampered with, and his sister's, clean. He thumbed it open. His mother greeted him with a scold, that he had gotten them into this, and then told him his brother John was conniving with King Philip to steal Normandy.

He balled up the letter only half-read. Philip would not even heed the Pope, and why should he, if Richard could not take Jerusalem? He stamped around the rough little hall, the urge rising in him to attack again.

◆ ◆ ◆

In Jaffa, Johanna could not leave the palace without meeting a crowd that jeered her and cursed Richard; she went by ship back to Acre, there being now a busy stream of ships up and down the coast, and in Acre it was the same. The great city was full of brawling men, drunks, cripples, beggars and whores, Crusaders trying to get back to the west, and local people selling them whatever they wanted at ridiculous prices. She traveled through the streets in a litter, to avoid these howling mobs, but when they got to the church her guard had to form a circle around her to force a way through the press of bodies.

In French, in Syrian, the people screamed curses on Richard, on the Crusade, on her.

"Frankish dog!"

On the porch of the church, she left the litter and went quickly in the front door. There were pages, squires, all around, lining her way. Then in the dark aisle, while she was in the midst of her own court, someone brushed against her and thrust a flat stick into her hand.

She clutched it, knowing what it was without looking. In the dark she had seen nothing of whoever had given it to her. The pages around her herded her up three steps into the royal cabinet, and she sat rigid through a pious sermon about enduring trials.

It was not Richard's fault they had failed. She burned with this. She had talked to Humphrey, to Rouquin, to other lords, and she knew what had happened. She thought of ordering a charge of her knights into the crowd, to teach them how to see this, and at once knew she could not. Someone might be hurt, some innocent.

The reed had a star on it, steps, and three wavy lines. She showed it to Edythe, back at the palace.

"He will meet me at the sea gate, there by the steps, at Vespers."

Edythe said, "Yes, he's very clever."

"He will require something of me—what am I to do? Ah, God, I hate him. I wish—I wish I could get rid of him—"

Edythe said, "For the love of God, do not meet him. The King knows, Johanna. That's what my lord Rouquin meant, that time. The King knows everything."

Not everything. Edythe did not know everything, so how could Richard? Johanna lay awake, unable to sleep, remembering her mother's letters. He could build a castle of false meaning on those letters. By dawn she had decided not to meet de Sablé. Edythe was right about that. But she would send for Humphrey, who had long

before offered to help her with this, and who had just come back
to Acre.

•   •   •

Humphrey said, "I know a few . . . useful men. They would cast
some fear into him. Let him know you are not to be trifled with. But
they will need to be paid."

"Oh, money," she said. "The bane of the Plantagenets. Would
there were Jews here, I would pawn my gold chains."

Sixteen

JAFFA

Edythe knew where Rouquin kept his horses, in a long stable against the city wall, and as soon as she came into Jaffa she went there and found him hitching his roan stallion to a ring in one corner.

"I have heard you are going to Jerusalem," she said. "Take me with you."

Rouquin hung the bridle on the wall. "What are you doing down here? You're all supposed to be in Acre. What are you talking about?"

"Ayberk brought me. I told Johanna that Besac needed me at the hospital." She shrugged that off. "I'll dress like a man. A squire, I've seen enough of them. I can get the clothes. I'll work. I'll keep up." She watched his eyes. "I've done a lot for you, and for Richard. He won't let me, but he doesn't have to know. I realize it will be hard. I was in the camp at Acre. Can it be worse than that?" She said, carefully, "I'll do anything you want."

The gray eyes narrowed. In the spiky red beard his wide mouth twisted into a crooked smile. "Anything I want, huh? He's got me riding rear guard. All right. I'll take you. If you mean it. Come with me, right now, and prove it."

She swallowed, unnerved. Her legs quivered. She had not meant this to happen so suddenly, but she had promised. She followed him around the end of the stable and out to the yard.

It was broad, paved in old bricks, with an orange tree growing in one corner, and a fountain. On three sides were the low stone houses where his men were quartered. He said, "I'm surprised Johanna let you go." It was the heat of the day and except for three boys brushing down horses, and Mercadier lounging under the orange tree, no one was there.

She did not say, *Johanna has another plot. She wants me out of the way.* She said, "She knows how important the hospital is. Richard must think I'm still in Acre, though." Another boy rolled a barrow full of horseshit and straw out of the stable and around a corner. Rouquin took her into the middle building.

They went through a long hall, dark, smelling of dirty clothes and stale chamber pots, littered with blankets, to the south end, where there was a door, which opened on a narrow closet. This was his room, she saw, his helmet on the crossbar, his mail, his shield against the wall.

"Sit." He put a stool down in the middle of the room.

She had no idea what was going to happen. She swallowed, and rubbed her palms on her skirt, and sat. He pulled off her coif, and her hair came down over her shoulders and back.

She saw then he had the shears in his hand, and she cried out, but before she could defend her hair he took the whole long swag, rolled it over his hand, and in one chop cut it off.

She gasped. She put her hands to her head, the short hair bris-

tling, scratching her neck; she had never cut her hair. He pushed her
hands aside and began to crop away even the rest, as close as he
could, down to her scalp, like his.

Mercadier had come into the open doorway and was leaning his
shoulder on the jamb, his eyes quizzical. He made a gesture with his
hands.

Rouquin said, "She's going with us. Keep it tight."

"With us." The Brabanter's round face creased in a smile. "A
pretty knight she'll make. In a dress?"

"She'll need a jerkin. Our colors. Shirt, hose, boots, small clothes."

She said, "I have my own . . . ," and blushed, clamping her lips
shut.

"She can wear her own small clothes." Rouquin ran his hand
over her cropped head. Her scalp felt cold. She was bald. She looked
up at him, and he smiled at her, pleased with himself.

"You still don't look like a boy."

"I'll grow a moustache," she said, and Mercadier laughed.

♦   ♦   ♦

She had expected a different demand of him. He had felt her hand
tremble in his grasp. When she had gone, he stood under the orange tree in the dusk, thinking about that. He could have had her,
right there. She would have let him.

It would have been the price she paid for going with him. An
obligation, a trade. He wanted something else. He wanted her free,
willing, eager, coming to him joyously. He remembered kissing her,
how she had lifted her face to him, her eyes closed, trusting in his
arms. She would give herself utterly to him, freely, for his own sake,
when it happened. He could wait. There would be no chances on
the march, but maybe in Jerusalem.

. . .

Richard had chosen his army carefully: the remainder of his Poitevins, Rouquin and his men, several local barons and their companies, who knew the ground well. The Templars and Hospitallers, Guy and his men, Henry of Champagne, and the last of the French. They had brought a supply train of six wagons. Leaving Jaffa, Edythe rode on one of the wagons, dressed in a dark jerkin and hose and old shoes too big for her, a long cap. Under the shirt she wore a band of cloth bound tight across her breasts, to hold her flat. Richard led the army; the wagons traveled well behind him, and Rouquin behind them. The army stretched out along miles of the road.

The first day went along easily enough. The sky was bright blue, a single bird floating in high circles overhead. It was dull sitting on the jouncing wagon seat; the driver snored. She noticed the other pages and squires of Rouquin's company picking up wood as they went and stowing it in the wagons, and she got down and ran around gathering with them. It was easier moving in the jerkin than in a long dress. The wood was sparse, thorny, low to the ground. She came into camp at sundown worn to exhaustion. She slept on the ground by the fire, Rouquin on one side of her, Mercadier on the other.

The next night as they made camp, she watched Mercadier chop kindling so fast she couldn't see precisely what he was doing. The others moved around her, bringing wood, dumping their saddles and other gear on the ground around the fire to mark their spaces. When they met, they banged their hands together and said, "Jerusalem."

She helped the cook spit mutton. The chatter around her was full of laughter. Richard rode by and they all cheered him. She stacked wood, hauled water, part of this. She felt suddenly warmer. Someone began to sing a marching song, and the others picked it up. The tuneless growl of voices spread from campfire to campfire. She turned the meat and greased it and the fire crackled; she backed quickly away. She began to pick up the words of the refrain. Settling by the fire to keep the spit turning, she began to sing along. She was one of them, going to Jerusalem. Nobody cared about anything else.

The next day, as they moved up into the first low hills, suddenly a shower of arrows came pelting down from the slope beside the road.

Edythe was out looking for wood; she heard someone yell, and turned back to see the front wagon abruptly stop, its lead team slumping down in the harness. The wagons coming along the road after ran up on one another, the drivers cursing and ducking the arrows, crawling under their seats and jumping to the ground. Another horse was down, kicking. Another reared in the harness and fell sideways. She started toward them and a second shower of arrows pelted into the wagons, each arrow carrying a little cuff of fire.

She stopped. A yell went up from the rear guard. The pounding hooves warned her, and she flung herself under the wagon; all she could see was a wall of horses' forelegs driving toward her. They divided smoothly around the wagon and crossed the road on either side. She crawled out and stood up.

The mass of horsemen was charging up the hill toward the unseen bowmen, and from the vanguard another stream of horses came galloping after them. She lowered her hand. Now she saw that the wagon she had just hid under was burning.

That was their food, those barrels and bales. She scrambled up the wheel to the driver's seat; two other squires were climbing on, and another ran to the horses. The two boys on the wagon were crawling across the covered top toward the burning arrows.

She shouted, "Be careful—" The whole load of the wagon was

covered with this sheet of canvas, and so far only that was burning. She cried, "Help me get this off." She pulled her belt knife and slashed the cords holding the canvas down.

The boys bounded around and together they threw off the burning cover. The third squire had freed the living horses trapped with the dead ones, and they pulled the wagon out of line. Behind them the next wagon burned, past saving. Three squires were trying to loose the pitching, screaming team.

She ran to help. They saved the horses, but the whole wagon was on fire. They dragged the rest out of the way, hauling them close together, in case there was another attack.

Abruptly the knights were galloping back around them, arrows in their mail and shields, roaring. They howled at each other and made their horses rear and prance. Their faces blazed. They had fought the Saracens in some blind draw and crushed them. A little rain began to fall, and with the other squires she crept in under the wagons, watching the knights whoop over their victory.

The boy next to her said, "They are hot, look at them." His voice was wistful. "I'll be such a knight as that."

She made some indefinite sound. He was one of the squires to Rouquin's company; his name was Walter. He seemed familiar and she knew she had seen him before, probably often, but only now she paid attention. Now that they shared the Crusade. She turned to watch one knight rear his horse up and make it leap four great bounds on its hind legs along the road, and the others cheered.

They stayed where they were, built camps around the wagons, in the rain. The fire sputtered and the meat was raw and turning bad. Sometime just before sundown, when she was halfway dozing, she looked up and saw Richard dismounting from his horse on the other side of the camp.

She crouched back among the other squires. Richard came into

the middle of the camp, on the other side of the fire, his eyes steadily
on the squires. He wore no helmet, no sign of rank, only a dirty
white surcoat over his mail. His blue eyes blazed. He said, "Your
masters say you saved these wagons. By God's spurs you are worthy,
and I love you for it, I shall dub each one of you by my own hand,
when this is done."

The boys all cheered, and some stood up, and said their names
and bowed; Walter leaped to his feet and bowed and bowed, grinning all over his face. She stayed sitting, hidden among them, but
what he had said swelled in her mind. He had meant her, too. He
had praised her, too. She would have done anything for him. She
deserved Jerusalem.

They slogged on. The wagons that had burned had held most
of the fodder for their horses. Besides the constant search for dry
wood, now they were looking also for grass, for hay, anything in this
desert country that the horses would eat. She thought the army was
growing smaller. She saw little of Rouquin, who was in the saddle
before she woke up until after she was asleep. She asked Walter if
there were fewer men, and he shrugged.

"Probably they're leaving. They did last time." He had an armful
of grass; she had found a narrow meadow in a draw just off the road,
along a creek rapidly filling in the rain, and they were cutting all they
could before the rising waters drove them out. The wet grass was
soaking her jerkin. He said, "You're a girl, aren't you."

She mumbled a denial. He said, "It's all right. There've been other
girls. There were girls the first time. At least I've heard. Like that
song." He began to sing an old ballad, about a woman who followed
her husband to the Holy Land.

She thought probably he had seen her before, too, back at Jaffa,
at Acre, but he had not recognized her, not paid attention, until they
shared this. They went back up to the camp and fed the snorting

horses; the roan tried to bite her. She went to help the cook. Walter sat by the fire, yawning. That night again she never saw Rouquin come into camp, and he was gone when she woke up.

Plodding on through the mud, she grew hungrier. In the higher hills, they took another assault of arrows, and again the knights drove the Saracens away. The wagons were empty anyway, except for lances and shields.

Walter said, "I'll keep going. Won't you?"

"Yes," she said. "Yes, of course."

"Yes, but then you have—" He nodded toward Mercadier. With a start she realized that he saw her lie down each night beside Mercadier, and so he thought her the Brabanter's woman. She said nothing.

They trudged on. There was nothing to eat. The horses neighed with hunger. The sun could not break through the low clouds; it would rain again soon. She thought she should pray. She plodded along beside Walter, her head down, afraid she would give up. A drop of rain hit her nose. Another, and another.

Then the foreguard was yelling, and the rear guard dashed by to help them. She caught a glimpse of the great roan bolting past, its long ugly head stretched forward, the mailed rider drawing out his sword.

The shouting up front became clamorous. Ahead the road topped a saddle ridge, and they labored, panting the last few hundred yards, and from the summit looked down into a long, wide valley. As the wagons rolled onto the down slope, they could see the valley floor, where the knights had surrounded a collection of laden animals: donkeys, and many camels and some horses, and a flock of sheep and goats. Walter thumped her back.

"A caravan! We're saved!"

She let out a yell. They had found food. The rain even lessened awhile. The knights let the handful of Saracens driving the caravan leak through their circle. They unpacked the camels and let them go and slaughtered the sheep and goats, built fires, put meat over them, and they began eating; they were eating well past sundown, when Rouquin finally came in.

"Hah, you like that, hah?" He sat beside her. She saw Walter's eyes widen, and the squire slide away. She gave the dripping haunch in her hands to Rouquin.

"Eat. There's plenty. It's delicious." There was blood running down her chin.

"Yes. Nothing like a fast for seasoning."

The singing began again, but this time they were singing Christian hymns, and she only listened. They were going to Jerusalem, all together, that was what mattered. She lay down, and he lay next to her.

The rain began again. She hunched down under her cloak, and then he spread his cloak over them both and drew her close to him. He slept in his mail and he was cold and damp against her, but he kept the rain off. She pressed her face into the shelter of his body. Surely the caravan was a sign. God favored them. This time they would come into the Holy City.

· · ·

They moved on through driving rain. They had abandoned most of the wagons and she rode one of those horses now, first by herself, then with Walter up behind. They rode bareback, the harness reins chopped short. She had never ridden astride before, and it surprised her how different it was. Eleanor, she remembered, had ridden astride.

Behind her, Walter crept closer on the horse's back, put his arms around her waist as if to hold on, and began to move his fingers toward her breasts. She looped the reins into one hand and gouged the nails of the other across his wrist.

"Ow," he said.

"Oh, did I hurt you?" she asked, looking to see who noticed. Nobody paid them heed.

"Slut," he said, under his breath, but he withdrew his hands, and just held to the back of her belt. In the afternoon, they dodged another spray of arrows. Several of the knights lost their horses, and one took their horse, so they were walking again.

Rouquin whispered, "Are you sorry you came?"

"No," she said, amazed that he asked. "No."

But there was no food anymore. All night the hungry horses neighed and her stomach hurt and she dreamed of eating. In the bleak wintry hills nothing grew but thorns and scrub. On the up and down road, she saw Richard riding ahead of them and realized how many had deserted, how small the army was becoming.

She saw him again when they came to a river, and he pulled off to the side to watch them all cross. She caught only a glimpse of his face, but that was enough. His eyes were hollow, his skin a bad color. She knew, with a knot in her stomach, that he was getting sick again.

She thought, *In Jerusalem, he will get better*. She thought of the tincture, back in Jaffa; she should have brought it. Maybe she could find some in Jerusalem. She should have brought it.

Then he would have known. But she should have brought it.

The next morning, in the driving rain, she was helping break the camp when the chief men began to move up toward the front of the army. She saw they were having a council. Walter said, "This is what they did when they turned back the last time." Her stomach rolled. They must be close, she thought. It must be only over the next hill, beyond the next bend in the road. But the men were gathering, up there, and she could hear them shouting.

. . .

"Sire, we cannot go farther. There's nothing to eat. God knows what lies ahead of us. Saladin and all his troops—"

"And us so weakened, Sire—"

Richard stood with the cloak pulled tight around him, shaking. The corruption of his body was more to him than the arguing around him. De Sablé came at him again. "How can we even mount a charge if we are attacked? We have lost half the horses."

He thought, *That hardly matters, since we've lost half the men.* Gerald of Nablus, the Hospitaller, rose up before him, adamant here as he never was against the Saracens.

"Sire, we must turn back. There's still the long way to the coast and we have no food."

They had food. Not much. It was the horses he pitied. He felt cold all the way to his bones, as if each stroke of rain pierced him like a lance. He wanted to lie down, but they were miles from any bed.

Rouquin was there, his face streaming in the rain, his eyes hard, accusing. "In the great Crusade, they never turned back. They took Jerusalem."

Guy said, "My lord, I am low minded saying this, but the Grand Masters are right. We must go back."

Richard held his jaw fast, to keep his teeth from chattering. Around him were men who owed him their swords, their power, even their lives: Guy whom he maintained as King, Henry of Champagne who was his cousin, Guy's brother Hugh whom he had made lord of Ascalon, the orders whose coffers he filled regularly, and they were curling their tails up between their legs and getting ready to run.

But he needed them. Without them, he himself could not go forward.

He bent his head. "Go tell the rest, then. We will go back." His muscles hurt, every part of his body throbbing.

Rouquin surged up in front of him. His gray eyes were wide with fury; Richard thought suddenly of his father, raging like this. Rouquin's voice spat at him.

"You can't do this. You swore to lead us." He wheeled toward the men already hurrying off to retreat. "I will go on; who will go to Jerusalem with me?"

Mercadier stood there, but Rouquin's voice stretched to reach the others, already gone into the haze of the rain, their backs to him. Nor did they heed him. No one turned to join him, but all rushed away.

Richard clutched the cloak around him. He had to get somewhere warm and safe. With his doctor, and her gentle hands and her potions against the pain. He looked at Rouquin and said, "I order you to retreat."

*   *   *

She was sheltering under a wagon when Rouquin came back, and from his face she saw what had happened. She turned her gaze down. His voice was bitter, the words chopped, broken in her ears. The Crusade was over. They would not see Jerusalem. The old beggar was right: Nobody won.

She had known this. She had known this, she thought, since the massacre at Acre.

He said, "Now are you sorry you came?"

She lifted her face to him. "No." She put her head forward, her forehead against his mailed chest. At least now she had a measure of the task. "No." She pressed closer into his warmth, his arms around her.

. . .

All the way back to Jaffa she ate only a piece of bread, an old apple, a bone she gnawed down almost to nothing. The army fell steadily apart, men going off in all directions. Rouquin and his company and the few Poitevins left reached Jaffa with Richard almost falling out of the saddle. Edythe went into the palace and watched over him for the next three days while he thrashed and shivered and burned with the fever.

She hardly slept. She put aside Jerusalem and set herself entirely to tend the sick King. She ate what she could and put on fresh, dry clothes, which did much to restore her, but Richard had tumbled away into the dark and she could barely keep her hands on him, much less bring him back.

She gave him the tincture, but he vomited it up. All his muscles cramped. She stayed by him, talked to him, rubbed the knots in his back and arms and washed him, brewed potions by the bed and fed them to him drop by drop, cleaned him up and kept him warm.

Once, he lay on the bed and laughed. He said, "I see it, there, there, the peaks—all shining, they shine like gold."

She sat beside him, uneasy, remembering the old wives' whisper that dying people saw heaven. He sang to himself, or maybe he was just breathing loudly. Then he said, again, "This city in the clouds, there—there's no way to it. I can't fly."

She put her hand on his wrist; the pulse there was stronger than before. He was not dying. He was somewhere else, but he would come back. He started under her touch and turned his face toward her.

His eyes stared, wide and full, seeing something entirely other. "What is there? What do I have to do?"

"Ah," she said, wondering what she was talking to, "I hope you will be well, my lord King."

His eyes stared at her, unblinking, still huge. "They say the Jew knows the answer," he said. He turned his head again and shut his eyes.

She gave him the tincture again, this time with a sour water the apothecary said would soothe his stomach. He kept it down, and from then on he seemed to get better.

She slept a little. But she dared not leave him.

Day by day he grew stronger. The dark handsome Saracen, Safadin, came with a letter. Richard had them move him out to the hall to meet him. He needed help even sitting down on the throne, but when the crown was on his head, his back straightened, and his shoulders squared, he shook them off and sat alone.

The place was full of braziers, too hot for comfort. All along the walls stood the people of the court. Edythe stayed in the corner; the Saracen had looked at her once and she had seen hatred in his eyes. She searched among the crowd along the wall, but she did not see Rouquin. He had not forgiven Richard, then. Walter was there, and Henry of Champagne. Humphrey de Toron passed the words back and forth between Richard and the Saracen.

He read out loud the letter from the Sultan, and Richard said, "My lord Saladin hears I am sick, and offers me his own physician. Very generous of him."

Safadin spoke.

"The Sultan's physician is a very famous and learned Jew from Cairo. He has magic herbs and amulets unknown to you in the West."

Richard laughed. He said, "Tell him I have my own physician. As it happens, I have meant to write my lord the Sultan, and if my lord Safadin will wait, I shall have this done."

Safadin bowed; Richard bowed. He sent for a scribe, and Edythe went out of the hall.

She walked down the stairs, to the courtyard. Since they had come back she had not gone to the hospital, for fear of leaving Richard in his extremity. She could not go now, either. He was holding together for Safadin's sake, but she knew he would not stay upright very long. The discord still raged in his body. Yeshua had said to give him the tincture as soon as she knew he was sick. She had done it too late. For her own selfish purpose she had failed him.

She went around to the kitchen, meaning to find something to eat, and came upon Rouquin there. Her heart quickened when she saw him.

He said, "How does the King?"

"Well enough," she said. "He thinks too much."

He got her hand, and she followed him into the shadow between the kitchen wall and the vine-covered back of the palace. The air smelled sweet of flowers. Spring was coming. She felt his arms around her and lifted her face, and they kissed.

His hand got swiftly into her clothes. "I want you. Now. This time."

She said, "We can't—not here—" She coiled her arms around his neck. "Yes. Take me someplace." She shut her eyes.

He had her lip between his teeth. He had pulled off her coif and his hand stroked over her cropped hair. Then he stood back.

"Go make sure he has someone with him, and come back. I know where."

She went out, quickly wrapping the cloth around her head again, which was much easier, with her hair only an inch long. She went up the hall, empty except for a guard at the door. A table stood by the throne, an inky goose quill lying on it.

At the end of the hall was the King's chamber, where she found

Richard back in his bed, asleep. A half-full cup of wine stood on the floor beside him. A page dozed at the foot of the bed. Her heart was pounding. She tried not to think what Rouquin was doing. She listened to the King's back and felt the pulses of his liver and of his brain; he murmured at her touch but did not waken. She went out and back down the steps to the courtyard.

•   •   •

He took her to a shed behind the kitchen, where on the dirt floor there were some rugs in a heap, a lamp, and a cup.

The room was dark and smelled moldy. He said, "Light the lamp." While she fumbled with a tinderbox, he threw off his shirt and boots and hose. She got the lamp lit in spite of her trembling hands. Before she turned back to face him, he was unlacing her kirtle.

She took off her coif, her eyes on his nakedness, and her woman's part clenched. His part was already swollen hard. She lifted her gaze to the heavy muscles of his chest, but her eyes wandered down, over the slab of his belly, to the club thrusting straight out, its tip like a helmet.

"Your hair's coming back darker." He fingered the short curl beside her ear and pulled off the kirtle. "I have wanted this—so long." He stroked his hands down her sides, up to undo the clasp at the back of her neck.

She stood before him, her arms out, so that he could pull her gown down around her waist. "Yes," she said, although her voice shook. Her breasts tingled, only her thin shift covering them, the nipples poking out the fine cloth. Her blood hammered in her ears. She did not know what she wanted, but she knew what was happening.

"No bells this time. Nothing about honorable." He slid her clothes down over her hips to the floor.

"Yes." She stepped out of the heap of cloth.

He knelt and drew her down onto him, so she faced him, straddling his great horseman's thighs. Lifting her thin underdress, he took it off over her head. She shut her eyes, as if then she would not be so naked.

"Do you want me?"

"Yes. Yes."

She put her arms around his neck, and he slid his hand between her legs. The touch made her shiver. His fingers parted the folds of her body and the round head of his club poked up into the opening.

She was too small. She clutched him, gritting her teeth. He drove himself up into the middle of her, tearing in, tight and burning. She laid her head on his shoulder and sobbed.

He pulled her around, up and down, whispering to her. Her arms around his neck, she clung to him, trying to move the way he wanted, her chest against his, rocking together with him. The pain became an aching need for more. He moved faster, sucked on her shoulder and with his arms under her knees curled her legs up between them. He gasped and groaned and held her fast, a deep pulse in the middle of her. Breathing hard, he was still.

She shivered. She straightened herself slowly; she felt as if she had never noticed her body before. As if she had never been naked before. Something else was supposed to happen. Something needed to happen. He was still inside her, and she moved against him. He laid them both down on the rags, his weight against her, kissed her, tipping her head back.

"My dear one. My dearling." His tongue flickered into her ear. He pulled her leg up over his hip. She moaned, her arms sliding down his hips, her hands running over his backside. She was climbing, climbing. Then for an instant everything was perfect, warm, and sweet.

He put his head down next to hers, face-to-face, and they were both silent awhile.

"I want to marry you."

She wept. She rubbed her face against his. "Don't say that."

"You were a virgin. Look at all this blood. We should marry."

"No, we can never marry."

He looked at her, puzzled, but did not ask her why. He stroked her belly, the inside of her thigh, streaked with blood and seed. She lay against him, tired. She would think about all this later. For now this was enough, to have him in her arms. But nothing lasted.

"I need to go back to Richard."

"Yes, I know."

"I love you." That seemed so extraordinary. She had not known what that meant before. She felt as if a door she had never seen before had opened, as if she had been locked all this while in a little room, and the walls had suddenly fallen away, and now the world lay open to her. She never wanted to leave him. She would take whatever she could of this wonderful thing. Maybe that was what Yeshua had meant, about being the woman she was, not wanting more, just that.

"I love you." He played with the curl by her ear; he kissed her. "I don't need to marry. I'm a bastard."

She held him, her hands on his hair, and he bent and kissed her collarbone and set his teeth against her skin. She had to tell him. He trusted her; that was why he did not ask for reasons. He didn't want to know, either. She arched her back so that he could reach her nipple with his tongue. His hand slid down between her legs again. This was delicious; her whole body throbbed. When he found out, everything would be over. Better a dog than a Jew. He would never touch her again. So she would never tell him. But it could not go on forever.

·   ·   ·

Richard was getting steadily better. He exchanged some more bantering letters with Saladin, who was staying in Jerusalem, and sent the Sultan a gift of Byzantine silk. Promptly there came back some very fine horses. The King showed them off for the rest of his court; one of the squires who trotted them up and down the courtyard was Walter.

His face was bruised, and he ran with a limp. She wondered what had happened to him. He saw her, and smiled, and then led the gray mare away. Behind her, somebody said, "That's Walter. As much as he gets beaten up, he won't hear a word against Richard."

A few days later, as she waited by the kitchen door for Richard's meat, the Templar de Sablé came up to her, casual, as if he himself were there for his dinner.

"I would have some words with you, Lady." He said this out of the side of his mouth.

She shivered. It had come to her now. Almost she said, *Then why not send me a reed?* Instead, she said, "No."

He could not linger; someone would remark on it. But he gave her a foul look and went off. Rouquin was gone again on a raid; she was alone.

With Richard better she went to the hospital in the afternoons. Coming back one evening she thought someone followed her, and turned into a lane, and went by crooked ways back to the palace. But she knew who it was.

So she was relieved when Johanna wrote from Acre, demanding she come; the Queen could not sleep, and Berengaria got headaches. Rouquin would come there soon anyway. Richard sent to his sister that he was going up there sometime in the spring, for yet another of his councils, and in the meantime, now that he was well, he would send Edythe.

Seventeen

ACRE

Edythe said, "Oh, but it's beautiful." She walked down the path, now paved with white rock. "My lady, what you have done. It's like needlework."

Her small thin face shining, Berengaria stood proudly looking around at the garden. The vine that covered the wall was sprouting red trumpets against the deep green of its leaves, and tall blue cornflowers stood like stars against them. Red and yellow dragonflower filled the space between the pistachio trees and the rosebush, the whole so lushly overgrown that the earth hardly showed. The rosebush was a mass of deep red. Little white daisies bordered the whole like a hem.

Edythe had never seen such a garden. Berengaria had no rosemary, no pot herbs or onions or garlic, no medicines; she had even rooted up the yarrow. Instead she had grown flowers, in masses and clusters, all for their gaudy color. She thought, *Who would spend so much care on mere flowers, except a Queen?*

Johanna was sitting down on the stone bench in the middle. "Yes, it's very pretty." She dismissed it with a toss of her hand. She gave Edythe a quizzical look. "What happened to your hair?"

Edythe put her hand to her coif, which had slipped back on the short curly mass of her hair. "Umm—" She felt herself grow furiously hot.

Johanna laughed. "Well, then. Such a blush." She made a knowing face. "I shall not ask to whom you gave this favor. You know Richard is sending us back to the west."

Edythe had not heard this before. The garden disappeared from her mind; she put her hand in her lap. She blurted, "To France, you mean."

Johanna gave her a keen look. "Yes, to France. To Poitiers, really. Mother will want to see us all at once." She reached out for Edythe's skirt and pulled her down beside her on the bench. "Sometime this summer. I would you came with me, but I think he intends you to stay." She picked the edge of Edythe's coif over her forehead.

Edythe sat stiff on the bench, hardly hearing this. She could not go. She lost everything if she went back to France.

Johanna went on, not noticing. "You should ask him. He would let you come if you asked. He owes you much. He likes you, as much as he likes any woman. And he's not sick anymore."

Yet she could not think how to stay here, either, if Johanna left. Her place in the Queen's court gave her a home, fed her, protected her. The hospital. She swallowed. At least she would have that. Without Johanna's purse or Richard's, how long would that last? Johanna said, "Now they will let me marry again. I promise you— what I promised you, before."

"My lady," she said. If they went back to Poitiers, could she still be a Jew? Certainly she could not be with Rouquin anymore. Her heart cracked. She said, her voice feeble, "So much has happened here."

"What?" Johanna cried. "What has happened? Except to ruin my poor brother, sicken him body and soul, and muddy up his name? He did everything they asked of him, but they will not honor him for it, not an ounce. Little men. They are such little men. I cannot abide it here. I hate it here."

Edythe hardly heard this. She could make a hospital, she thought, in Poitiers. There was no such place in Poitiers. More likely, she would go back to tending Eleanor, who ached and wheezed more as she got older, and like her son loved to have her back rubbed; she would spend her afternoons mixing potions for the other court women. Sewing and spreading gossip. They would marry him to an heiress. She would see him, Count of this or that, only in crowds. They would marry her to some stranger.

"Of course," Johanna was saying, "then I might have another baby."

Edythe turned to her, intent. That had occurred to her, although not about Johanna. "I hope so, my lady. I do hope so."

◆　◆　◆

Richard came up from Jaffa, and they met him at the wharf. Only four ships had come with him, and he was shouting to his sister from the small boat even before he landed.

"I had to leave the rest of the fleet back there. Saladin tried to sneak in—" He leaped up onto the wharf, still wearing boat shoes but in his mail and with his helmet under his arm. The court dipped and bobbed into its homage of bows and murmurs and bent necks. Standing behind his sister, Edythe recognized his high color, his snapping excitement; he had won some fight.

His voice sang on. "When I was on the boat but still in the harbor. I'd only left a little garrison, everybody wanted to get up here, I guess the stews are cheaper here." He bent and kissed Johanna's

cheek. Edythe looked past him, at the men coming with him; Rouquin was not one of them. Richard's exuberant voice continued.

"Saladin never quits. He sent his first ranks into the city before
I was even out beyond the surf. He must want Jaffa very badly. But
he isn't going to get it." He bowed to Berengaria, and started off
down the wharf. "Rouquin pulled all the garrison into the palace
and sent a priest to swim to my ship. I had to wade back and clear
the bastards out. We chased them halfway to the hills." He strode
away down the wharf, and they all pattered after him. Edythe hung
back, looking at the galleys.

Johanna said, "So you left Rouquin back there? You're still not
getting along?"

"He's in one of his fits." He turned his head, looking for her. "He
needs Edythe to give him a potion, to change his humor." His eyes
glittered.

She said, mildly, "My lord." She could feel her cheeks burning;
she lifted her skirts to go after them, disappointed. The grooms came
forward with their horses, and they rode away to the citadel.

Halfway there the street filled with shouting men. Richard raised
his hand, as if to greet a welcome, and a shower of rotten fruit
bounced around him.

"Traitor! Oath breaker!" The crowd screamed up and down the
street. Swiftly the knights formed up around the court in a tight
wall, and a charge cleared the way. Richard's hand was at his side.
His face was like a stone. They fought their way through the jeers
and volleys of dung and offal to the Citadel of Acre.

⋅   ⋅   ⋅

"It's actually very pleasant out here in the evenings," Johanna said.
"And far from the street." She led him down through the yard toward the old garden.

Richard hardly heard her, his ears still full of the shouting back there, not the words, but the noise. His nerves jumped. As if he were carried outside himself and looked back he realized what the street mob saw: a man who had failed the Crusade. All those fine, stupid words. Jerusalem the impossible. Here around him his sister, still laying her adoring look upon him, his stranger wife.

"There's another letter from Mother. Bad news."

And that. He sat on a bench and tore the letter open. "From Her Grace the Duchess of Aquitaine to her beloved son Richard Duke of Aquitaine and King of England, greeting." No sweetness of inquiry after his health, the weather, God's blessings on him. Straight into the gut.

"I have warned you about John and now it is coming to pass. My spies tell me he has promised Philip the great fortress of Gisors if Philip will recognize him as Duke of Normandy. They are gathering an army. And worse: They are in constant consult with the Duke of Austria, whom somehow in your charm and wisdom you have succeeded in giving a deadly insult, and who says you are cut down now, and will pay like any other man."

Richard said, aloud, "If I ever tremble at the Duke of Austria, put me out with a bowl to beg."

"Therefore, my dear son, come not home in any way to put yourself within his reach, or Philip's either, for that matter, but come home while there is still a home left to you."

He tossed the letter down. Everything was falling apart. The women talked around him, but in his mind he still heard the shouting in the street.

He could not even leave now. He had to get some arrangement from Saladin, some formal acceptance of his gains, or everything he had fought for would go up in the flames of these little local feuds. There was Guy, who without him had nothing, and whom, in spite of himself, Richard had come to like. Humphrey. He began to plot the way home—by ship, perforce, maybe to Rome, or southern France. Damn the Duke of Austria, whose face he could not even remember, although he remembered at the fall of Acre telling Rouquin to tear his banner down.

Johanna chattered on beside him. He whipped his gaze around to her. "Do you never shut up? Send for something to drink."

Her face crumbled. With a sniff she leaped up and went off. Now he would have to deal with that, too. He saw that everything happening to him was of his own making; he was damned, the devil in him well pleased at all his ruin, damned and hopeless.

He lifted his head, and for the first time the color around him burst in on his attention. He looked dazed around him. This garden had not been here before. The living colors, reds and blues and streaks of white, flooded his eyes, magnificent, overwhelming. For a moment, even his mood lightened.

Some idea about this lay in the back of his mind, and he turned to Berengaria, on the next bench.

"Did you do this?"

The girl blinked at him and smiled. "Yes, my lord. Do you like it?"

"You are very clever," he said, his greatest compliment to a woman. But he did not look at the garden again; he looked at her, as if he saw her for the first time, and after a moment, he leaned toward her and kissed her.

•   •   •

In the morning, after he had cozened his sister back to sweetness, Edythe came in to give him a potion. She felt the pulse in his throat, one hand on his shoulder, handling him, as she often did, as if she were plumping chickens in a market stall. No King at all, but a skinful of humors. He said, "Johanna says you want to ask me something."

She stepped back, her eyes wide. "I—I don't know what."

"She says you would ask to go back to France with them, but you are too dutiful. Her word."

Her eyes widened; she had interesting eyes for a woman: dark, prominent, the heavy upper lids fringed with black lashes. She whispered, "I would stay here, my lord."

He nodded, pleased; but he knew why, and it was not for his sake. He said, "I am going to Jaffa again, once they're seen off. You come with me."

"Thank you, my lord." She lowered her eyes. She put her hand on his wrist; he thought she was listening, as if her fingertips had ears. He shut his eyes. Maybe then he would hear what she heard, his body talking, wiser probably than his mind.

•   •   •

The sun was just rising, the air pink and warm already, the ships rocking at their anchors on the bay. Richard led Johanna down the quay, her hand on his arm. The galley captain himself waited for them above the small boat.

Johanna turned to him, resolute. She wore a traveling cloak of green, her best color, her skin warm against it, her eyes like sea jewels. She said, "Richard, you must take care. Come quickly."

"I will." He held her hand. In spite of her meddling, he was sorry she would be gone; he would be much alone, with her away and Rouquin in a temper. He said, "I will come soon after."

"I hope so." She kissed him. Her eyes were damp. But she looked away, over his shoulder, not meeting his gaze. "Richard—I—I—did wrong, I think. I made a mistake. Something awful. Forgive me. I hope it comes to nothing."

He held her hands. "Whatever it is, it doesn't matter. Tell Mother about it when you see her; she's got all the advice."

She hugged him. "I will. Please come soon." She turned and went down into the little boat.

He turned to Berengaria. "Take care, little wife."

"My lord, I will."

Then she too was gone, rowing toward the galley standing in the bay. In a few months they would reach Poitiers. The rising sun beat on his back. It would be hot here, in this strange place, where somehow he could not find a way to win. He turned and went back to the citadel.

From the top floor, he watched the galleys stroke out to sea, and he crossed himself. God who hated him, please watch over his sister.

Now he had other problems.

As he had anticipated, nobody wanted Guy to be King. Without Richard there for his champion, Guy would have nothing. He might as well admit that. He called a council, which sat for one day and named Conrad the King, his heirs by Queen Isabella to follow him to the throne.

Throne of a few cities, a kingdom with a false name. Even so, it gave a man like Conrad room to strut.

"I told you the Crusade was dead. You see, in the end, who comes out best." The Italian thrust his chest out, pranced and preened around him in his curly-toed shoes, his diamond-crusted ears, his greased hair. "You have to work with the real matter, see, not dreams." He shot a look at Humphrey, across the room. "Of course, for some people, that's hard." He laughed as if he had made a joke and went away. Across the room, Richard caught Humphrey's glance, and held it; now that the Crusade was over, he had no reason anymore to be chaste. He smiled, and Humphrey, his eyes bright, flushed and smiled back.

He would give Guy Cyprus. A bigger, better kingdom than Conrad's. Let the greasy schemer strut then.

* * *

But only a few days later, before he could deliver this thrust, a courier from Tyre said, "My lord, the King is dead."

"King Conrad," Richard said. "What happened?" He had met the courier rushing up the courtyard steps as he was coming down from the hall. Behind him on the staircase, de Sablé and Guy de Lusignan overheard this and began to chatter, and Richard waved a hand at them impatiently to shut up.

"My lord," the courier said, "it was the Assassins. Two of them came upon him in the street in Tyre; one gave him a letter, and while he was reading it they both stuck knives in him."

"Assassins," he said. "Who sent the letter? Did they take the killers alive?"

"My lord," the courier said, and sank down on his knees on the step below Richard, his hands together. "One was taken. They put him to the test."

In the fear of the messenger, Richard saw what news was coming; he glanced over his shoulder at the other men, on the stair above him: de Sablé, who was as always thinking about something else, and Guy frowning in bewilderment. Richard faced the courier praying to him. "What did they find out?"

"He said it was you, my lord. He said you paid the knives." The courier was white as bone.

Richard stood a moment, not surprised, not even, really, angry. He said, at last, "Pity I didn't think of it." He beckoned to a page. "Give this man a bezant." He went on down the stairs.

* * *

In the pulpits of Tyre, of Acre, of the fat little towns that throve because of him, the priests cried shame on him, murderer, oath breaker, the man who turned back from Jerusalem and then killed the King. Whenever he rode out in Acre, people gathered to jeer and curse at him. He remembered what Johanna had said when she left.

His beard itched and he wanted it off. He sat on the balcony, where there was good light, so the ham-handed barber would not slice his face to pieces. The razor scraped against his throat. Down the way, his pages loitered, a few other men, waiting to catch his notice. Through them came the doctor, slender as a palm tree, wearing a dark gown and a plain white coif, bowing before him.

"You sent for me, my lord," she said.

"Yes, come here." Richard waved the barber out of earshot. She came to the side of the throne and he studied her, up and down; when he wanted to be bled, she did it, not the barber, and he began to think he would have her shave him, too. He said, "You have heard all this about King Conrad."

She said, "I have heard only street gossip, my lord."

"Yes, now that my sister's gone, the brew here must be thin as whey. Did she do it?"

Edythe twitched all over. Her eyes went elsewhere and her voice grated. At her temple a dark curl escaped the edge of her coif. "Conrad was not her enemy."

"Could she have done it for his wife's sake?"

"His wife's sake," she said, in a true voice, and looked at him. He saw that the words had quickened some connection. She gathered in a deep breath. When she spoke he had the feeling she was changing the subject, although it was the same wife. "She and Isabella wrote, but he caught them at it. She was trying to help her escape. You know that. That led to what happened last winter here, eventually."

"The Assassins killed him. How could she have reached them? How likely was she even to know they exist? Do you know who they are?"

"No, my lord. Only—" She shrugged. "They kill people."

"They kill people for hire. Unlike righteous folk who kill them for God." His eyes narrowed. "Why Conrad, though? She had enemies—which did she want dead?"

She said, "No one, my lord, no one, she would not have done this."

"You told Rouquin already. You women, you keep and break faith at the same time. It was de Sablé. Who is still alive."

"Oh, God, my Lord, she would never have—killed him. My lord, I pray you, you must know her better." Defending Johanna, she was urgent, swift-spoken.

"No. But de Sablé was devilling her. I know my sister. She cannot keep her fork out of the pot, and so she is ever being burned. She got help to discourage him. Or at least she thought that was what she was doing. But whoever helped her turned her purpose to his own ends. Which was to kill King Conrad." For his wife's sake.

"I don't know." She rubbed her hands together. "It was not my lady Johanna, ever."

He rubbed his finger over his clean-shaven chin. The barber had left a rasp of stubble under his jawbone. He said, at last, "I know." He nodded at her. "Go get ready to sail for Jaffa. We should be able to leave tomorrow."

She dipped him a curtsy. "My lord."

·   ·   ·

He sent a page for Humphrey and met him in his small room at the end of the hall. The young man came in smiling. He was beautiful, his face smooth, young, happy; he would be a boy when he was fifty.

Richard sat down and did not tell him to sit. He said no greeting. His voice was stony. "You betrayed me. You used my sister in your plot against Conrad; you made my sister guilty in his murder.

Everybody thinks it was me; I don't care about that, they all hate me anyway. But I love my sister, and you corrupted her. She trusted you because I trusted you. Go; I never want to see you again."

As he spoke, Humphrey's face slid down out of its smile, and the creases along his nose grew deeper. He was suddenly not beautiful anymore. He turned and went out the door. Richard sat there awhile, until he knew Humphrey was gone, and no one else saw him, and put his hands over his face.

He remembered how he had set out on this, the glorious words, the high promises, round oaths taken with the fullest confidence. What had been golden once seemed like tin and paper now. Under a fraudulent banner he had led his people into the desert, and the wind had blown them away. He lowered his hands, empty as an old wineskin, wretched.

．　．　．

They sailed back to Jaffa, and that night Edythe went into the hall, where the court was gathered around to hear music. Rouquin was not there. She slipped back out onto the windy terrace, looking toward the sea. A storm was blowing in, and out as far as her gaze could reach the waves jumped in dashes of foam, vivid in the dark. She went down the stairs into the courtyard. It was empty; she could hear the men talking in the hall above her. Then, by the wall, someone hissed at her.

"Stand where you are, witch."

She wheeled. It was de Sablé, his back to the blank wall.

He said, "I have found your secret." He held up a book before her.

It was her father's book. She let out a cry, and reached for it, and he threw it down at her feet.

"A Jew book. You are a Jew."

She stooped and picked the book up. He must have snooped

through the hospital. She straightened, clutching the book, cold all over.

"Do you dare deny it?" he said. "Do as I wish, and no one ever need know."

She looked him in the face. She said, "I am a Jew. Let all know it, I will hide no longer. You are a lecher, a murderer, you killed Lilia, you threatened the Queen, you spied on the King, you dirtied your vows and the cross you swore them on. I will never do your bidding, ever."

He straightened as she spoke, moved away from the wall; he seemed to swell, to give off some foul vapor like an adder. He reached to his belt. "Ah, you know too much. You need a bleeding." He drew a knife.

She gathered herself, to run, to scream, and then, behind her, Rouquin's voice growled out.

"She is not alone, Grand Master."

The Templar tipped his head back. "You defend a Jew against one who wears the cross."

"I'll cut a slice out of that cross, if you don't get beyond my reach." He came up beside her. In his hand, low, his sword was a streak of wavering light in the darkness. She could not move. He knew. Surely he had heard what the Templar said, and he knew. De Sablé was backing away; he turned and strode off across the courtyard.

Beside her, Rouquin ran the sword back into its sheath on his belt. He did not look at her. He said nothing. She said, "You heard."

"Yes," he said. "I'll take you where you're safe." He let her go ahead of him up the stair and across the balcony to Johanna's empty chamber, and there he left her without a word. It was over. She stood for a long time, in the dark, not thinking or moving. It was over.

Eighteen

JAFFA

A Jew was almost worse than a Saracen.

He thought to himself: *Everything is a lie.* He was going to get drunk and find a whore. But he did not; he walked around the town until he was exhausted enough to sleep.

. . .

In the afternoon, the court gathered, to watch Richard eat, and then to eat themselves. Waiting, they all milled around, chattering. Everybody went to Henry of Champagne, who was now to marry Queen Isabella, and shook his hand and kissed it. The new King of Jerusalem. He was laughing, delighted, drinking to his wife-to-be with every cup. It was rumored she was pregnant, that he was getting more, or less, than he might have.

When Edythe came in, she saw Rouquin standing behind Richard, and he turned his face away.

She lingered by the wall, her head so flooded with memories, with pleas and excuses, that she saw nothing. No one spoke to her, although she saw the sideways glances. She should leave, and make them serve her in her room, which had been Johanna's room. Then suddenly, behind her, a bellow of rage went up.

It was Rouquin. He shouted, "Do you tell me you're giving him Cyprus?"

She jolted back to the moment. Up there in front of the throne, Richard and Rouquin stood face-to-face. Richard said, "Guy was a king. I will not let him be disparaged—"

Rouquin shouted, "He's a fool. He's incapable." They were so close they almost touched. The whole hall had fallen still, breathless, watching.

Richard's voice cut, almost a sneer. "Did you want it? What's the matter with you?"

Rouquin was still shouting. "What about the Crusade? Everything we did—the marches, the wounds, the men who died—so you could give it all to a pretty face?"

A general gasp went up. Richard's lips pulled back in a snarl, and he lifted his right hand and struck Rouquin across the mouth. No one in the watching crowd moved. Rouquin was flushed dark as raw meat and his hair bristled. Edythe gripped her hands together. He clenched his fist, and she held her breath; she could not move, it seemed even her heart was stopped.

He said, "You hit like a woman. You're still half-sick. I don't fight invalids." Then he wheeled and strode away, headed for the door.

"Rouquin!" Richard took a step after him. "Turn and draw your sword!" Rouquin burst out through the door and was gone.

The crowd murmured, people bending together, their hands moving, and their voices rose to a general racket. She drew a deep breath, and another, dizzy. Richard had gone back up to his throne. In a moment he would send them all away. She turned toward the door.

De Sablé stood there, watching her. She made herself walk by him without a word.

·   ·   ·

Later, in the evening, when she heard he was in the hall, she went to Richard and said, "My lord, I need to talk to you."

He was sitting on a bench at a table, two men beside him with a handful of papers, and a paper on the table between his hands. An inkwell and a quill lay on the table before him, and he picked up the quill and signed the bottom of the paper, handed it to the man on his left, and sent them both away. He gave her a surly look.

"What is it? I'm busy."

"The Grand Master of the Templars came to me; he wanted me for a spy, and when I refused, he threatened me."

His face altered, the temper smoothing away. Leaning back, his hands behind his head, he studied her up and down. "You are loyal enough. How could he get you to spy?"

"He knows about me. What you know."

"And you refused, even so. You have more honor than a Templar."

She said, "I would not have come to you, except he threatened to kill me. I will not ask a Christian king to defend me against a Christian knight, but if he kills me, I want you to know that he did it."

Richard said, "You know, in this, for once, I can do as I please. I don't want you to die, and he's done me in, time on time, as you know. I'll send him to Cyprus. The Templars managed it very ill while they had it, and they have accounts to put in order so Guy can pay me for it."

She said, "Thank you, my lord."

"No, you're my good little monster, I'll protect you." He looked down at her from a great height of understanding. "I cannot help you, though, with Rouq', who won't talk to me either."

◆   ◆   ◆

The days passed, the heat of the summer on them, the nights so hot the whole court often slept out on the balcony. She went down to work in the hospital, but it was as if her mind had jammed; she did everything wrong. She forgot what she was doing in the middle of a treatment, sorted medicines into the wrong jars and spilled bedpans, and when Besac squeaked at her in front of everybody she raged back like a fishwife. She was alone. There was no one to talk to. She felt thinned out, faint, and useless. Some plague had struck the town and many children were sick and she went from house to house, dosing them with lemon and oxymel, but a lot of them died anyway.

◆   ◆   ◆

Rouquin had kept the long plume of her hair, tied with a thong, under the cushion of his bed; he burned it. He gathered whatever else he had of hers—a coif, a letter, a bit of linen—and burned them also. He went to church. Usually he could not endure even half a Mass, but he knelt and prayed and stood and knelt again with everybody else, all Sunday, until the final Missa Est.

None of this worked. He could not stop thinking of her. How she moved, how her mouth tasted, how she laughed. A Jewess, forever damned, Christ-denier. Creature of magic and devilish powers. No wonder she was a good doctor. She had enspelled him, polluted him. That was why he couldn't stop thinking about her. She had made him soft. He struggled himself back into the hard, cold man he had been, who cared only about overcoming other men.

He could not remember how to be like that. Maybe he had never been that way, just an empty coat of mail with a bad temper. He needed his temper. When he was riding, when he was fighting, then he moved fast and sure, without thinking, without maddening himself with thinking. He rode out every day, to get away from Richard.

Richard had known, all along, damn him, the devil's trueborn son.

He could not get away from Edythe, clinging there always in the back of his mind. She had sunk her claws into him like the monster Richard called her. He needed a woman, any woman, any other woman, to drive her out. But when he found a whore, the thought of touching what so many other men had touched made him sick.

She was his, he had broached her, virgin sweet, she belonged to him alone. He would kill her before anyone else had her.

He rode at the head of his column up the flank of a ridge, and across the way he saw the flash of a white robe.

He reined the roan horse back and cut along quick below the spine of the ridge, but he thought they had probably seen him. The roan bolted over the low brush, sure-footed on the slope. Where the dry wash cut the ridge, he slid down and bunched his men together and led them fast around the foot of the hill toward where he had seen the Saracens.

They were gone. The obvious trail led off down a seam through the lumpy sandy hills, where they would have to ride single file. He divided his men, sent Mercadier with half down the gully, and took the other half in the same direction, but up and over the ridge.

He was in the middle of the Saracen ambush almost before he saw them. Their backs to him, squatting in the brush, they were strung out along the lip of the gully looking down, their bows ready. He charged along the top of the bank, his men pouring after him; they pounded through the brush and across the sandy slope, the horses scrabbling for footing on the dry ground.

The Saracens fired a wild flock of arrows, bounded to their horses, and raced on ahead of them. He saw the sock-footed bay mare ahead of him and yelled, hot.

To the left the slope pitched off suddenly. The narrowing crest of the ridge was funneling the Saracens toward the plain with Rouquin on their heels and Mercadier coming out of the gully to their right. He spurred the roan to a flat run. For a moment, as the big horses bounded and slid down the slope and bolted out onto the open ground, his front ranks and the last of the Saracens galloped side by side.

He slashed out with his sword at a rider; the Saracen flung up a bow to fend off the strike and the sword cut it in two. Then the bay mare galloped up on his other side.

He saw Safadin's dark face over the round target of his shield and lashed out with all his strength, blow on blow. The Saracen's blade smashed his shield until his arm was numb. The swords rang together with a shower of sparks. Then the mare was pulling away. The roan horse, his neck lathered, faltered, and Rouquin reined him up.

All the knights slowed with him; they had learned that much anyway. The gap between them and the Saracens widened. The white-robed riders disappeared into a crack in the hills. The last to go whirled his bay mare and looked back.

Rouquin was still panting, soaked with sweat, his blood racing. He raised his sword over his head. He thought, *This is our one true faith, the House of War*. Across the plain, Safadin lifted his scimitar in answer, spun his mare on her hocks, and rode away.

Rouquin gathered up his men. They were scratched and banged up, a few wounded, and he turned back toward Jaffa. The fighting rage left him, and he rode along remembering what had happened, making a story of it. He liked Safadin a lot better than he liked some of the Crusader lords. That was heresy, but he believed it. She had said that to him. He remembered how lightly he had answered her. Bragged of being born half out of the church. To one wholly outcast. She must have thought him a fool.

He had lied to her, from the beginning, the devil's bastard brat. She had not understood that, or how lost he was himself. And he wanted her, with a longing like hunger, to love, to be one with. To tell his truth to. Yet she had lied to him; how could he trust her?

He had to see her one more time. If there was nothing to her but a lie, then he would kill her, and put an end to this. He would know when he saw her again. He spurred his horse back toward the city.

. . .

Late in the day a Syrian woman brought a child to the hospital. Drawn by the child's screams, Edythe met her at the door; when she saw the blood all over the side of the little boy's face she gasped, and took them in to the nearest bed.

The mother babbled at her in the local tongue, which she understood very little, but she heard "ear" over and over. She made her sit with the child on her lap and brought vinegar and a cloth, but the howling baby would not let her touch him.

She went into the back and found a piece of honeycomb and brought that to him, and his mother sang to him and Edythe made faces and he settled and let her touch the bloody mess around his ear. She was afraid to use the vinegar, for fear of hurting him again. Drawing his hair aside, she uncovered his ear.

She snorted, relieved. The blood was all from shallow cuts around the outside of his ear; something pale and bulbous filled the canal. She looked at the mother.

"Earache?" She pulled her own ear. "His ear hurt, so you put garlic into it?"

The mother smiled and spread her hands. Edythe stroked the boy's head with one hand, and groped for her pincers with the other, and in a single stroke she drew out the garlic. The gashes on his ear were knife cuts. The mother, failing other ways, had tried to dig out the garlic with a knife. Edythe pressed her lips together to keep from saying anything. She cleaned up the dried blood, tended the cuts on his ear, kissed him, and sent them away. She heard them singing off down the street.

Everything, she supposed, seemed reasonable at the time. She wiped her hands on her apron, looking around.

Besac had already left. She went to the people in the beds, making sure they would rest. There weren't many: an old woman dying, a man with no other place to go who was pretending he had a headache. Night came while she was doing this. She stood in the doorway looking into the dark and thought of staying the night in the hospital, rather than going alone through the rough streets of Jaffa.

Whatever Richard did, she could not trust in it; there were Templars all over Jaffa.

She went out, and just as she stepped out the gate someone seized her from behind. She jabbed back with her elbows and kicked, but he held her effortlessly fast. She thrashed, afraid, feeling the knife coming, but then suddenly she knew who it was, by that touch, that strength.

"Rouquin."

He lifted her quickly up and set her sideways on his saddle. She grabbed the cantle to stay on. The light from the lantern above the hospital door shone on his upturned face. She said, again, joyful, "Rouquin." He leaned forward, his arms around her, and buried his face in her skirts.

· · ·

Later, they lay side by side, in the little room in the middle house where his men were quartered. He said, "I have something to tell you."

She stretched herself against the warmth of his body. "Tell me, then."

"I've never said this before," he said. "Not to anybody. That—you know they say my mother was the queen's sister."

"Yes," she said. She had heard this for years. "The lady Petronilla—"

"No. Eleanor was my mother. My father was the king. But I was born before they married, when they were not queen nor king."

That jolted her; she said, "How do you know?" She touched the star-shaped scar on his shoulder, where he had taken the arrow. In her mind bits and pieces joined together and now made more sense.

"I just figured it out. Little by little, it seems, I understood it, growing up."

"Are you sure?" she said. She was sure. She laid her palm flat against him, her head on his arm.

"Even my name is a lie. My aunt christened me Philip, but nobody calls me that. De Rançun was not my father. My—my aunt—Eleanor called me Rouquin. She said when I was angry I looked like a little redheaded hedgehog." His voice stopped.

She waited, thinking he would say more. His mother had given him away. She had taken him back—in act, at least, if not in name—but she had sacrificed him, the eldest son, on the rock of her ambition, and he could not forget it.

He said, "I've never told anybody before. It feels different now, saying it."

The pallet was too narrow for both of them; she had to lie half on top of him, her leg between his. It was too hot to be so close, but she loved to lie so, touching him all the way. Her clothes were strewn everywhere. The men out in the main hall must be watching the door for any sign they were coming out. They would get a jeering then, whistles and whoops; there would be no chance to lie. Richard had said, once, "My brother."

"Then you should be King," she said.

"No, I am baseborn. I could not be such a king as Richard, anyway. But I am their true brother, his and Jo's, and Mattie's and Nora's and John's. They all know it. No one says anything. We all lie." He burst out, "You can't trust any of us."

"They love you."

"Oh, we love each other. We hate each other, too."

Her cheek against his shoulder, she nodded, having noticed this.

"It's like everything else in this family," he said; "it's double-tongued. It was twisted from the start, when the first one murdered his way into the first title. So not even Richard could make the Kingdom come." He put his hands over his face. "I am sick of lies. I will live the truth or nothing."

She thought of Yeshua ben Yafo and what he had said to her. "People think in one world and live in another." *But it is the dream that saves us,* she thought. *Isn't it? Which is the lie, and which the truth?*

He said, "What's your real name?"

"What?"

"I want to know. You didn't escape from a nunnery, and you weren't named Edythe, were you?"

"No," she said. "No." She had not heard her own name in more than twelve years. She said, "My name is Deborah." She went hot all over, her skin tingling, as if she woke up.

She felt him smile, his face against her face. "Deborah," he said. "My Deborah." He kissed her again. "My truth."

* * *

She lay against him as he slept; she wanted him again, right away. There was still so little time. They were still doomed. Richard was talking things over with Saladin; and when he did, even if it took a year, they would go back to the west.

Let it take a year. In the dark she touched his chest, the broad muscle covered with curly hair, and tried not to think past the time they would go to France. He woke enough to put his arm around her and went back to sleep.

What would happen, back in Poitiers? Would he love her there? How could they be together? What he said—about the truth—that would not work in France. Truth did not carry well from one place to another. In France it would be impossible for them. Unless she went back to being Edythe. Which would not be the truth anymore.

* * *

It was near the full moon, and Richard had begun nagging her to bleed him. She saw the Saracen horsemen in the courtyard and came up to the hall as Safadin was leaving. She drew back out of the Saracen's way; he ignored her, although she knew he saw her. Richard called her into his little room.

She looked Richard over, felt his pulses, and listened to his back. He was strong as ever, his long body lean and white. Maybe bleeding him was a good idea, to keep his humors active. The lance slash under his right arm had healed well, in rows of little dots where the needle had pierced his skin, a narrow white scar between, no puckers or proud flesh. He had a bruise on his shield arm, another argument for bleeding him. He was putting his shirt back on.

"You saw the Saracen there. We have agreed on a treaty, Saladin and I. I have now officially failed."

He paused a moment, as if she might argue, or burst into applause. She knew nothing to say and kept still. He said, "We are monsters, you and I. God has one idea, and we are not it." He pulled his shirt straight.

She said, "What is the treaty?"

"Three years with no war. And unarmed Christian pilgrims can go to Jerusalem. That's what I have won, a handful of days."

"What does your treaty say of Jews?"

"There is nothing about Jews. The Jews have nothing to do with this."

"Then I can go to Jerusalem," she said.

He flipped his belt around his middle. "No, dear little fool, it is still too dangerous. You're a woman. The place is full of bandits. You wouldn't last a day alone. You'd have to find company, and pay for that somehow, and even then . . . You'd be dead, or in a slave market, too old for anybody to want you. I am leaving, very soon, for the west, and you're coming with me."

"I am going to Jerusalem," she said.

He looked puzzled. "I command you. What about Johanna? And my mother surely wants you back."

She paced around before him, so that he had to turn to watch her. "But I am outside your Christian realm, my lord. Your treaty has nothing to do with me."

"Edythe," he said. "You're mad. I'm the only one who can protect you."

"That's not my name anymore. I have to go. Besac has the tincture," she said. "Find the Jew Yeshua ben Yafo and he will tell you how to take it." And she went.

* * *

She walked in quietly through the barracks, to the room where Rouquin was asleep; the door was open a hand's breadth. She stood there awhile and looked through the crack at him. In the morning when she left the whole pallet to him, he had stretched out and his head was cradled in his arms. She could not bear to wake him. If she told him what she was doing, and he wanted her to go with him instead, she would, even to the farthest reaches of the world. She would be Edythe again to keep him.

She went out again to take the road. She had to go through the gate before Richard decided to stop her. She went by the hospital first, and put her books and the pouch of medicines and some food she had packed in a big bag to carry on her shoulder.

At the gate no one challenged her. Maybe she had given herself an excess of importance. She walked out through the new gate-house, to the beginning of the long road east. A wave of uncertainty rose around her. She started out, one foot in front of the other, the bag already heavy.

                       ✦ ✦ ✦

Mercadier said, "Your woman, she was here, and then she left." He filled the narrow doorway.

Rouquin washed his face in the basin. "Where did she go?"

"How would I know? She is like a wild mare, that one; she goes where she will. It's all over the city that the King has made a deal with the Sultan."

"Really. And what do you think this means?" He reached for his swordbelt, hanging on the wall.

"I think we are going home, my lord." Mercadier shrugged, but one hand rose, palm up. "Whatever happens, there will be some war. I am your man, whatever comes."

Rouquin bopped him with his fist. "I think from now on you will be Richard's man."

"The King!" The Brabanter's eyes widened, awed. Then, loyal, he said, "No other, though. No lesser would I ever follow."

Rouquin laughed and went out of the house to the yard. A squire brought him the roan horse, and he rode up to the palace and found Richard pacing around the hall, eating a chicken and giving orders. Rouquin had not seen him in days, since Richard hit him. The King chased everybody else out of the hall and turned on him.

"So you finally show up, do you? Over your sulk? What, do you want me to apologize? After what you said?"

Rouquin said, "I don't want much of anything from you, actually. I hear you sorted it out with the Sultan."

Richard flung down the carcass in his hands. His eyes blazed; his voice snapped like ice cracking. "What has come over you all, some plague of defiance? I should have whacked your damned head off. We are leaving. Philip and that damned German are apparently waiting for me, but they won't be looking for you. I want you to go straight back to France and start raising an army."

Rouquin sat down, folding his arms over his chest, enjoying this. "Actually, I am not going back. There's nothing for me back there, and I'm done with following you."

Richard flung his arms up. He gave Rouquin another furious look and stalked away. Rouquin sat where he was. Someone came in the door, saw the two of them there, and went away. Finally Richard had to walk back toward him.

"So, you're deserting me too? You can't do that. I need you."

Rouquin said, "I can do exactly that. I'm your brother, but it's not my kingdom. I've given you everything due you. You have no power over me."

Richard stopped, silent. He put his head to one side, and said, in another voice, "So that's what this is."

"Yes. I'm done lying. I'm done with the whole family. I am not going back to France. Take Mercadier, pay him and my men, and they'll never leave you. But I'm going to find my woman, and then go to Jerusalem, which I swore to do."

Richard walked away again, and came back. "You can't carry a sword. The treaty says, unarmed pilgrims. What are you without your sword?"

"Let them find out," Rouquin said, "who try to stop me." He stood up.

The King faced him, and their eyes met. There was a long silence. Richard said, "Well, you'd better start soon, she's already left. She's on the road now." He put his hand out. "This was no choice of mine. I always loved you. You were always my true brother to me."

"I know that." Rouquin gripped the King's hand.

"Better than a brother. God forgive me for the times I failed you." Richard pulled him into an embrace. "Go find her. With you some of me goes to Jerusalem." He stood back. "Go. With my blessing."

Rouquin said, "Maybe we will come back." But if she had already left he had to hurry. He went out the door, down to his horse.

◆　◆　◆

At first the road was full of people, going in both directions, donkeys and carts and barefoot porters carrying loads in and out of Jaffa. Along the side of the road eight monks were creeping along on their knees, chanting as they went. She thought of Rouquin and put him firmly out of her mind. A few moments later she was putting him out of her mind again. By noon there were fewer people, the land broad and flat still, the hills beginning to rise before her, gullied and seamed. On the slope above her she saw two Saracens on horses. She remembered the road from the winter march, although now it was dry and hot and the brown grass tall. A group of pilgrims, with their hats and staffs, walked along ahead of her singing, and she tried to stay within range of them. The bag on her shoulder felt full of rocks.

Other people passed her, and she saw a few heads turn, taking notice of her, a woman alone. She ran to get closer to the pilgrims. They might not defend her anyway. She had her knife in her belt. She found a big stone and carried it in her free fist. But night was coming; she wondered how she would do that. She would ask the pilgrims if she could sleep in their camp. She had enough food, she could even barter some for room by a fire.

She heard the jingle of harness and the jogging hoofbeats and moved off to one side, to let the horse pass. It dropped to a walk up beside her, and she wheeled, warned of the attention.

"Deborah."

The name rocked her; she looked up, astonished. He smiled down at her from the height of the roan stallion's back. He wore mail, but no sword, only a long dagger in his belt, and instead of his helmet he had wrapped a white cloth around his head like a Saracen. His eyes were startlingly bright.

He reached his arm down to her. They needed to say nothing. She dropped the stone and held up the bag of her things, which he hung on his saddlebows. He reached down again and she grasped his arm, and he swung her up behind him. She sat astride, her legs spread wide on the broad back, and put her arms around his waist.

"Tighter," he said.

She leaned against him, her cheek against his back, and clasped her arms tight as she could around him. They jogged off up the road to Jerusalem.

Afterword

The First Crusade in 1096 was not the first Crusade. By the end of the eleventh century, Christians and Muslims had been fighting for more than four hundred years. At first the Arabs had things pretty much their own way, taking Spain and Sicily, Sardinia and the Holy Land and everything south of there from Morocco to India; there was an Arab emirate at Bari, on the heel of Italy, for thirty years, and Arab fleets raided Rome and Marseilles. Only hard-fought Christian victories at Constantinople in the late seventh and early eighth centuries and in central France at the Battle of Tours in 726 kept Arab armies from romping through backward, poor, and feeble Europe. There are those who, viewing the brilliant civilization of Umayyad Spain, still think that would not have been a bad thing.

By the eleventh century, however, the Arab conquest was over and its fragmented empire was in retreat. Under the duress of having to defend itself not just against Arabs but against Vikings and Magyars and Avars as well, Christian Europe had grown into a powerhouse: strong, organized, numerous, and rich. Especially, they had learned a formidable new way of fighting: mailed knights, mounted on powerful horses, whose massed charge mowed down everything in its path. With such knights in the eleventh century, the Christians recovered Sicily and a lot of Spain.

Constantinople, however, had suffered a terrible defeat at Manzikert in 1076 at the hands of the Seljuk Turks, recent converts to Islam coming out of central Asia. Subsequently the Seljuks overran Anatolia and the Holy Land. The emperor in Constantinople appealed to the pope for help against them, and the so-called First Crusade was what he got.

That sudden attack on the disorganized Levant won the Crusaders Jerusalem, as well as a number of other valuable places, which they held for almost a hundred years. But the Turks recovered, and in 1187 at the Battle of Hattin the great sultan Saladin crushed the Crusader army and swiftly rolled up the rest of the Christian domain, except for the cities of Tyre and Antioch, on the northern coast of the Holy Land, and a few other isolated fortresses.

The Christian west reacted with shock and horror. At once the great monarchs of Europe—the emperor Barbarossa, the king of France, and the king of England—pledged to go to the rescue of the Holy Land, and although practical politics delayed their leaving for years, in which one king of England died and another took up his vow, eventually they all set out for the east. Barbarossa, the legendary emperor, drowned in a mountain stream. The kings of France and England reached the Levant in 1191.

Theirs was the Third Crusade, the Kings' Crusade, in which Richard the Lionhearted defeated Saladin but could not take Jerusalem.

There were nine numbered Crusades and a variety of smaller ones, but by the end of the thirteenth century, the Holy Land was completely lost to Christendom. Nonetheless, the long, bloody struggle continues to this day.

The public events of this novel are based on the primary sources of the time, including Muslim sources, for the siege of Acre, the massacre of Acre, the battles of Arsuf and Jaffa, the infighting among the Crusader lords, the murder of Conrad of Montferrat, and the eventual settlement between Richard and Saladin. Richard, who was the superstar of the twelfth century, is often quoted directly in these sources; he is one of the most vivid characters in medieval history, a true knight and a great general. He could not take Jerusalem back, but the territory he did conquer, including Cyprus, allowed the Levantine coast to stay in Christian hands for another century.

The issue of his sexual orientation remains a big argument and may be impossible to resolve, since the ideas of the twelfth century about such things are much different than ours. I'm more convinced by the evidence for rather than against his being what we call homosexual. Humphrey IV de Toron was viewed by his contemporaries as "not a knight" and "a boy who is almost a girl," which seems less controversial. His contemporaries respected his wit and diplomatic ability, and Richard liked him and spent a lot of time with him. He died sometime after the end of the Third Crusade.

Henry of Champagne, who married Isabella and became king of Jerusalem, fell out a window in 1197 and broke his neck. Isabella soon married her fourth husband in ten years, Amalric of Lusignan, another of the tenacious upwardly mobile clan from Poitou that included King Guy and Hugh of Ascalon. Amalric became king of Cyprus, which he made into a coherent and stable realm. He and Isabella both died in 1205, and her daughter by Conrad of Montferrat, Maria of Montferrat, inherited their titles.

On Richard's way home from the Crusade he fell into the hands of the Duke of Austria, who sold him to the emperor Henry VI, who freed him only on receipt of a ruinous ransom. Richard's mother, Eleanor, raised it, thus beggaring England, not his brother Prince John, as Sir Walter Scott would have it; John did offer the emperor a sum of money not to let Richard go. Even in captivity Richard managed to make allies, and when he was finally free he quickly drove John off and recovered his property.

He spent almost none of his reign in England. The core of his power was in western and southern France, where he died in 1199, still fighting. His sister Johanna died only a few days later; they are both buried in Fontevraud Abbey with Eleanor.

Richard and Berengaria never had children, and the youngest of Eleanor's children, Prince John, succeeded him. He was half the king his brother and his father had been, lost all his continental possessions to King Philip Augustus, and then was humiliatingly forced into signing the Magna Carta by his infuriated barons. Some generations on, another great Plantagenet king laid claim to those continental possessions again, beginning the Hundred Years' War.

The private story is fiction. Edythe, or Deborah, and Rouquin are imagined people; Richard had a number of commanders, of whom Rouquin is a sort of distillation, most obviously of Mercadier, the great captain of mercenaries who served the Lionheart for most of his kingship.

In the twelfth century there were a number of types of medical practitioners, many of them women. The great medical school at Salerno accepted female students from its founding. Lest anybody think I am making a leap here with Edythe, please note that the personal physician to Louis IX of France on his disastrous Crusade was a woman.

The Crusades benefited the practice of physicians and hospitals, bringing ideas from the Byzantines and the Muslim world into the

West; Galen, Maimonides, and Ibn Sina were the primary theorists. Most of the details in the story are drawn from the primary data. The medical practice strives to describe Galen's humor theory, a lovely intellectual construct, part of the neoplatonic idea-world of the Middle Ages, like Ptolemy's cosmos.

The name Plantagenet is parlous. It does not appear in written records before Edward I's day, although it was Henry II's father, Geoffrey, who first wore a sprig of broom in his hat—the *planta genet*—and absence of evidence is not evidence of absence. The alternative, the House of Anjou, has no magic in it. The greatest family of the Middle Ages deserves its flamboyant name. *J'adjust.*

READERS GUIDE

The King's Witch

DISCUSSION QUESTIONS

1. Discuss the relationship between Edythe and Rouquin. They both feel like outcasts in their respective worlds—how does this affect their relationship? Do you think that, had they not been able to move outside of their regular worlds, they would have been able to connect the way they do?

2. Did you enter into reading *The King's Witch* with an understanding of the time period and of the reign of Richard the Lionheart? If not, did the author's research into this time period help you develop a better understanding of the Crusades?

3. How do you think Edythe's background as a Jew, and her desire to learn more about her heritage, affect the decisions she makes throughout the course of the novel?

4. On page 138, in regard to the Crusades, Rouquin states, "This isn't about God, whatever Richard says. This is about power." Do you agree or disagree with this statement, based on your own knowledge of the Crusades? Do you think other wars were fought for which the motivation may have been power instead of religion?

5. Edythe decides to go with Richard to Jaffa in order to possibly learn more about her Jewish heritage, as well as to care for the injured soldiers. How does her journey compare to other religious pilgrimages?

6. King Richard is believed by many historians to have been a homosexual. Do you think Richard's relationship with Edythe is influenced by the fact that he's a man not attracted to women, leaving him free to treat her as an equal?

7. Edythe is referred to as a witch by Richard's men at various points throughout the course of the novel. Do you think that they truly believe that she is capable of witchcraft? In what ways do their reactions to her abilities to heal act as a precursor to later instances in history when people were persecuted as witches?

8. Throughout the course of the novel, the Templars also play a significant role in trying to shape the outcome of the attack on Jerusalem and the installation of a new king. Why do you think Edythe seems to have an easier time standing up to them than Johanna does?

9. Toward the beginning of the novel, Edythe meets an old beggar whose words haunt her throughout the novel. In what ways does the novel suggest that in war, no one wins?

10. Why do you think Edythe chooses to go to Jerusalem and live the rest of her life as a Jewish woman, an arguably harder life than she would have had if she returned with Johanna to Eleanor's court?